MW01015639

The Maypo Lea Forever

The Maypo Lea Forever

- STORIES OF A CANADIAN CHILDHOOD -

Kathreen A. Nash

© 2002 by Kathreen A. Nash. All rights reserved.

No part of this publication may be reproduced, stored in a retrieval system, or transmitted, in any form or by any means, electronic, mechanical, photocopying, recording, or otherwise, without the written prior permission of the author.

Front Cover Photo: Nash children, 1935
L. to R.: Alberta Rose, Kathreen, Donald, Mildred, Howard, Harvey, and our horse, "Darky", with our first school cart.

Fairy Godmother was written in 1993 for Nancy Fraser
[March 8th, 1910 - October 25th, 2002] and is included here in tribute to our sixty-year friendship.

National Library of Canada Cataloguing in Publication

Nash, Kathreen A. (Kathreen Amelia), 1928-
     The maypo lea forever : stories of a Canadian childhood / Kathreen A. Nash.
SBN 1-55395-202-2

     1. Nash, Kathreen A. (Kathreen Amelia), 1928- --Childhood and youth.
2. Farm life--Alberta--Huxley. I. Title.

FC3699.H89Z49 2002   971.23'3   C2002-905050-2
F1079.5.H89N37 2002

 *PRINTED IN CANADA*

This book was published *on-demand* in cooperation with Trafford Publishing.
On-demand publishing is a unique process and service of making a book available for retail sale to the public taking advantage of on-demand manufacturing and Internet marketing.
On-demand publishing includes promotions, retail sales, manufacturing, order fulfilment, accounting and collecting royalties on behalf of the author.

Suite 6E, 2333 Government St., Victoria, B.C. V8T 4P4, CANADA
Phone   250-383-6864   Toll-free   1-888-232-4444 (Canada & US)
Fax   250-383-6804   E-mail   sales@trafford.com
Web site   www.trafford.com   TRAFFORD PUBLISHING IS A DIVISION OF TRAFFORD HOLDINGS LTD.
Trafford Catalogue #02-0916   www.trafford.com/robots/02-0916.html

10   9   8   7   6

For Howard
who contributed so much,
to the stories and to
my childhood.

Acknowledgements

This book *is* the acknowledgment of the many who, knowingly or unknowingly, contributed to my childhood experiences and perceptions. Remembered especially are several exceptional teachers, among them, Roland M. Ward and Miss Marion Hodgson (later Storey) in Alberta, and Ida N. Vyse in British Columbia, all of whom gave consistent, indispensable encouragement to my early writing.

I thank my sisters and brothers for help with various memories and my many friends for their faith in waiting for this book. I feel continuing gratitude to my good friend, Don Rees (1929-1998), for his insistence over the years that I get on with publishing my work.

For some specific facts about people in the Huxley Community, I have relied on their own stories in *Our Huxley Heritage*, published in 1983 by the Huxley and District History Book Committee. For more general facts and understanding of the years between 1928 and 1939 I am indebted to Pierre Berton for his fascinating and enlightening book, *The Great Depression 1929-1939*, McClelland and Stewart, Inc. 1990.

The expertise of many people helped bring this book to publication. I especially thank Dr. Jim London, of *Classic Memoirs*, for not only his practical and professional advice, but also for his discerning and skillful editing. I am most grateful to Alison Makkinga, who not only typed the manuscript, but whose quiet patience and efficiency guided the work expertly through the final maze of technical requirements. Barbara Munzar turned my vague ideas into a beautiful cover and the friendly staff at Trafford brought it all together.

I send a special thank you to Maeve Binchy (*The Copper Beech, The Lilac Bus*) who, speaking at the 1998 Vancouver Writers Festival, scolded three hundred of us for not following her previous specific instructions on how to write and publish a book. I take her at her word that she doesn't exactly expect a *dedication*, but that an acknowledgment would be quite acceptable.

Village of Huxley, Alberta 1940

From *Our Huxley Heritage,* Huxley and
District History Book Committee 1983.

Huxley School, middle right
Community Hall, upper right
Nash farm was northwest of grain elevators, upper left

Contents

Preface

As my children and grandchildren were growing up, a realization crept slowly to my consciousness. I began to understand that, when I told them small anecdotes from my own childhood, they really had no way of relating to the early experiences of my generation. Our worlds had become radically different. If they asked why we didn't, as children, go to a certain event, and I replied, "We had no money," I could tell that they thought I meant we didn't have five or ten dollars to go out that Saturday night.

How could they know about living with coal oil lamps, horse drawn transportation, food rationing and no telephones? To me, as a child, these middle class children with coins in their pockets would have been "rich kids," far beyond reach of friendship with me. This revelation became the beginning of these stories, written primarily to provide a child's viewpoint of those years for succeeding generations who, it is to be hoped, will never experience first hand the desperate circumstances, and often hopelessness, that affected hundreds of thousands of Canadians in the Great Depression of the 1930's.

I offer this collection, first of all, to my children, Christine, Trisha and Avril, to my grandchildren, John, Myra, David and Jennifer, and to my great-grandchildren, John and Sara.

Not all can be remembered. Of that remembered, only a small part can be written. People will have experienced life and situations differently; memories will vary. These are a few of mine.

Kathie Nash
Victoria, B.C.
Canada

Our Gracious King

To a young child the concept of a King is pretty difficult, and to a seven year old farm child on the Canadian prairie in 1936 it was almost unfathomable. Television was years in the future, radio in our world was brand new and, to me, mostly unintelligible. In any case, in those first days it was switched on and off only by our father for the news, *The Lone Ranger*, and *Lux Family Theatre*, and no one else touched it, except to dust it. Furthermore, chores and homework had to be finished before any of us could sit in the livingroom to listen. Weekly and monthly farm newspapers and magazines reached us, *The Family Herald, The Free Press and Prairie Farmer, The Country Guide, The Western Producer* and *The Farm and Ranch Review,* but if there was ever anything in them that would have enlightened me about the definition and function of royalty, I never heard of it.

True, there was the King's picture, high on the wall at the front of the schoolroom, a solemn and kind-looking man with a dark beard, in a dark blue uniform, and by his side a stately, rather imposing looking woman dressed in white, wearing a high crown and many strings of pearls – King George V and Queen Mary of England. We knew they were *our* King and Queen, but probably

1

none of us really knew, at least until grade five or six, what that actually meant. We did know that the King was important, and we could see that he was rich. We also knew that he was to be greatly respected. For one thing, at every school function, even the really important ones like the Christmas Concert, we all, not only children but adults, too, stood to sing *God Save the King,* and everyone was very serious about it. No one dared giggle or whisper. We all stood straight and solemn, arms by our sides. This was so instilled in us that fifty or sixty years later most of us still leap to our feet, arms rigid, at the first strains of *God Save the Queen.*

No one ever explained the words to us so I, for one, did a lot of puzzling about what God was to save the King *from.* Having listened well and with fascination to all my fairy stories, I finally decided that it must mean in a great battle, which certainly fit well with "our noble King" and "send him victorious," though this last seemed rather poor grammar to me. I never did figure out "our gracious King." Even at that young age I thought it was a phrase that would more fittingly be applied to a woman. It seemed like a mistake on the part of the songwriter. However, it was all very stirring and inspiring and I sang out as loudly as I could on every occasion. He was definitely "Our King," whatever it might mean, and if he needed saving then it was important to get the message through clearly.

Since I was somewhat fuzzy about the order of hierarchy of

"King" and "God," it seemed best to just believe the song. Obviously if God was to save the King and send him somewhere, then God must have more power in some ways than the King. On the other hand, the King was important enough to have his picture up in the schoolroom, whereas God apparently was not. As well, the King had a song written for him and it was played and sung lustily and frequently. What God got each day was a mumbled and ritualistic "Our Father Witchart and Heaven, Hello be Thy name---." In fact, it took me until grade three to realize that this Father Witchart (also known as "Hello") and God were one and the same.

It is not surprising then, that the most impressive thing that King George V did in the short time I knew him, was to die, thereby incidentally diminishing my impression of God's power even more, since the King had obviously not been saved. If the concept of "King" was difficult, death was only a little less so. As might be expected, there was a fair amount of death on a farm. Small chickens and turkeys died and got thrown away. Sometimes a baby pig or a larger animal would die. Farmers routinely raised and butchered their own meat, but at age seven I had had minimal exposure to most of this, and certainly had not had any experience that would help me to apply the idea of death to people.

This then, was the somewhat confusing background of information with which, early in 1936, I attempted to understand our teacher's solemn announcement that "The King" had died. We knew as soon as we arrived in the schoolroom that something momentous had happened, or was about to happen, because the teacher had brought a radio to school! It was sitting on her desk, shiny and brown, and the students in the upper grades, four, five and six, and those younger children who were not shy, were crowded around it. It was not turned on, of course. We took our seats, hushed and waiting, and the school day began. The teacher then stood at the front of the room and made her Important Announcement.

I don't think she expected or got any response. What could we say? There he was, our King, still looking down on us from the front of the classroom, eternally ageless, and our teacher was telling us that the King had died. The two facts were totally incompatible. I heard her words, I knew the event was grave and significant in some way, but I had no understanding of what it meant to me and my world, if anything. If any of us were inclined to give the situation less weight than it merited we soon realized our error, as we were then told that we would be sent home at noon for a half day holiday. Through Alberta blizzards and storms, and forty below weather, we travelled to and from school, though many of us had three and four miles to drive or ride with horses and sleighs. It was taken for granted that we could deal with these things, and we did. The only time, possibly in the history of the school, that we were ever sent home early was on the day of the annual Christmas

4

Concert, which far out-ranked, both in preparation and performance, any other event in our school year. Now it became apparent that the King, or at any rate his death, was at least as important as the Christmas Concert!

At ten o'clock we were all instructed to put away our work and the teacher turned on the radio. We heard a great deal of crackling and some men speaking in dialects we could not understand, with voices that sounded like they were coming through water, all wavy and bubbly. This, of course, seemed quite logical to me, since we had been told that the voices were coming across the ocean from London. We knew what the ocean was – water. All that blue on the map. And then, at the end of the noise and crackling, and people talking through their noses, came one clear and astounding sentence, "The King is dead! Long live the King!" Then, anti-climactically, finally something we recognized – the familiar, if somewhat watery, strains of *God Save The King*.

I gave up. Never would I understand the completely contradictory statements of adults. We had been told The King was dead. I believed it totally. Our beloved Miss Hodgson would not lie to us. Now someone from the King's own town had just told us the same thing and then immediately shouted, "Long live the King!" It was beyond all logic and reason and, try as I did to fit those two statements together into something that made sense to me, I could not. When I finally became enlightened a few years later, I really

5

thought it was a callous custom, to dismiss the poor old King so immediately and turn all attention to the new one. It seemed disloyal, even traitorous somehow, and ungrateful. And even though, a year later I, like children and adults all over the world, fell passionately in love with the beautiful new King and Queen, George VI and Elizabeth, I still missed the protectiveness of my first King, "Our King," looking solemnly down on us with his blue eyes and his beard, from the front of the schoolroom.

.

_____

Our Gracious King first appeared as an award-winner in *A Writer's World,* Surrey Writers Conference 1999.

The Pigpen Roof

At the far south end of the very large, very full farmyard, beyond the kitchen yard, the weather-beaten garage, and the spreading accumulation of broken farm machinery, abandoned in the long dry grass; at the very end of the dusty trail where the fields began, and almost out of calling distance from the house, sat a low, grey stone building. Inside were an old well, musty and mysterious – its water no longer used for humans, great mountains of dusty, choking, sneeze-making ground chop for the pigs, and many families of mice. We went into this building occasionally, but there was no room to play and nothing of interest, only sometimes the drifting, chaff laden shafts of sunlight slanting through a small, dusty window. The chaff seemed never to settle.

On the other side of this building (called "the pumphouse" by the adults), and inside the pagewire fence extending west into the grove of maple and poplar trees that provided a protective rectangle around the farmyard, were the grunting, squealing pigs, jostling for place at their feeding troughs and sleeping shelters in the muddy yard. Beyond and around these low sheds, sharing the same field, were hundreds and hundreds of gophers, the mounds of dirt from their underground runs pockmarking the scrubby land that sloped down to a fenced hayfield. In the distance, beyond the hayfield, a wide field of grain away and a mile from the pigpen, lay "The Bottom Road," with telephone poles running east to west marking its location.

Except for the one or two summers when we had our small creature cemetery in the corner of the pigpen field (before the pigs rooted it up), or when there were new baby pigs at the pigpen, only the roof of the stone building held significance for us. Though it wasn't really part of the pigpen, we called it "the pigpen roof" and in our minds it did define one of the several animal areas of the farm from the living area of the humans.

Our parents worked long, hard hours in those Depression days of no conveniences, and Sunday was the day that work was kept to a minimum while they and the horses took some much needed rest. Except for the rare special happening, like a summer picnic with neighbours, or a family walk to the slough to pick wild peppermint, the only things expected of us children on Sundays were to be around at chore time, to otherwise amuse ourselves, and to keep out of our parents' way.

Though there were six children in the family, in many ways it was lonely for us. We four youngest, especially, had many things we liked to do together as well as individually, but visitors of any kind were the exception rather than the rule and we often longed for contact with other people. On hot summer Sunday afternoons in particular, free for a few hours from our own share of the farm's never ending work, when we had tired of holding concerts on the roof of the cowbarn, and no one felt like playing Red Light or hunting wild birds' nests, an aimless and vague restlessness would begin and someone would finally say, "Let's go sit on the pigpen roof."

We all knew what "sitting on the pigpen roof" meant and we didn't talk about it, although we must have at some early date, or perhaps our game just evolved. In my memory it was just something we had always done. Furthermore, there was the unspoken childhood superstition that if the desire was voiced the "magic" would be spoiled, and the thing itself would not happen.

Silently, two, three or four of us would troop down the trail, past the old dirt-floored wooden garage, which shared space across a wall with our father's harness, metal and forge filled workshop – dark, oily-smelling and also mysterious. On we went, single file, between the "machinery cemetery," on our left and, on our right, the gigantic garden of corn, cabbages, cauliflower, squash, pumpkins, cucumbers, and marrows, stretching all the way back to the trees on the west and south sides, and bordered on the north along our driveway by a long row of tall sentinel sunflowers.

I don't think any of us ever went alone, though we often left at varying times, as one or another became bored or tired of the activity. By climbing up the big wooden pigpen gate, it was easy

9

for us to get onto the sloping roof of the pumphouse and there we sat. From this position, facing south, we had a clear view across the rolling fields to the town four miles away. The roads that led from our farm to Huxley looked like steps of a staircase lying on its side – one mile south on the dirt road that ran past the farm, then along "The Bottom Road" one mile east, one mile south on the gravelled Edmonton-Calgary highway, then a short mile east into the town.

Few people had cars yet, especially in the years before I was about eight or nine, and those of us with the best eyesight could sometimes spot them on the first mile out of town, or coming along the highway from north or south of town. I seldom saw one until it had turned west onto The Bottom Road. Most of the infrequent cars we saw on the highway went on by that corner and this we expected, as it was the main road between Calgary and Edmonton. When a car occasionally turned west onto The Bottom Road our anticipation and excitement grew, though we were masters at containing it, and spoke casually and a bit pessimistically about where it might be going, to show that we didn't care.

We kept our eyes fixed on the car, holding our collective breath for a few minutes when it disappeared into the gully, just in case it had turned in, out of our view, to Jensen's farm. Even when we knew that must have happened, we would still keep watch, telling each other that it could have broken down, or had a flat tire – not an uncommon occurrence!

10

If the car did appear on the near side of the gully, emotions surged and the nonchalant betting began, "I bet it's going to turn."

"No, it's not."

"I bet it's going straight on."

"I knew it would go straight on."

The instinctive and perhaps unconscious rule of childhood seemed to be that it was not permissible to show or acknowledge any longing, anticipation or excitement and, having obeyed this rule, disappointment need not be acknowledged either, and perhaps might even be minimized. I'm not sure how well this actually worked. Most of the time the cars didn't turn onto Our Road at all, or even onto The Bottom Road, and it was not unusual for us to sit for a whole afternoon without seeing even one car, on any of the roads. With one exception, the yearly visits of our special "Auntie" and her family, I can't recall ever having a car actually come to our house while we were watching, though people in cars did come occasionally at other times.

Many times the only thing that got us down off the pigpen roof was the call to come set the table for supper, or do other evening chores. Once in a rare while, however, a car *did* turn north on the last mile past our farm and then all rules flew to the wind! Several, or often all of us, would run shrieking to the house, "There's a car coming up OUR ROAD!" And in those early days, before cars became more numerous and ordinary, even the older

11

family members would come out to see if they knew who it was.

Over "The Little Hill" it came, and if it was recognizable by then as one of the two neighbours whose farmhouses were further north along that untravelled, dead-end road, excitement dropped, faded away. Adults went back to their Sunday rest; children must find new occupations.

If the car was not recognized the ritual sometimes held out a bit longer and we might half-heartedly go back for a little while to the pigpen roof. Even if it went on by, as it most often did, we made do with a sort of compromise thrill. SOMETHING HAPPENED! A car came up Our Road! Most often though, the game was finished. Everyone knew that there was no possibility of another car coming up Our Road in the same day, and we didn't usually have the courage to go back to the pigpen roof, thereby letting the others know how really important it was and how great the longing to have that car come. What I always knew was that a car *would* come, if only we could wait long enough.

"Star light, star bright, first star I see tonight; I wish I may, I wish I might, have the wish I wish tonight." Childhood belief in magic ought not be altogether discarded just because one reaches "adulthood." We believed earnestly in our solemn and secret wishes on wishbones and stars, and I knew there was a pot of gold in the middle of my father's yellow wheat field at the end of the brilliant rainbow – our mother had told us so. It was puzzling and disappointing to me that I was not allowed to go tramping down the precious wheat to get it. I thought the adults were terribly short-sighted. Didn't they *want* the gold? I also, each time, made a firm, inward resolution that when I was grown up I would go through the field and get the pot of gold. *And* – the wristwatch I fervently and secretly requested every single clear evening for several years, did indeed materialize, when I was twenty-two! (But what is ten or fifteen years to a star?)

Little Red Lunch Pail

Oh, how I wished for a little red tin lard pail to carry my lunch in! Many children at school had them, and they came into homes with three pounds of Burns' lard in them. They were shiny apple red, with a big green shamrock on the side, a lid that fitted easily over the rim and a bail handle. There had been at least one in our farm home in my very young years. I don't know who got that one, and I don't know whether I had been promised the next one, or whether it was just my great wishing, but somehow I came to assume that the next one would be mine – a not very realistic assumption with six children in the family!

I waited silently for my mother to buy that kind of lard again, but she never did. It never occurred to me to ask about it, then or later. A few times she bought the kind that came in yellow, blue and silver tins, but mostly our lunches were packed in four pound jam tins that had no handles. The lids fitted into the tops tightly and were really hard to get off, especially if one had small fingers and bitten fingernails. I really hated those jam tins, and I hated what they did to my lunch. Square sandwiches packed in a round tin and bounced with horse and cart over four miles of rutted prairie road did not entice a finicky eater, as I was then.

15

The sandwich filling was usually jam, which soaked through the bread, so the sandwiches came out squashed, wet and soggy. Added to that, in the hot summer weather the tins and contents would be warm and steaming when we took the lids off. In the winter they sometimes froze. If there was a bit of brown paper in the bottom of the tin, it soaked up some of the moisture, but paper of any kind was not plentiful and was carefully saved for essentials. Plastic wrap and waxed paper were conveniences of the future. My mother's excellent baking fared only a little better than the bread. Cookies crumbled and chocolate cake got damp.

By June, and sometimes into early fall, sandwich fillings could be more varied, as there were the good fresh vegetables from the garden – lettuce, watercress, and a few times nasturtium leaves. Cheese was expensive and bought only occasionally, cut in wedges from the huge yellow round which sat under a glass cover in the Red and White grocery store in town. At our house it was used only for cooking, most often in Mother's delicious macaroni and cheese casseroles. Sometimes as a treat we got bologna. Of course, on the farm there were plenty of eggs, and we could take a boiled egg to school anytime we wanted. My problem with this was that the smell in the classroom with everyone cracking boiled eggs destroyed any possibility of my eating one. After World War II had begun in 1939 and we had ration books for things like sugar, tea and coffee, many substitutes for scarce foods came on the market and

Mother tried several. In my memory we never had peanut butter at our house, but one time our mother bought a wonderful substitute spread which we were allowed to use in our sandwiches. To me it tasted like pure chocolate icing with nuts in it, and I remember my surprise at getting such a fantastic treat. I waited for that to be repeated, too, but it never was.

In any case, since school lunches were, in good weather, eaten unsupervised in the schoolyard, I am sorry to finally make public the fact that nearly all of my jam sandwiches went over the caragana hedge. I did my best not to have to take them home. Wasting anything in those years of struggle was not permitted, and wasting food was a major crime. Occasionally one of the "town kids," enticed by our mother's good homemade bread and jam, would trade us a sandwich of store bought bread, which we thought tasted wonderful. More often though, they traded with the Andreassen kids for Mrs. Jensen's Norwegian pancakes or big cookies.

It is possible that our school principal, Mr. Ward, saved me from a certain level of malnutrition. He certainly saved me from soggy jam sandwiches. While I was still in the grades one to six classroom – known by us as "The Little Room," Mr. Ward, who taught "The Big Room," grades seven to eleven, instituted a program of hot school lunches in the wintertime. Who knows? Maybe he had seen a few jam sandwiches going over the fence. He

17

must have worked hard to get it organized and supported. Part of the girls' basement was partitioned off, a wood and coal stove was installed, as well as long trestle tables and benches. This lunchroom doubled as a typing room and a science lab for students from The Big Room.

The lunches consisted of hot soup and cocoa on alternating days. Families of the children donated what they could. From the farms came milk, potatoes, carrots, turnips, and other vegetables from root cellars, or beef bones when butchering was done. Town children's families also gave from their gardens or the grocery stores, and anyone who could gave money for cocoa, sugar, dishes, utensils and soap. Various mothers provided, and took turns washing, a supply of dishtowels. The girls and boys from The Big Room made the soup and cocoa (the first Home Ec class?) and dishwashing was assigned among all of us on a rotating basis. I thought it was marvelous! I loved soup and I loved cocoa, even *burnt* cocoa, if it meant I didn't have to eat jam sandwiches! There was lots of milk at our house, and it felt good to know that we were able to contribute, as we took our turn at carrying it with us to school.

Sometimes in the winter, when the coal furnace was on at school, we would take whole potatoes with us and put them just inside the furnace door. If we were lucky we had a really good baked potato for lunch, but if the furnace was too hot and the potato too small, all we had was a little black lump. I'm sure the school janitor turned many a potato through the years and kept it out of the flames, but probably a few fell in along with the coal. If the potatoes had frozen on our way to school they tasted terrible, even cooked.

Sometime in those years Mr. Ward also tried to actualize our collective mothers' optimistic dreams of instilling some hygienic habits into our heedless lives. One of the long former cloakrooms was turned into a washroom, with a row of enamel washbasins on a long bench and a bucket of water brought by the "big boys" from the schoolyard pump. Each family of children brought a towel and soap, and Mr. Ward installed large metal buckets under each end of the bench for the dirty water, to be carried out in turns by strong boys. At lunchtime we would line up to wash our hands. The expectation, or at least the faint hope, was that we would stand in line without too much pushing and shoving – or at any rate with no bloodshed – actually *pick up* the soap, wash *both* sides of *both* hands, *take the soap out of the water,* carefully empty the water into the slop bucket, then dry our hands on our own towel and hang it back on the nail. This fantasy continued with each child entering the classroom in a reasonably civilized manner, sitting at a desk and eating lunch, with clean hands.

I am sure I would remember if I had ever seen it actually work this way. Everybody was hungry. Nobody saw any reason at all for washing hands that *looked* clean, and all of the boys plus some of the girls had one prime and immediate goal – to bolt their lunches as fast as possible and get out to the ball field. The rest of us wanted to be first on the swings. So, people pushed and shoved and intimidated to be first in line. People grabbed their own or other people's soap, dipped it into the closest available water, fingertips sometimes getting wet incidentally, flung the water in the general direction of the nearest slop bucket, took a swipe at a towel in passing, if there was one left that was not on the floor, and rushed into the classroom yelling, "I'm pitcher today! You got to pitch yesterday!"

Poor Mr. Ward! Though he tried his best to supervise all of this, he could not be in several places at once so, after we were all settled down to eating, he would go to survey the day's ruin in the washroom. It was *supposed* to work like this: when a slop bucket was full, whoever had put the last basin of water in it would carry it out and empty it in the yard, or (ha ha) find a "strong boy" to do it. Invariably, at least several times a week, portly Mr. Ward would return to the classroom looking grim, no doubt barely hanging on to his tolerance and his ideals, glare through his glasses at the roomful of barbarians gobbling their lunches and say in his slow, dry manner, through clenched teeth, "Who tried to heap up the slop bucket?"

When I talked recently to my brother, Howard, about the

little red lard pails, wondering why we never had them, he thought they probably didn't stand up to rough use as well as the jam tins. They were softer, and when they got battered the lids didn't fit very well anymore. I had not thought of that. Over the years I have been in many antique, junk and "collectible Canadiana" stores. I always look for a little red tin lard pail, but I have never seen one. I still wish I had one.

Chickens Little - - and Big

Chickens, to me, always seemed to be very stupid, and as a child I never understood why some people, my mother for one, appeared genuinely fond of them. The only way I liked them was when they had just hatched out of an egg, clean, cute, fluffy, yellow or black – or on the Sunday dinner table, fried, roasted, or boiled with dumplings, as only my mother could ever cook a chicken. There must have been something different, too, about chickens roaming freely over the farm, fed with grain raised on the farm, killed on the farm, as part of the natural and necessary food chain, and cooked in a big wood and coal range. Try as I have, *I* have never been able to make a plastic wrapped, store bought chicken taste like that, and neither has anyone I know.

When I look at the paintings of the Canadian artist, William Kurelek, I am always in awe that he seemed to paint so many accurate pictures of me and my family. I think most prairie Canadians growing up in that era must feel this way. There I am, in one picture, at seven or eight years of age, bringing the cows up the lane, seemingly along the same dirt trail, the same fields on either side, the same willow bushes in the same places, every detail perfect except the colour of my hair. And there we all are in another, just

23

home from school, big black clouds boiling up on the horizon and skirmishes of wind beginning to lift twigs and whirls of dust in the yard, with our mother hurrying us in, exclaiming, "Quick! Get out and get the little chickens and turkeys in! It's going to hail!" She was always right.

Out we all rushed, trying to round up and corral baby chickens and turkeys before the hail crashed down on their heads and killed them. Some of the grown poultry were already in the chicken house, but most of them, big or little, seemed to have no innate sense of self-protection. They acted confused and stunned and as though *we*, instead of the storm, were the enemy to be feared. Maybe their innate sense of self-protection was stronger for the possibility of getting their heads chopped off than it was for danger from the elements!

The storm came down in a matter of minutes, first high wind and cloudburst rain and then the hail. We were all soaked in the first thirty seconds. The small chickens and turkeys ran in every direction except toward the chicken house. Big ones stood stupidly, getting wet, or else flapped into a tree branch just out of reach. We herded in as many as we could find and dashed for the house as the hail began, the next necessity being to grab pillows and blankets to hold against the windows in an attempt to prevent the hailstones breaking the glass. If our dad was at the house he helped with all this, but more often he was still in the fields and we'd see him

24

dimly, his tall figure striding through the hail in his big, battered cowboy hat, leading the horses in their harness.

Our dog, Teddy, a part border collie, had a much more highly developed sense of self-preservation than the chickens. At the first clap of thunder we would hear the slap of the screen door, see an almost instantaneous blur of black and white streak across the kitchen as Teddy, tail between legs, dashed into our bedroom and under the bed, where he huddled in the farthest corner and would not be coaxed out, until all was again peaceful and quiet, usually some ten to twenty minutes later.

Then came the survey of the damage, an apprehensive time for everyone. If we were lucky, we would find at most one or two tiny dead chickens under a bush or in the garden. This always distressed Mother. Each one represented dollars and cents, a lot of work and an eventual meal on the table. Often there was crop damage. In the spring when the grain was through the ground, the tender shoots could be demolished quickly, but sometimes there was the possibility of reseeding. If it was late summer and the grain was ripening, the stalk heads containing the precious grains of wheat could all be broken off in a matter of minutes, destroying the farmer's work and livelihood of a whole year. It was not unusual then, as now, for hail to completely devastate the crops of one farm while leaving a neighbouring one untouched.

There was always, for me, a feeling of lightness, of renewal

25

and refreshment after a storm, as opposed to the heavy, foreboding oppressiveness that preceded it. If damage was slight or there was none, everyone breathed easily again. Sometimes we would be sent out with pails and pans to collect the hail from where it had piled up behind the sheds, barns and machinery; Mother would get out the big wooden ice cream freezer and we'd have homemade ice cream. Depression farm wives were, by necessity if not by nature, the world's best opportunists!

In my very young years, there was always some excitement when Mother started "setting" her hens in the springtime. It wasn't until I was older that I really understood the reasons for all that she did, but I knew the special feeling of waiting for baby chicks to hatch. When a hen began clucking, strutting around the yard with feathers puffed up and sitting on a nest for long periods of time, (called being "broody"), Mother would provide her with ten or so fresh eggs in a clean nest of straw in the henhouse. She always marked these eggs with a lead pencil, in case any were laid in the nest later, so she could keep track of when the chicks would hatch. Mother tried to teach me to reach in under broody hens to see if they were sitting on eggs or empty nests, but I never learned to do that. The hens were cranky and didn't want to be disturbed, so they'd peck my small tentative hands sharply.

It was a slow process raising chickens in this manner. Some hens, when overcome with the instinct for motherhood, would make

26

hidden nests around the farm, in the grass among the grove of trees that surrounded our yard, or under the old machinery that dominated the barnyard. These nests were seldom very productive, since the hen had only her own eggs, one a day, and chicks would be hatching at various times, if at all. Often weasels or other animals would get either the eggs or the chicks. We used to be sent to search out these nests. It was fun to try to creep secretly after the hen to see where her nest was hidden.

Mostly the hens eluded us but occasionally we came upon a nest, with the hen quietly crouched in the grass, trying not to be seen. Mother would then take her back to the henhouse and give her a fresh "clutch" of eggs. Often this worked but sometimes the hen would not stay, trekking daily back to her original nest, even though the eggs had been removed. We also would occasionally find an abandoned nest in which most of the eggs were rotten. We knew this because we broke them with sticks and then ran, as not even a skunk could rival the smell!

One of my warmest memories is the thrill of seeing a hen emerge from the henhouse one day, or sometimes as a surprise from among the trees, having fooled everyone, with her newly hatched brood of babies, fluffy and yellow, and proudly introduce them to the chicken yard. We always liked it when there were a few little black chicks among them. I thought the chicks were the cutest things I'd ever seen, along with little ducklings, which Mother also

27

sometimes raised.

Before I was of school age, one of my chores was to scatter a pan of table scraps, to which was added a handful of rolled oats, in the yard for the chickens. I really wanted to pick up a baby chick and I often tried, but never could. I wondered why my mother could do it so easily. She liked her chickens and the hens possibly trusted her. She always stroked their feathers and talked to them, and they didn't seem to intimidate or peck at her as they did me. There were times when she had to help a chick out of its shell if it was too weak or tired, or if the shell had become too dry inside. We watched this in fascination, hoping that the little creature would survive. If it did not, and if we were given the egg to throw away, sometimes we children picked off the rest of the shell to see the formation of the unhatched chick inside. The adults did not seem to care or perhaps, being busy, did not know about these early practical biology lessons.

I liked gathering the eggs from the nests in the chicken house, especially if there were no chickens on the nests. Sometimes we would actually see the chicken stand up and lay the egg all warm in the nest. It was more fun, though, finding unexpected nests in the hayloft or the horses' mangers, or even in the doghouse. A chicken's instinct is to be very secretive.

One year Mother decided to expand her chicken raising, and she bought an incubator with a circular metal hood, able to be regulated to the right temperature. This must have been done with batteries, since there was no electricity. The incubator was installed on a table in a corner of the livingroom and two or three dozen eggs were placed in it. I don't know how successful this venture was. I remember watching some chicks peck their way out of shells and I also remember a lot of concern on my mother's part and a lot of discussion with Dad as they tinkered daily with the incubator.

Eventually Mother got into her chicken business in a big way, and began buying chicks. A special treat for us was to drive our buggy to the railway station after school to get the boxes of baby chicks that had arrived that day on the train from Calgary. Because we had no telephone, this all had to be arranged by mail. All the way home we heard the little "cheep, cheeps," and we would peek into the little round air holes in the boxes, poking our fingers in to touch the soft little chicks. We knew we were carrying precious cargo. The chicks were put in a "brooder house," a room in a shed set up with heat lamps under a hood, water bottles that dripped into trays, and feeding space. There they stayed until they were big enough to be put into the chicken yard.

I think it would have been easier for Mother if any of the rest of us had shared her enthusiasm for her project. Dad helped her, of course, in setting up the buildings, fences and any repairs, but he was already working long, hard hours with the rest of the farm. We children cleaned, watered and fed as directed, but I don't think any of us ever got really excited about raising chickens. One year, Howard, perhaps twelve at the time, had some chickens of his own to raise. All I remember about that is that he didn't have much time to play with the rest of us anymore, and that our older sister, Milly, made up a song about him and his chickens, a parody on the cowboy song, *When The Work's All Done This Fall.*

One year, Mother also encouraged her four youngest to raise some ducks, which we then might sell to earn ourselves a bit of Christmas money. The ducks got out of every pen and fence and were always eating up the garden; none of us had salesman instincts, and were too timid to go door to door in town offering fat lettuce and cabbage fed ducks. I think we went bankrupt. And probably ate a lot of duck meat that winter.

I missed the mother hens scratching around the yard with their own babies. I also found it puzzling and disappointing that bright yellow chicks grew up to be scruffy white chickens. I didn't think these long legged birds were proper chickens at all. I had seen from earliest childhood Mother's Barred Rock hens, fat little ladies in black and white checkered feather dresses, and later her Rhode Island Reds. Just the name promised something special. The pretty reddish gold chicks grew up to be fat fluffy chickens, with shiny red-brown feathers covering much of their legs, like pantaloons, glistening in the sunlight. Those big roosters with their red and blue tail feathers really ruled the chicken yard.

30

My guess is that the most unpleasant of my brothers' farm chores was cleaning out the chicken house. There could hardly be a smellier, messier job, and I knew I was fortunate that in our household it was not considered "girl's work." That might not have been true had I not had brothers. The most unpleasant chore for me was preparing chickens for cooking. I hated the smell of the feathers, as the newly killed chicken was dipped into a pail of scalding water. This loosened the feathers, which then had to be plucked out as quickly as possible. I never could do it fast enough and the cold feathers were nearly impossible to get out. I hated the smell as the pinfeathers were singed by lighting a twist of paper and passing the naked chicken quickly through the flame. I did not like the tedious chore of picking out the pinfeathers, made more difficult with my bitten fingernails. Most of all I disliked removing the insides of the chicken and washing out the cavity. Since there was little that I could identify, I spent a lot of time in the washing, picking out bits of this and that, fat or membrane, lest I later inadvertently get something in my mouth not meant to be eaten.

All of this, including the cooking, my mother taught me to do before I was twelve. Then, on one unfortunately too memorable day, she decided the time had come for the final stage of my chicken education. I was twelve years old and, said Mother decisively, "It's high time you learned how to kill a chicken. Come on outside."

I was horrified. I had not seen this coming. Without hope

31

and rather weakly, I objected, something I almost never dared do. In those days *no* children I knew of questioned or argued with adults, definitely not with parents or teachers. To do so would bring, not only a very public reputation as "the bad one," but also the immediate threat, if not the actuality, of "a good whack alongside the head." There were no "troubled" children in that era, only *troublesome* ones.

I had seen chickens killed lots of times, and had seen farm animals butchered. It was not my favourite part of farm life and I avoided it as much as possible. My objections were overridden. I am sure Mother couldn't see how I would ever become a proper farm woman if I couldn't kill a chicken. She knew it was her chore to teach me, so out we went for the lesson, my whole being in silent but violent revolt. Someone selected and caught the chicken, probably Mother, to save time. My reluctant efforts would certainly never have succeeded. I hoped the chicken would get away, and when that didn't happen I hoped hard for a miracle to save us both.

Different people had their own methods of execution, and my mother's was by wringing the chicken's neck, probably a more instantaneous and painless method than many. She showed me how to hold the chicken by the head and I was then to swing it round in fast circles near the ground, breaking the neck. Unfortunately for Mother's goal, both my hands and my heart for the task were weak, and after one pathetic swing the chicken flapped out of my hands

32

and into the nearest tree, squawking and probably trying to unkink its neck. I fled to the house, tears streaming, making as much noise as the chicken, heedless of my mother's insistent calls to come back and get it. Whether she finished it off, caught another one, or whether the family had something else for supper that night I don't remember. I knew that I was in some disgrace, but for once I didn't care. Though I didn't actually recognize this as the manifestation of the miracle I had asked for, the incident, or my inadequacy, did make a sufficient impression upon the household that I was never again required to kill a chicken, or anything else.

My mother tested me, mildly, one more time later that summer. She and Dad had gone out for the afternoon. Howard, fourteen, was off somewhere, probably working in the fields, and I was left with instructions to get a chicken ready and cook it for supper, with the help of Bertie and Donnie, eleven and seven. Nobody had said anything about who was going to kill it. I knew it was not going to be me. I also knew I would be in big trouble if there was no chicken cooked for supper, so somehow, among the three of us, Bertie and Donnie got appointed executioners. The details of that dispatch are best left unrelated. Suffice it to say that I was eventually presented with a dead chicken, ready for plucking and cleaning.

Now, I easily recognized heart, liver and gizzard, all treats for various family members, but I had not been taught to identify any of the rest of the innards. They were always just rolled into a paper and discarded. This time, however, as she was about to leave, Mother apparently thought of something she had neglected. She came into the kitchen where I was washing the lunch dishes in the big enamel dishpan, hurriedly pulling on her gloves. " Do you know what the gall bladder is in a chicken?" she asked.

"No." I had never heard of it. She explained to me carefully where it was located, I think assuming that I knew more about a chicken's insides than I really did. I guess she didn't know that I never actually *looked* at them. I just pulled them out and got rid of them and started scrubbing out the cavity, to me the most important part of preparation.

Anyway, she was in a hurry, and after emphasizing several times that this organ was like a small green sack, and that I must be really careful not to break it or the whole chicken would taste bitter, she left. I was then obliged to look at things. I didn't see anything small and green. Bertie and Donnie were presented with various anatomical parts as each appeared, which they took to the yard, broke and examined. (*They* say they were delegated; *I* say they volunteered.) Nobody found any little green sack. I scrubbed that chicken like none had been scrubbed before, and in some apprehension fried it up. I watched in more apprehension as the family sat down to supper, and I tasted my piece of chicken cautiously. It tasted fine, and though Mother made no comment, I took that to mean that she felt I had done all right.

I have always thought that the author of *Chicken Little* must have had a close experience with chickens. How else could he have described so accurately the chicken's typically paranoid and hysterical behaviour at a leaf falling on its head, flapping off in all directions, yelling that the sky was falling? I have not had any personal contact with live chickens for a long time. That seems best for all of us.

The Maypo Lea and the Pig List

The maypo lea, far emblem dear,
The maypo lea---forever!
God save our King and heaven bless
The maypo lea---forever!

What a wonderful song! And most of it made sense, too, in spite of Wolfe the donkless hero. At least by grade two I knew it was a maple leaf, and by grade five I understood a little of Wolfe and his dauntlessness. No cumbersome sentences here to bewilder young minds as in *God Save the King* and *O Canada!*

How I looked forward to the mornings when we got to sing *The Maple Leaf Forever* instead of *O Canada!* Not that I didn't like singing *O Canada!* I still do. I consider it one of the more attractive national anthems of the world. Well played, the music has a lovely flow to it that easily evokes visions of tumbling rivers and waterways, wide plains and mountains rising to open skies. A sense of pride in country was certainly instilled along with the learning of the song.

It always felt to me though, more of a "duty" song. Just look at the words "– True patriot love in all thy sons command." What could that possibly mean to a six year old? The only word in that sentence that caught was "sons," and it certainly made me feel left

37

out. What about all us daughters? Didn't we count? Putting "sons" and "command" together, I decided they must be talking about soldiers. No less confusing was " – we see thee rise, the True North strong and free." Rise? Like the sun? Like bread dough? And the True North? Eskimos lived in the True North. We knew that because we had made a little flour, salt and water model Eskimo village in the sand table and learned all about them. Obviously the song was not written for us, a group of prairie children in the True West. Left out again. " – We stand on guard for thee." Well, that confirmed it. Who stands on guard? Soldiers, of course. So here we were, singing dutifully every day, a song that was written for Eskimo soldiers, and I had no idea why.

When our teacher was sick and Mrs. McMillan came to substitute, we always got to sing *The Maple Leaf Forever*. It almost made up for the thing we *didn't* like about Mrs. McMillan coming to teach. Mrs. McMillan always made a "Pig List." I think, besides *The Maple Leaf Forever*, she must have liked art and drawing very much, because on her first day she would come early, and on one side of the blackboard she would draw, in a variety of coloured chalk, the most beautiful fairy imaginable. On the other side she would draw a large and handsome pink pig. When we were in our desks she would come around to inspect our faces, our hands, our hair, and our fingernails for cleanliness. This was called "Health Inspection." She would also ask each of us if we had brushed our teeth that morning. Of course, everybody always said they had. In our family often nobody had, and I suspect it was so with at least half of the thirty or so children.

In town, though there were electric lights, nobody in the early years had running water. Those who didn't have their own wells got their water at the town pump with a bucket. On the farms there was no electricity. We used coal oil lamps for many years, and later gas lamps. Water came from wells, or sometimes from a fresh spring bubbling out of the ground somewhere on the farm. There was such a spring on our farm, a mile and a half away through the fields, and we were considered quite fortunate. Our water for drinking and cooking was hauled from this spring by horses pulling a "stoneboat," a large, heavy flat sled on two big wooden runners, on which three or four wooden or metal barrels could be placed. It sat outside the kitchen door and we carried water into the house in buckets as it was needed. Hauling the water took a lot of time and was very hard work, both for the people and for the horses, and we were taught early to make do with very small amounts.

Brushing teeth was a major operation. This is the way it was done at our house, after we got toothbrushes at around six years of age. In the summertime, just before getting ready for bed, we would get a tin cup and a half cup of water from the pail in the kitchen. We then got a bit of baking soda or salt in one hand (toothpaste was a few years down the road), went out and stood by the caragana bushes and brushed our teeth. I liked the soda, but the salt always scratched my gums and made them sting. One time my mother told us that the Indians used to use the charcoal end of a burnt stick to brush their teeth, so I got a piece of charcoal out of the ashes and tried it. Once was enough!

With five or six children brushing teeth and one or two tin cups, it took awhile. In the winter, of course, things got a little lax. Nobody was going out in below zero weather to brush teeth. It was bad enough having to go to the outdoor toilet, an exercise we delayed as long as physically possible. Sometimes, if our mother was not too tired to nag us into it, we would brush our teeth in the kitchen and spit into the slop bucket.

At school, however, nobody was going to be stupid enough to say they had not brushed their teeth, and deliberately get themselves put on the Pig List. The next hurdle was having to produce a clean handkerchief. While the motives were sound, the expectations were unrealistic. Who had handkerchiefs? Sometimes the girls got a box of handkerchiefs for a birthday or Christmas present, not a coveted gift, by the way, but they were kept for "good," which meant the Christmas Concert or the rare occasion when we managed to get to Sunday School or some other church function, and then we usually lost them. Living four miles from town, with horses for transportation, limited our social activities.

40

When we had colds, which were chronic winter afflictions, our mother tore up worn out flannelette sheets and nightgowns into squares for handkerchiefs. These could then be burned in the stove. Sometimes we managed to save or find a small white rag to take to school. Mostly we mumbled what everyone else mumbled, "I forgot my hankie," and we were let off with a reminder to remember tomorrow. Actually, the only person who *always* had a clean handkerchief was Jean Clarke, who always had clean everything, from her shiny hair and her pretty white blouse and tartan skirt to her knee socks and shiny brown oxfords. Little Mrs. McMillan, who, to us seemed very elderly, never put any of the girls on the Pig List anyway but I, at least, was full of terror at the thought of the humiliation if I *should* get put on it. The most fearful times were when the teacher let the children take turns doing Health Inspection. *Then* watch out for the ones who didn't like you!

The boys did not fare so well. I don't think they often got hankies for presents, and if they did they tried to be as vulgar as possible about them. They certainly never called them "hankies" except to mothers and teachers. As well, any of the farm boys over the age of seven, and some of the girls too, were out in the barns doing chores before coming to school. Nobody at home had time to clean or check fingernails and ears. Fingernails were often our downfall. I can't imagine that any of us had particularly clean ones – except Jean. Our mother had a nail file, but she guarded it pretty

41

closely, no doubt with good reason. I don't remember a nail brush, and I do remember several brothers and sisters washing up in the same few inches of water.

So, what usually happened was that all of the girls got put on the Fairy List and most of the boys got put on the Pig List. This, of course, led to great persecution of the Fairy List boys by the Pig List boys. (They'd have a ball with it these days, wouldn't they? In those days "fairy" and "gay" meant what the dictionary said, and if the word "homosexual" had been invented I suspect that even some of our teachers had not heard it.) What I never understood then was that the Pig List boys didn't seem to care that they were on it. I knew *I* would have cared, and I also knew that I probably should have been on it lots of times, and that didn't feel very good either.

I guess the boys did care though, in spite of the way they acted, because one day they erased the Pig List. The rest of us were stunned. Some of us were also very scared about what would happen. I was in grade three, and even though it was the grades five and six boys who had erased it, we all thought that all of us would be punished. There weren't even any names on it yet, as the teacher had drawn the fairy and the pig the day before, after we had gone home. She was not at school yet when most of us arrived, and I watched with a mixture of anxiety and sadness as the beautiful fairy disappeared. I thought that they *could* have left the fairy. It really was very lovely. Mrs. McMillan must have spent a long time

42

drawing it.

The teacher arrived and classes began. We waited in various degrees of the traditional fear and trembling. We waited all day. Not one word was said, at least to us, not that day or the next, or ever. There was never another pig on the blackboard, and though I waited with dwindling hope, not another fairy. Nor did we ever again, with Mrs. McMillan, have Health Inspection. I mourned the fairy for a long time, and I still think of Mrs. McMillan when I hear *The Maple Leaf Forever.* Mostly I hear it when I sing it myself, as it was banned from Canadian schools in the 1950's or '60's, because some French-Canadians objected to parts of its lyrics.

I was quite upset about that and I still am, and I have made sure that my children, and anyone else I could coerce, have learned *The Maple Leaf Forever.* There are some traditions that are a part of our heritage, and just because they don't quite fit anymore does not mean they should be thrown out. They fit once, and that makes them valid. (*Lots* of us don't fit so well anymore!)

The Maple Leaf Forever

In days of yore, from Britain's shore,
Wolfe, the dauntless hero came
And planted firm, Britannia's flag
On Canada's fair domain!

Here may it wave, our boast, our pride
And joined in love together,
The Thistle, Shamrock, Rose entwine
The Maple Leaf Forever!

The Maple Leaf, our emblem dear,
The Maple Leaf forever!
God save our King and Heaven bless
The Maple Leaf forever!

Now *there's* a song to stir the imagination and rouse patriotism in the heart of a grade one-er!

Raised on Meat and Potatoes

When, in a recent year, I visited my cousins, Joyce and Glen, on their large Alberta farm, Glen backed his big, new combine out of its shed to explain its workings to my friend and me and tell us how much it cost. "It cost more than my house!" I said later to my friend.

"It must have cost him fifty dollars just to back it out of the shed!" Shirley responded, awe in her voice.

While Glen explained the operation to Shirley, I climbed down from the cab, as modern as my kitchen – and began looking underneath the machine. What a surprise I got, to immediately recognize, under the classy exterior, the shape of the old threshing machine of early farm days. Farming changed radically when farmers, my father among them, were able to have motorized equipment. I certainly remember the first big green John Deere tractor with the huge metal wheels, and later a "modern" one with rubber tires. Howard tried to teach me to drive that one when I was about thirteen. It was quite different from "steering" a horse and I managed to get the back wheel between two strands of the barbed wire barnyard fence. Howard's comment was, "Well, I've seen a horse get its back leg caught in the barbed wire fence, but never a tractor!"

Nineteen thirties farm implements, some of them still lying around behind old barns and sheds, some in large machinery museums like the one in Wetaskiwin, Alberta, certainly appear now much more picturesque than their modern, efficient replacements, but I have never found anyone still living on a prairie farm with the least bit of nostalgia for the old methods and the old machinery. As my cousin Edward used to say, "That old stuff? It's out behind the barn. Come see the CB radio I just put in my combine!"

Given the short prairie growing season, the delays caused by weather, damaged implements, harness (or horses!) and many other unforeseen circumstances, it is close to incredible that farming people ever got fields and gardens planted, grown and harvested in time and with enough produce to feed even the smallest of families. Our dad sat on the rusty iron seat of the old sod-breaking, backbreaking plough, driving the horses round and round the field from daylight to dark, while the heavy steel ploughshares turned last year's wheat stubble into long black furrows, or broke through untouched prairie grasslands to make way for new fields of grain.

There was also a one horse walking plough, which he used often to turn up the rows of potatoes when they were mature, walking along behind, controlling the direction and depth of the blade with two long handles and a lever at the back. The ploughing process, called "the breaking" if the land was previously

46

uncultivated, was followed by discing, using a machine with a long row of circular steel blades that cut through and broke the furrows of turned sod. Then a harrow, with its spike-like teeth, further refined and leveled the soil, breaking up clods of dirt and gathering uprooted weeds, much like a giant comb through tangles of hair.

Before motorized machinery, children could be much closer to farm operations, since all of these implements were pulled by horses. It was fun, before I was of school age, to run along in bare feet behind the seed drill in the newly worked soil. There were narrow platforms at the back of the drill that we could climb on to ride along and we liked to open the long box containing the seed grain to watch the kernels dropping into the row of little metal coils that distributed them into the waiting earth. Attached at the bottom were short lengths of chain that dragged along behind, covering the seed from the hungry crows and gulls that followed, sharp-eyed for a free meal of worms or wheat.

Four horses pulled the seed drill and we could easily catch up if we jumped off to examine an interesting rock, or even sometimes the remains of a poor bird's nest that had been overturned in ploughing. This all changed with the arrival of the tractor. Suddenly the fields of machinery became dangerous places for small bare feet, even if the noise and smell had not been enough to keep us away. While they were a welcome benefit for farmers, who were now able to open up larger tracts of land – though never

47

seeming to work any fewer hours, tractors changed the lives of children in a different way. I had a vague sadness, even at that young age, as of something having gone out of my life, though I was not able to identify it until very many years later.

Once the seeding was done, farmers hoped and prayed for rain, not a deluge that would wash the grains out of their shallow beds, but gentle, warm and nourishing showers. Meanwhile, there was much to do. Though our main crop was wheat, Dad also planted, most years, some oats and barley, which he usually stored in the wooden granaries and ground into chop in the winter, as feed for pigs and horses. A little cash was sometimes brought in by also grinding chop for neighbours. In the early 1940's, Dad planted flax for a few years but, I am told, found this very hard to cut.

"I don't care how good your sickle is, if your ledger plates aren't sharp, it won't cut," said our father, aged eighty-seven, out of the silence of the car, as my sister and I drove him back for a visit to Alberta relatives in 1983. Since this pronouncement did not follow any conversation of the last few hours, I had very little idea of what he was talking about, though I did know it was farm machinery, probably from the era of our childhood. I was also beginning to be aware of his habit of suddenly verbalizing a thought, far along in his process of thinking through a subject, seemingly with the assumption that his listeners knew what had gone before. (This is not a characteristic limited to the elderly, by the way, as I had a child who frequently did the same thing at a very young age.)

I knew what a sickle was – the long blade with the triangular shaped segments that was part of the mower, used for cutting hay in the field. Dad used to take it off after a day of mowing to sharpen those pointed metal teeth on the grindstone, turning the big stone round with foot pedals as he sat on the bicycle-style seat. Sometimes a child would be required to stand in front dripping small amounts of water on the turning stone to help the sharpening process.

Hayfields were wonderful places for children. Walking through the waist- or shoulder-high growing grass, sometimes planted, as with Brome or Timothy, but often just the natural, rich wild grass of the Canadian prairie, "prairie wool," always brought a sense of freedom and adventure. We pulled the green stalks from their sheaths and chewed on the sweet soft ends; we went to the edges of the boggy places each year to search for the rare and beautiful Shooting Stars that flowered there. If we were *really* lucky we might even find a meadowlark's nest, with its secret eggs hidden low in the grass. If we did, we always told our parents, hoping Dad would be able to go around it while mowing.

I liked the activity surrounding haying time. Perhaps adults were a little more relaxed after the pressure of getting the spring seeding finished, even though cutting and taking in the hay at exactly the right time also depended almost totally on perfect weather conditions. Mowing was usually started around the first of June, while we were still in school; we would come home to the wonderful smell of cut green hay lying in the fields, where it would be left to "cure" for two or three days, hopefully in sunshine. When I was about thirteen my father taught me how to operate a hayrake and I loved it! I had no problem at all in driving a team of horses (I'm sure he provided me with some very elderly ones) and round the field we would fly on this lightweight contraption, Howard on one rake, I on another, gathering the sweet smelling hay into the long row of semi-circular tines on the backs of our rakes, tripping the lever at the right moment to dump it, leaving field-width windrows of hay, ready to be picked up by pitchfork or by haybuck and made into large haystacks. These sat in farmers' fields like gigantic loaves of bread, as winter feed for livestock.

The haybuck, probably a little more complicated than my memory of it, seemed like a long plank, with a team of horses hitched to either end. This was used for making the haystack; dragged around the hayfield, gathering the hay we had left in windrows and bringing it all to centre field. As the stack got higher, the horses would be driven, one team to each side, pulling the haybuck and hay to the top of the growing pile (sometimes on a slide) where someone waited with pitchfork to shape it into a stack that would dry without falling down in the first winter gale.

One year, Dad was not using the haybuck. Maybe it was

broken. We now had to gather a rake full of hay, driving our teams right up and over the growing stack, tripping the load out at the top. I was horrified that I was expected to do this, frightened that the rake, with its big metal wheels, would tip over on top of me or that the horses would sink totally over their heads and completely disappear into the soft hay. The horses were not too thrilled with the whole idea either, but Dad, anxious to get the work done, and not very patient with our, from his perspective, needless fears, urged us all on. So up and over we went, clanging down empty on the other side, until the stack became too steep for the horses to climb.

If weather cooperated, often a second crop of hay could be taken off the fields in August, before the grain harvest began, near early September. As well, the rich slough hay was cut later than the rest, after the sloughs had mostly dried up.

The huge hayloft above the barn had to be filled with the drying hay and the large, open frame racks were mounted on wagon wheels and loaded high by hand in the fields, with pitchforks. The refreshing scent of new hay suffused the farm air. The mountainous loads, with drivers perched high atop the hay and the teams of horses looking miniscule below as they strained to pull their heavy burdens from field to barn, looked beautiful, scenic and picturesque. It was, however, extremely hard work for those pitching the hay into the loft far above, where someone else worked in the choking dust to distribute it. Whatever its satisfactions, haying time was also a time of blistered hands and aching backs. We were sometimes allowed to ride on the empty racks. I especially liked the more leisurely winter rides out to the field on the hayrack, now on sleighs, to replenish the supply in the hayloft. If there was a sled in the household it could be tied with a rope to the back of the hayrack for a free sleighride, but I preferred coming home tucked in the hay, sitting on the top of the world.

Howard has now explained to me what ledger plates are. These are the stationary serrated metal plates on which the blade of the sickle runs, low to the ground, back and forth, back and forth, similar to the action of a pair of scissors, cutting the hay.

In spite of his many years on the prairies, I have wondered, in recent years, whether Dad really wanted to be a farmer and whether, had there been no Depression, he would have stayed with it and found satisfaction in it. Certainly, after his marriage in 1919, he would know that he could not raise a family on cowboy's wages, but that was the life he obviously loved, talked most about and sometimes romanticized in his later years. No one knew things were going to get so bad; perhaps, as a young couple, our parents had dreams and plans for a little ranch of their own someday.

Young children usually just accept that their parents do what they do and, if they think about it at all, assume that it is what their parents have always done and will go on doing. In reality, our father's prairie farming days were less than twenty-five years of his long life, though in later moves he often had a few pigs or chickens around and always a bit of land.

It was not only difficult for me to understand, when he sold the farm in late 1943 and moved those of us still at home back to his childhood habitat in the Fraser Valley of British Columbia, it was really outside my comprehension. Other people sold their homes, auctioned off their belongings and moved away, not us. I had never even been to an auction sale until our own. It was disturbing to see each horse that we knew so well, the milk cows that we had petted, our beds and furniture disappear. It was depressing to come upon people digging through boxes in the yard, commenting on the worth of Mother's familiar household items, knowing by our parents' faces that these were not bringing the prices they had hoped for.

It was not that I *minded* moving away so much; I just did not understand where we were going or why. B.C.? The "Coast?" Where was that? The move was really precipitated by an altercation with a horse, resulting in a badly broken leg for Dad, that never healed properly, leaving him with a stiff leg, a problem for the rest of his life. However, as the accident happened in March (dramatically, as typical of the prairies, during one of the worst blizzards in years) and the move was in November, and also because no one ever explained things to us, I at that time did not connect the two events.

Our father, fifth child of an eventual eight, was the first of

53

his family to be born in North America. His young parents had come from England with four little boys, the youngest only a few months old, in 1895, and after a year of working around Victoria, B.C., and Bellingham, Washington, settled near the Canadian-U.S. border south of Aldergrove in the Fraser Valley. Here, on the original eighty acres bought in 1900, the new house that their father, John A. Nash, built his family in 1908, still stands at the corner of 256th and Zero Avenue – originally Coghlan and Boundary Roads.

There the six brothers and two sisters grew up, learning the small mixed farming methods their parents had acquired from a long ancestry of English farmers. The children helped take the produce many miles to market with horses and wagons over rough country trails to Abbotsford and New Westminster. Our father, christened "Bernard" and called "Billy," spent any spare time fishing, trapping and hunting with his brothers, along the Bertrand Creek that wound through the border country. As adults, we children heard many stories of that era from this born story-teller, usually beginning loudly, "One time, me 'n Geoff," or "me 'n Ed," but mostly, "me 'n Frank." Small, gentle and mild-looking, Frankie was apparently the daredevil in the family, obviously greatly admired by his brother Billy, one year younger.

They walked through the bushes to the old Patricia School on County Line Road (now 264th Street) and they dug clams on the empty beaches of what are now the towns of White Rock, Crescent

54

Beach and Birch Bay. Their father supplemented the farm income with carpenter work – building houses, barns, coffins, churches and whatever else his pioneer neighbours called upon him to do.

The situation of the brothers and sisters was perhaps rare in that they, themselves, were the only relatives that they ever really knew. There were no cousins, aunts, uncles and grandparents to visit; everyone else was in England and, though letters and cards were encouraged and travelled slowly back and forth across Canada and the Atlantic Ocean, only one child, Edgar, would ever be seen by those left behind, he as a young soldier sent overseas in the first World War, 1914-1918.

In 1916, my grandfather, John Nash, traded all or part of his Boundary Road property for three hundred and twenty-two acres ("more or less," says the Certificate of Title!) in central Alberta. He had never been to Alberta and knew nothing about prairie farming, but it must have sounded like a good deal, and his sons were growing up and leaving home. Near the same time he acquired a few acres in Fort Langley, B.C., where he built the home he and our grandmother lived in for the rest of their lives. John Nash immediately sent his oldest son, Philip, to Alberta to take the hay off the new acreage. Young Billy, then twenty and working at various jobs around Vancouver, the Fraser Valley and Washington, promptly followed his brother, began to work on ranches and found that he liked that life.

Our Dad occasionally told us, as children, "Once there was a cowboy who worked on a ranch. One day a pretty girl came to cook on the ranch and the cowboy threw her over his horse and rode off with her!" (Old pictures attest to the fact that it was not a horse, but a Model T Ford.)

John Nash only ever saw his prairie property once, on a train trip to Alberta before my birth, and none of his children stayed on it for long, moving on to make homes and raise families in widely separated areas of North America. As children, we did not know our far away grandparents, John and Alice Nash, except for one visit from our grandmother with Uncle Frank when I was about eight. She was then in her seventies and, though shy with her, I was fascinated by this brisk little dark-haired, dark-eyed woman with her English accent and her wonderful hearty laugh.

John Nash's Alberta acreage lay almost a day's journey to the north of our home, near The Imperial Ranch where our father had worked as a cowboy and our mother had cooked, before their marriage in December, 1919. I grew up unaware of the existence of my grandfather's land, and it was with great surprise many years later, that I learned it had been sold as late as 1943 by Dad, for his parents, before our move to British Columbia. It had not been a good investment, only providing our grandparents from time to time over the years with a little rental income.

The colour of autumn is gold and green,
And yellow and brown and rust and red,
With the crunch of dry leaves underfoot,
The cry of wild geese overhead - - -

I was four or five years old when I was lifted up to the high wooden seat at the front of the wagon box and allowed to ride with my dad the four miles, to take a load of wheat to the big red grain elevators in town. It seemed a long way and a heavy burden for the horses over the dirt and gravel roads. If Dad took me for company he was probably disappointed as I was timid and didn't say much. I was not at ease with adults. They all seemed large, loud and powerful, and usually dismissive of children. He didn't say much either, but he did buy me, in the Red and White grocery store, a one cent plug of licorice "chewing tobacco." These were little squares, made, I assume, like the real thing, each with a small round red metal tab stuck on top (nothing fancy like packaging or wrapping paper).

What a long time it must have taken to get the grain harvested, even with several men hauling loads. First, the ripe standing grain had to be cut. The long, horizontal wooden slats on the reel of the reaper, commonly called "the binder," went round and round, bringing down wide swaths of yellow wheat, feeding it into the sickle which cut it off and pushed it onto a canvas table. From there it was carried to the top of the machine, tied with twine

57

by a mechanical "knotter" into a bundle, or sheaf, thence onto the bundle carrier. This the driver controlled with a foot lever, dumping the bundles, a few at a time, into the windrows he was creating in the stubble on the cut side of the field, ready for stooking.

I thought the binder looked beautiful as it travelled round the field, horses moving at a leisurely pace, the area of standing grain in the middle becoming smaller and smaller. I'm sure farmers, working against time and weather, seldom saw it in this way. They laboured long, hot days on the hard iron seat and it seemed that binders were always breaking down in one part or another, necessitating precious hours out of the fields for repairs. If the knotter was not working properly, the grain would fall out loosely and have to be tied into sheaves by hand. Dad seemed to spend a lot of time at his forge in haying and harvest seasons. Our father, as most farmers in that era, mended and repaired everything possible himself – machinery, harness, tools, fences, barns, home and household equipment. He sewed up or half-soled his own and his children's boots and shoes, and shod his own horses. There was no one else to do these things.

For awhile, some of us had a yearly "secret" with a binder. Dad's conglomeration of old machinery, used for parts in repairs, took up several areas of the large farmyard. Among these were a few rusty skeletons of old binders, partly hidden in the long grass growing up around them. Binders had, attached quite low on one

58

side, a round, tall tin canister with a hinged lid. This was for the roll of brown binder twine, which threaded through a small hole and into the mysterious innards of the machine, where it tied itself around the correctly sized bundles of wheat, oats, rye or barley.

Into one of these unused, rusty containers, one year a mother bluebird found her way. "What a wonderful place for a nest!" she must have thought. "Look! Just the right size, and a roof over my head at last! Best of all, no way for those horrible, vulturous crows to get at my beautiful eggs or babies. I think I'll start building right away!" And she did. And we, who looked into everything, discovered her. We saw the nest, we saw the pretty mother bird, the precious eggs and the newly hatched young ones. For two or three years we saw them and then it all became too much for the poor bird. Mountain Bluebirds are by nature very shy, preferring to build and live in open spaces, well away from human populations.

Of course we thought we were being very quiet and careful, not wanting to frighten her away, but with several of us sneaking off at various times to look, wanting to be the first each year to tell the others, "The bluebird is in the binder!" I'm sure her anxiety level reached its limit, sending her back to open fields. ("Well! So much for apartments, crows or no crows! Let me tell *you*, Mabel - - -.") We continued to look each year but she didn't come back.

Stooking was begun, if there was enough help, while the binder was still cutting. It was important to get the sheaves upright

59

quickly to prevent mildew and rot until they could be threshed. There was also the danger of rain, which did less damage if the water could run down the straw stalks to the ground. There were usually hired men around at harvest time and, before my brothers were old enough to work full time in the fields, also at other of the busiest times for farm work. These were men, sometimes from other parts of the country, who found plenty of work moving from farm to farm, or perhaps they were sons from neighbouring farms, not needed right then at home.

One year, for whatever reason, we were all, even Mother, out in the field, trying to stook. "Trying" was my experience; I'm sure others were more successful. At nine or ten I had difficulty lifting the heavy bundles and I certainly could not get two of them to stand at the same time, with their tops leaning against each other. Quickly, several more were to be gathered and propped against the first two (which by now had fallen over), forming, theoretically, a nice little tent, with the sheaf heads toward the sun. Besides not having the necessary skill and practice, a hampering factor for me was the liberal number of large thistles and other scratchy weeds in many bundles.

If someone could have travelled by train or bus at that time, through those prairie fields, all he would have seen for several days, for hundreds of miles, in all directions, would have been thousands and thousands of acres of stooked yellow grain, dotting the rolling

60

landscape. It really was very beautiful and it is staggering to think of the labour that produced it, every single stook in every field put together by a pair of hands.

Then came the most exciting time of all! It was threshing time, the final work that was the culmination of all the months of sweat and labour. In came the awesome big silver-coloured threshing machine (also called "the separator"), pulled into the field below our house, in early years by a steam engine, later a tractor. In came the horses pulling hayracks, in came the men, some with their own teams and racks, some on foot or on horseback. In came the bunkhouse on its little wheels, parked just beyond the kitchen yard, very basic sleeping space for six or eight men (bring your own blankets). And in came neighbour women each morning to help Mother with the monumental task of providing five meals a day for up to fifteen hardworking, hungry men.

Traditionally, a threshing crew consisted of, first, eight drivers with hayracks and teams of horses to gather the stooks from the field. Two more men worked at the separator, one being responsible for any minor repairs needed and for greasing parts, fueling the tractor, and in general having everything ready to go. There was also one field pitcher, who walked around the field, helping to load racks where needed, and a spike pitcher, who stayed at the machine, helping to unload the hayracks.

Work began early, with sleepy men coming out of the

bunkhouse, or out of the hayloft, where some of them preferred to sleep. They fed and harnessed their horses, washing up at the bench outside the kitchen door, where two or three enamel washbasins, soap, towels and a pail of water with dipper had been provided. They then sat down to breakfast at the dining table, lengthened to its maximum with many boards in the front room, and were in the field by 7:00 A.M.

The belt was connected from the tractor engine to a cylinder on the separator and the great noise of the great machines began; orders were shouted, and off went hayracks and drivers into the field. Threshing crews, except for the farmer and the men who owned the machines, were largely made up of very young men; anyone robust enough, by the age of fourteen could usually drive a team and hayrack, and being allowed on a threshing crew was regarded by all as a privileged rite of passage. Though crews were kept working hard, there were lots of hi-jinks (not necessarily limited to the younger men) and often some lively competition to be first back to the machine, to get in the most loads in a day, produce the highest load, or whatever else they could dream up. Since time was invaluable, these activities were probably not discouraged, though sloppy loads, half loads or exhausting horses and damaging racks by too much galloping back to the field when empty was not tolerated.

The sheaves were pitched, heads first, into the feeder at the top of the separator where knives cut the twine and the main cylinder chopped up the bundles and sent them through sets of shakers. The wheat went through a sieve which took out most of the weed seeds, was then carried to the top of the machine by an elevator and into a weighted bushel sized container, which automatically dumped itself when full, into a much larger bin, or hopper, on the machine. This held about thirty or forty bushels. A wagon or a truck could then be driven alongside this bin where a slide on the sloping bottom would be opened, pouring out the grain into the vehicle box, ready to be driven to market.

As the sheaves went through the thresher, the straw and chaff from the chopped up bundles would come blowing out into the sky in a great stream from the big metal pipe, the blower, at the top of the machine, arching over to fall in a large yellow pile, building to a big, clean new strawstack. Even Mother, in the midst of more work than was possible, would take an unspareable moment to watch the beginning of this. "There it goes!" she would exclaim, as the first yellow cloud erupted, and we would be hustled back to our work, peeling endless buckets of potatoes, washing endless stacks of dirty dishes, with a feeling that Harvest had now truly begun.

Probably our mother never fully realized her reputation as one of the finest cooks in the large farming community. We certainly did not at the time; we ate at other people's homes so seldom that we had little with which to compare. It was only as we grew older that we younger ones began to hear the stories of the threshing crews' voluble comparisons of the meals they received as they moved from farm to farm. Many of them were not shy about voicing their praise, "You sure make good apple pie, Mrs. Nash!" which always flustered Mother, but we could see that she was pleased. Relationships, even with friends and neighbours, were more formal then than now. Threshers never came into the kitchen unless sent for something, and certainly not without knocking. One year, on the first day of threshing, the kitchen door opened and in walked our neighbour, Bill Wagstaff, probably then about seventeen. He went directly to the stove and opened the oven door. To Mother's surprised, "What do you want, Bill?" he happily replied, "I *knew* you'd have a big pot of baked beans for us!" [1]

Harvest was the only time our parents ever bought fresh meat from Mr. Musburger's butcher shop in town. Milly remembers huge slabs of bacon, "as long as the pig," but the main meats were beef, roasted or stewed, plus great mounds of fried chicken. For their early breakfast, threshers were served fried eggs and bacon, sometimes leftover baked beans, lots of homemade bread, platters of hotcakes, syrup and jam, or buns, biscuits or "johnny cake" (cornbread) and always both a big pot of oatmeal porridge with cream ("mush," as in "Eat your mush and go to

---

[1] Mildred (Nash) Michie, August, 2000.

school!") and fried potatoes.

Potatoes were a staple, served three times a day, in whatever way a potato could be cooked – boiled, scalloped, mashed, fried and in Mother's wonderful potato salad with its fresh eggs and homemade dressing. There were still lots of vegetables in the gardens and the ears of corn were ripening. Consequently, there would be many dishes of these on the table, both for dinner at noon and supper in the evening.

All meals for that many people, over the three to five days it was expected to take for harvesting, would be a challenge, but Mother excelled in her desserts, not the least important part of the meal for the men! Pies were probably the all round favorite, and pies came out of her oven by the dozen – apple pies, pumpkin pies, raisin pies, custard pies, chocolate, lemon, coconut cream, saskatoon, and rhubarb pies. Have I left any out? There were canned plum or saskatoon cobblers, and big pans of hot gingerbread served with whipped cream. Most desserts on the farm were served with whipped cream or fresh cream, which all of us poured on liberally. Between breakfast and dinner at noon, a plentiful lunch had to be taken to the men in the field, and another mid-afternoon. For these, many sandwiches were made with lots of eggs, or bologna, or there would be pans of fresh buns, biscuits or cinnamon rolls, as well as pickles, coffee, tea, milk, lemonade and, of course, always a large variety of cakes and cookies or doughnuts.

In spite of extra work it was an exciting time for us children. We didn't always get to eat the same things the threshers were having because generally they would eat everything provided for them, but there was usually the special treat of bologna in our school sandwiches for a few days and when we came home from school Mother would often cut an apple in quarters, one piece for each of us. There was always a box of apples bought at harvest time and it was the only time we had them. We could eat the peelings, though, as the pies were being made, and we did, watching hired girls, or other young women who were helping Mother, throw apple peelings over their shoulders, where each was supposed to land on the floor in the initial of the man the peeler would marry. I think there were many apple peelings very loosely translated.

The threshing crew rather fascinated us. We were not used to hearing the good natured banter that went on around the meal table and it seemed like fun. One time, after I had helped Mother set several pies on the dinner table, one for each four men, I believe, there was a little flurry of consternation when someone reported that we were one pie short. However, a big grin was soon noticed on the face of our young neighbouring farmer, Shirley Fawcett, in whose lap the missing pie was promptly found by his teammates.

We had strict instructions not to go near the bunkhouse but sometimes, when the men were all in the field and I was sent to the garden for something, I would peek inside – the door was usually

66

open. It was not very interesting, just piles of bedding and clothes everywhere.

It was pleasant at night, though, to hear them laughing and talking; sometimes one or another would have a harmonica or a guitar, or someone would sing. Occasionally one of the men would have to ride home at night, if he didn't have anyone on his own farm to do the chores; cows still had to be milked and animals fed. Everyone went to bed early; harvest days were long and exhausting. After the kitchen had been cleaned up, the cream separator and the milk pails washed, Mother would set the table for breakfast and organize as much as possible for morning, before falling into bed for a few hours.

Harvest was the only time I did not get really upset about missing school. Farm children were always kept home to help with harvest; that was expected and by the time I was eleven, with Milly, eight years older, away from home, I could be more of a help to Mother than just "doing chores." I loved the look and the feel of fall and I loved being out in it. It is still the most beautiful time to visit the prairies. The air was crisp and fresh, the leaves were turning colour, and the warm autumn sun turned the yellow fields to a burnished gold. I liked the things I was required to do, not just the usual old monotonous drudgery of housework but, "Do you think you can hitch up the buggy and go to town for some groceries?" Could I! I took the morning and afternoon lunches to the men in the fields, also in the buggy, unharnessing and feeding the horse afterwards, and I felt like I had been given a fantastic holiday.

With harvest completed and the crop either sold or stored in the old peak roofed, wooden granaries (which we loved to use for playhouses when empty), the pace slowed, but only a little. The big pile of weed seeds, shaken out of the grain and onto the ground under the threshing machine – buckwheat, stinkweed, pigweed and numerous others – had been loaded up and fed to the pigs and the shining strawstacks stood in the fields as testimony to the year's work. Frosty nights warned of winter's advent; garden produce had to be taken in, animals sent to market, and homes, farm buildings and all occupants prepared for the cold and snow to follow. Late fall and early winter, if mild, was a time of mending fences and machinery and shoeing horses. It sometimes even meant a day here and there for Dad to hike the fields alone with his shotgun or .22 rifle, occasionally coming home with a partridge, prairie chicken or duck, which he and some of the family considered a treat. Winter also saw him shooting or trapping an occasional coyote or weasel, skinning them out and nailing the pelts to the side of the barn to dry, before they were sold.

The old threshing machines were often owned by several farmers who had pooled their money; the bunkhouse and sometimes also a cookhouse on wheels were a part of the outfit. As farming, and life in general became motorized, methods changed. Threshers no longer rode in on horseback, but in trucks, and the bunkhouse disappeared. With the arrival of combines, also called "harvesters," farm work crews dwindled to a handful. We tend to forget now that most of the population of Canada, certainly of the prairies, used to be agricultural, with towns growing up around the grain elevators, to accommodate that circumstance. The city of Saskatoon discovered, in celebrating its centennial, that its population one hundred years earlier was 150! With less manpower needed, fewer sons stayed on the farms, and fewer men travelled the countryside looking for work in harvest time. Farms became much larger and towns, with their many conveniences, more accessible.

A modern combine, I now understand, is really a combination, refined, of many of the old farm implements and machinery – the binder, the threshing machine, even the tractor, as it moves around the fields on its own power, cutting the grain, separating the stalks from the heads, eliminating the whole labour of stooking. Though the beautiful fields of stooked sheaves have all but disappeared, along with the old laboriously slow machinery and much of the endless, bone-wearying work, harvest is still one of the busiest times of the year for farm families and, whatever the modern methods and implements, usually the weather still has the last word.

"Does this stuff have a name?" asked my eighty-five year old father, still eating heartily, but questioning the legitimacy of the supper I had served him.

69

"Yes," I said, "lasagna." Actually, I had prepared this meal in deference to Dad's lack of teeth. His dental plates had been relegated long before, after a brief trial, to his dresser drawer, to be followed shortly by a hearing aid.

"You weren't raised on this, y' know." Pause. "You were raised on meat and potatoes." We were.

Yellowleg Hall

When we were very young, before we were taught at around age five or six to ride the real horses on the farm, my sisters and brothers and I had learned to gallop around the yards and fields on stick horses. These were not the lovely painted hobby horses that are now available. Our stick horses were exactly that – sticks that we found in the sparse stand of trees that surrounded the farmyard. These horses were guarded, stabled and cared for; and they took on their own distinctive personalities and characteristics through the medium of our active imaginations. We would no more have thought of riding someone else's "horse" unasked than my father would have thought of walking into a neighbour's barn and taking a real one. And, of course, one of the most important and serious considerations was choosing our horses names.

In those days and in that setting the word "darn," as in "darn that cat!" was about the strongest expression acceptable around the house, and even so pretty much frowned upon if used by anyone under the age of ten or twelve. Stronger words were expected to be, and were, kept in the barnyard, used only by the men, or tried out by those who thought they qualified for that status and, certainly, never knowingly in the presence of women and children.

71

Our mother, a hardworking, capable farm wife from a large family, had been brought up in the somewhat sheltered existence usual for women and girls in that time and though practical and organized, was not what one would call "worldly wise." It is not hard to imagine her horrified reaction to hearing one day, her very small daughter galloping around the yard on her stick horse, slapping her thigh and shouting, "Git up, Sonofabitch! Git up, Sonofabitch!" Out rushed Mother to find out wherever her baby girl had learned such unthinkable language, to be innocently and logically told, "That's what Daddy calls *his* horses!" (I do believe there may have been some serious talk in the master bedroom that night.)

It seemed then that there was never time enough for play. In retrospect I think that perception came from the fact that our play, very serious and involved, was so frequently interrupted. If needed for work in the house, barns or fields, or for any of many other reasons, we were expected to go when called, not finish dressing the doll, not "unsaddle" our "horse," not complete the recitation in the concert on the cowbarn roof. Though the work was very hard at times and the hours often long, especially in the summer, in actuality we did many things on the farm that could be counted as "play," and we probably had as much play time as most other farm children of the time, perhaps more than some.

We thoroughly explored the windbreak grove of maple and

72

poplar trees that had at some much earlier time been planted around the large farmyard, climbing any we were able, learning where to find the yearly birds nests, checking regularly and carefully in anticipation, for the thrill of a nestful of beautiful blue robin's eggs, or the rare, secretive hanging baskets of the mysterious, brilliant oriole. We knew each tree and all the bird songs well, from the winter snowbirds, chickadees and varieties of owls in the night, to the robin's announcement of rain coming, or their bedtime song. We knew the lovely, intricate trill of the oriole and the voice of the shy meadowlark low in the grass – "I was here a year ago!" and "Mr. Mosquito, – *he ate* – a buttercup!" Many of the birds seemed to have two or more distinctive songs and we would creep quietly (we thought) through the trees or the hayfield, trying to spy the singer.

There was at that time a bounty offered to children for the collected eggs of magpies and crows, both predators of the young of many other species of birds, and also for gopher tails, as proof that this very prolific rodent, so damaging to farmers grain, was being exterminated. The bounties were very small, something like one quarter or half cent per egg, and crows nests in trees were very hard to reach; still, the search expeditions were hopeful and my brothers probably collected a few cents from time to time.

Drowning out gophers was a very much more popular, and certainly much more bloodthirsty, sport. It was often a noon hour or recess activity at school and consisted of crowds of yelling children pursuing a gopher through the yard until he dashed down his hole. Buckets of water were brought from the schoolyard pump and, with many shouted orders, poured down the gopher hole until the drenched and terrified gopher dashed out the back door of his run many yards away, only to be met, fatally, by screaming hordes of the enemy with baseball bats in their hands. All for one gopher tail. Gophers were also trapped, as were weasels and coyotes. Those boys saving gopher tails to turn in for money , if careless about their storage spots, were often in peril of having their cache thrown out by a wrathful mother who had tracked down the stench in her house to a dresser drawer or a young son's pocket.

We examined everything, we smelled and touched everything and we frequently tasted things, including the very bitter sap of poplar trees and bits of tar from under bridges and culverts, not to mention the tiny stinkweed seeds that Howard once conned Bert and I into biting! (Imagine a skunk in your mouth.) We climbed the inside barn ladder and played in the large hayloft, in summer empty and in winter full of hay, where we sometimes found new baby kittens, which either grew up to be more barn cats or mysteriously disappeared.

We planned and performed concerts on the cowbarn shed roof, I think with myself often as Director, and we occasionally tried to swim in "The Mudhole" in the creek. My brothers sometimes

74

dived and came up dripping mud, while some of us stood around in the heat trying to ward off horseflies.

One year Harvey, by then seventeen or eighteen, and often away from home working on other farms, built a raft which we floated on a large slough where the wild peppermint and watercress grew, in the field a half mile from the house. What a wonderful time we four youngest had with that! We "borrowed" a jar of canned peaches from the cellar and christened the raft "The Peach." Of course we ate the peaches first and filled the jar with rocks and muddy water before breaking it over the bow of our craft. We poled out to the middle of the high water and then had to quickly step over the top strand of barbed wire as The Peach slid between that and a lower one of the fence that divided two fields. Our destination was often "Gibraltar" – an old strawstack at the far edge of the slough which we could sometimes climb, a bit apprehensively, with an eye on our unanchored "tall ship," lest she float away and leave us stranded.

There were indoor games and outdoor games; summer games and winter games. While we were still quite small our mother taught us *I Spy, Button, Button, Who's Got the Button?*, *Hide the Thimble*, and later more complicated ones such as *Red Light* and *Mother, May I?* We learned many games from teachers: *Musical Chairs, Drop the Handkerchief, Go In and Out the Window, The Farmer's in the Dell, Here We Go Round the Mulberry Bush*. In the winter there were *Fox and Goose* rings in the snow, as well as the building of snowmen and snow forts. Sledding and toboganning were less frequent, as they were dependent on whatever makeshift equipment could be improvised by our brothers from scrap wood or tin lying around the farm. I think it was Harvey who also once produced a rather inefficient pair of skis from some old barrel staves. Ice skating was dependent upon outgrown skates of schoolmates or neighbours and, of course, the purchase price.

I was not athletically inclined and didn't like many of the outdoor games, especially the more boisterous ones at school, – *Run, Sheep, Run; Kick the Can; Prisoner's Base* – and since my sympathies were overwhelmingly with the poor wet gopher, I was successful often in my efforts to be allowed to stay in the classroom at recess, reading. This was not an asset to my social life and development, nor to the fulfillment of two of my long-held childhood fantasies – learning to swim, and becoming a world famous ice skater, whirling effortlessly around a rink in beautiful costumes like the glamorous Norwegian champion, Sonja Henie.

The once a year family picnic outing to Pine Lake, at that time an hour north by car, and my predictable resultant illness did not lead to championship swimming. I knew that I would get hives if I went into the water. Mother knew I would get hives and that she would have to nurse me, in bed for days. She nearly always gave in to my incessant begging. Last year was a *long* time ago; I had

76

forgotten or blocked out the misery. *All* the other children were in the water, having such fun! I always convinced myself, and maybe I convinced Mother, that I would not get hives *this* time. Unfortunately, I was always wrong. I did have my day of fun, though. The water was wonderful and, small mercy, the hives and accompanying illness did not manifest until we reached home.

A champion figure skater? Standing around in the snow by the flooded, frozen creek a mile from home, waiting my turn for one of the two elderly pair of skates which, even stuffed with many pairs of socks, kept me neither warm nor upright, resulted usually in my being sent back to the warmth of the house, making both me and, I'm sure, my brothers, a lot happier.

"My dear, dear, dolly came home!" So fervently declared our very small sister, clutching an old, worn, intricately turned wooden kitchen chair leg, which she kept wrapped in an equally worn piece of cloth. She had found the "dolly" somewhere in the large farmyard and the pattern of rings and ridges, with the rounded foot, no doubt suggested a simple head and body. Then she had lost it and searched anxiously, until finally Dad came upon it somewhere in the yard and brought it to her.

Bert, at that time "Bertie," and I had three dolls each. Our very earliest, except for my lovely little china baby doll that our grandmother sent for Christmas when I was three, (that Mother thought too fine to let me play with!) were our little sawdust stuffed dolls with what was called "composition" heads, hands and feet. Mine was called "Belle" and Bert's "Peggy," names either suggested by Mother or perhaps on tags with the dolls. I think we liked them better after they were thoroughly worn, their heads had got bashed in and Mother had glued on some pieces of the old buffalo robe. We were delighted with this alteration. It made beautiful hair, a rich auburn color that we could shampoo with soap in the wash basin and then finger wave. Later came Peggy and Belle's "big sisters," larger dolls with "real" hair. The tag on Bert's brown-haired doll said, "JOAN" and on my blonde one, "RELIABLE." It actually said "A RELIABLE Doll," but I only noticed the big letters, sounding them out, so, thinking that was her name, called her "Realy" for short. I got a lot of teasing about that but it was too late. Even though, when it was explained to me by Howard, I understood my mistake, she had become "Realy" to my sister and me and I couldn't change it. Eventually even our brothers just accepted and used the name.

Our dolls were very definitely our "children." We couldn't conceive of them in any other way. The third ones were our dear little "boys," Amos and Andy, fashioned after the popular black radio comedians of the day. They came to us one year in the Christmas parcel from our well- loved Auntie, who had made them from old black knitted stockings. She had stuffed them with soft cotton and embroidered smiling red mouths. They had button eyes and noses and nice thick fringes of black hair that looked suspiciously like the fur on our mother's overshoes. They each had little removable shirts and checkered pants with braces and they were absorbed instantly and with great happiness into our small "families," with not even a glimmer of awareness of ethnic differences. We would have been genuinely puzzled had anyone suggested such a thing. It is, I think, a mark of total absence of racism in our environment that no one ever did.

Though we were almost past playing with dolls by the late 1930's, what we really longed for, like every other young girl then, was an Eaton's Beauty doll. Eunice Lusk, an only child on a neighbouring farm across the fields to the northwest, had got one for Christmas and Bert and I couldn't understand, when our parents took us with them to visit, why she would rather run around outside with a piece of straw in her mouth, pretending to be a horse, than play with this wonderful creation. It was, indeed, a "Beauty" – large, with long curly hair, rosy cheeks, moveable arms and legs and, best of all, eyes with "real" eyelashes, that opened and closed.

We understood that since Eunice was the "hostess" and we were several years older than she was, we were supposed to be polite and play what she wanted to play, so we felt that we did a lot of galloping in return for holding Eaton's Beauty for two minutes. It wasn't the same at all as having such a beauty of our own.

One day, when I was not yet of school age, "Mamma," a roll

79

of binder twine in hand, took us with her into the grove of trees. I was curious and mystified as she went from tree to tree, winding the twine around each to form several rectangles at about our waist level. "There," she said, "is a playhouse for you." I was in awe that she knew how to do this, and we were all pleased and excited.

Of course we wanted more, one for each of us! We "built" several ourselves and our play in them became intricate and elaborate. We four youngest created a mini-society of our own. We furnished our "houses" with whatever scraps and discarded boxes we could find, with rocks or blocks of wood for chairs and tables, broken utensils from the kitchen, beautiful, broken pieces of flower-painted saucers and cups from Wagstaff's rubbish heap and, of course, our dolls.

My sister and I were "aunts" to each others dolls, and our brothers were the uncles. Throughout the long, hot summers, even when we were not actively at play, but busy with the many farm chores assigned us, our involvement in our play domains went on in our minds and with each other beneath all other activities. We managed our pretend households, baked the bread and churned the butter, sent our "men" to town for supplies (on their stick horses), fed and rocked and disciplined our "children" in sickness and in health, and visited each other frequently. "Pretend my little boy is sick and we have to come stay with you because you've got some medicine." "Pretend your child is bad and she has to have a spanking." The scenarios were endless. We built a large binder twine dance hall in another area of The Trees which we named "Yellowleg Hall." There we held many dances, though none of us had ever been to a real one.

Nor had any of us ever been to a funeral, with the possible exception of Howard, the oldest of we four and so our accepted authority for most areas of our inexperience. Many tiny chickens, ducks and turkeys died on the farm and sometimes small kittens, or even the occasional baby pig. Any of these small corpses that we managed to acquire was an excuse for a funeral. We used matchboxes, cocoa tins or shoe boxes for coffins, or sometimes Howard hammered together little rough wooden boxes. Our ideas of what went on at funerals might have been vague and not totally accurate, but we did know we had to have a burial and a gravestone; we also knew we were supposed to feel and act sad and we knew we had to sing.

Specific religious education and instruction were almost non-existent for us in our growing years. I never heard religion discussed in our household, though, as an adult, I realized that both our parents had come from homes where religious beliefs were practiced. Our father's parents had descended from a long line of Quakers in England, and in Canada his mother, at least, attended whatever churches were then available. In Dad's aging, story-telling years he once informed us that he had, in his childhood, "--

81

had enough church to last me the rest of my life!" Apparently he and his brothers and sisters were sent, each Sunday, to *two* different country churches within walking distance of their home. His preference, he told us, was the Lutheran Church, because of a number of rough-housing boys, whom he obviously admired (or joined).

Mother, I am sure, would have liked her children to attend Sunday School regularly, but it was difficult. The little white wooden United Church in Huxley (a former one-room school) was an eight mile round trip walk for us. Using the horses on Sundays was out of the question, and the nickel or dime for the collection plate often unavailable. At our mother's encouragement we did attend a few times, sporadically, but for me, with little previous knowledge, it was all quite confusing. I could tell that the other children had information that I did not.

My first introduction to God by name occurred in grade one, when we were required to stand by our desks each morning, bow our heads and recite The Lord's Prayer aloud with the teacher. I understood none of it. Having been told by Miss Hodgson that we were praying to God, I asked my best friend, Bertha, who God was. She told me confidently, "It's a man up in the sky who watches you and sees everything you do." Believing her, I found this reply very unsettling. I was afraid of men and I wished I hadn't asked.

When William Aberhart ("Bible Bill"), large, bald and

82

obese, came to power in Depression weary Alberta in 1936, with his Social Credit government and promises, his evangelical religion and his strange charisma, he offered free religious literature and Sunday School papers through his weekly radio Bible lessons from Calgary. Mother wrote away and got some for us. They were attractive little illustrated Bible stories for children and we liked them, but had no context in which to understand them. Thus, this small collection of random bits of information and misinformation, supplemented by the many hymns our mother sang, and the carols and Nativity scenes at Christmas concerts, comprised the bulk of my religious education until I was eighteen.

The singing at our small funerals was definitely the highlight, for me, followed closely by the loud and serious mourning. Our mother sang a great deal as she went about her work and we absorbed all those songs and hymns, and these we sang for the deceased, along with anything else we knew or thought appropriate. All of this took place by the miniature open grave in our graveyard in one corner of the pigpen field. We then buried the coffin, placed a rock on top and wrote a name and whatever we thought a suitable epitaph, or at least a date on the rock, with a carbon stick out of a discarded car battery.

One time we had just completed a funeral when unexpectedly through the hayfield came our friends, Ruby, Harry and Bertha Andreassen, from their farm a mile and a half away.

This was such a special event that we immediately exhumed the coffin and held the services again. Never had we had such a large congregation! Before the next summer the pigs rooted up our graveyard so we had to move it into Yellowleg Hall, which we weren't using much anymore. Of course, out of respect, we had to have all the funerals over again, before the reburials.

Under the clothesline on the north side of the house, near to the spot in the grass where we watched and searched each spring, noses to the ground, carefully parting the dead grass, for the first tiny buds of prairie crocus to push through, were areas of fine, bare black prairie soil. There we played "Little Farm," constructing long roads and miniature fields in the dirt, with cocoa tin garages, barns and sheds, blue Milk of Magnesia or vanilla bottle cars, trucks and machinery. These fragile little farms were frequently damaged or destroyed by older, unaware feet or by rain, hail and wind, so I think we often spent more time in the construction of them than in actual operation, an occurrence not uncommon, I have noticed, in the play of young children. We kept the same personalities as for our binder twine households, but these were very flexible and easily changed or modified to fit whatever circumstances might arise. When one of us was called by Mother for some chore or errand, or possibly even to go somewhere with her, that one might say to the others, "I have to go to town to get a part for the binder. See that the hired man gets that stooking done before I get back!" and off he or she would

84

gallop on a "horse," possibly not to return that day. Very much later in my life, thinking about our involvement in playing "Little Farm," I began to see why it is so difficult, perhaps impossible, for adults, even those doing careful observation and research, to really understand the complexity and importance of children's imaginative play.

When I was really very young my mother sang a song that made me feel terribly sad:

> I once had a beautiful doll, dears,
> The loveliest doll in the world.
> Her cheeks were so rosy pink, dears,
> And her hair was beautifully curled.
>
> I lost my beautiful doll, dears,
> As I played on the heath one day.
> And I cried for her more than a week, dears,
> And I never could find where she lay.

I didn't know what a heath was, but I felt very badly for the little girl whose doll no one had ever found. I thought the words were true and tried to think how I could help search for her. It was with surprise that I, many years later, by chance came upon the whole song and realized that my mother must have only known the first two verses. Though the lost doll had been found long, long ago, a fact unknown to me as a child, and the song ends happily, very early impressions last a lifetime, so that I have never been able to hear or sing *The Beautiful Doll* without still getting the childhood lump in my throat.

> I found my poor little doll, dears,
> As I played on the heath one day;
> Folks say she is very much changed, dears,
> For her paint is all washed away.
>
> And her arms trodden off by the cows, dears,
> And her hair not the least bit curled;
> Yet for old sake's sake she is still, dears,
> The prettiest doll in the world.

Charles Kingsley

Go Bite Your Belly Button

When small we called her "Mamma," spelled that way, though what we actually said was "Momma." By our mid-teens it was "Mum." Our father called her "Letty" or "Ma," as in, "Go ask yer Ma." Her own father was always "Papa" to her while ours was "Daddy" or "Dad."

I never knew where our mother's sayings came from, but she had many of them. I assume that they must have been common in her growing years with her family of eleven brothers and sisters. A few of these adages I still hear around today, such as, "Don't count your chickens before they're hatched," "Don't get your shirt in a knot," or less often, "Don't get your tail feathers wet!" I even heard one recently that I had not remembered, "Don't be a wisenheimer!" Most of the ones I heard as a child from Mother, however, seemed to be unique with her, as I never heard them used by anyone else, then or later.

A child's interpretations of adult communications are usually very literal and serious and, while I knew that there was often some joke in what our mother was saying, I seldom knew what it was, so did much puzzling over the meanings of her expressions. With several children pestering her with questions,

"What's that? What's that fer (for)?" she would often respond, "Cat fur, to make kitty britches. Wanta buy a pair?" It sounded like a riddle to me and I never understood it until I grew up. I thought she was saying, "Cat, fer (for) to make kitty britches." Maybe she was. I still don't know. The message that *was* clear was that she was in a lighthearted or cheerful frame of mind. It was her way of playing with us, in an age when parents didn't often do that.

Sometimes we recognized the nonsense and the fun, as in, "Go bite your belly button!" Definitely, in our limited world, these were very daring and risqué words for our mother to use and meant, we knew, in modern parlance, "Buzz off!" Giving something a "lick and a promise" only became clear to me when I had a home of my own and learned that often, for example, floors would have to get by with a quick dust-mopping, "a lick," when what they needed was a thorough vacuuming, therefore the "promise" to do a better job later.

Other expressions were also more adult oriented as, indicating time to get back to work after a break, "Well, this won't buy the baby a dress, or pay for the one she's wearing." I found that one very confusing, particularly because our baby was a boy.

While we may not have often understood the literal meanings of Mother's sayings, we learned to understand *her* meanings. If we were told our hair was "standing up, looking both ways for Sunday," we knew we were supposed to go brush it, and woe betide anyone who was told, "I could wring your neck!" A coughing or choking spasm while eating often elicited a sympathetic, "Oh, it's gone down the wrong throat," or "down your Sunday throat." The last child ready for anything, or to be finished chores, eating, etcetera, was "the cowtail," a label we hated, and anyone in a disorganized hurry was "running around like a chicken with its head chopped off." Having seen many chickens in such a state, that simile, though somewhat gory, was certainly graphic and understandable.

Mother's invariable and strongest term for someone she didn't much like or with whom she was annoyed was, "That old fool!" To Dad, on the other hand, irritating or not particularly desirable people – especially adolescent boys, when my sister and I got to the age to be interested – all came under one classification, "Who's that saphead?" This question seemed to fall into the same category as, "When did you stop beating your wife?" If we answered with a name we felt as though we were acknowledging that our friends or potential friends were "sapheads." We certainly did not feel free to say, "His name is so and so and he is not a saphead." (My best friend Maureen's father called all *her* boyfriends "goofs." "Who's that goof?")

We did hear a few seemingly more universal expressions from adults other than our parents. "Slow as molasses in January," and "too slow to catch cold" were common, though meaningless to me. The "whole kit and kaboodle" seems to have become "the whole kitchen kaboodle," as I noticed in a recent advertisement. The one I considered really idiotic was, "It never rains but it pours." Since I translated "but" as "however," it made absolutely no sense to me, like so many things adults said. They were going around saying that it never rained (in the first place, everybody knew that it did) and then contradicting that by saying, in the same sentence, that it poured!

I was startled one day recently while standing in line at a bank to hear a clerk say to someone, "I'll be with you in two shakes of a dead man's tail." I knew something was wrong with that and it bothered me until I remembered my mother's voice, "It's going to rain! Quick! Go get the washing off the line and do it in two shakes of a dead lamb's tail!" (Don't expect logic.)

Many of these adages seem to have fallen into disuse. I don't hear anyone anymore being told he is "talking through his hat" or is "full of hot air." New generations use stronger terms, people are "full of" more substantial material; the prunes and the beans my little brother was often playfully told he was full of have been digested and transmuted.

My most insulted moment in one of these situations came, not from my mother but from my older sister. Milly was around fourteen and I six or so. Her friend, Inga Jensen, was visiting and they were baking something. I very much wanted to turn the eggbeater so I stood around pestering and begging, in the manner of small sisters, "Can I beat it? Can I beat it?" until Milly finally said to me, "Yes, you can beat it! Go on! Beat it!" and they both then laughed uproariously. I certainly did not misunderstand that one and was highly indignant in my retreat. Mother would have just said, "Go chase yourself." My sister, Bert, remembers her telling anyone who made complaints, "You've got more troubles than your grandmother!"

Milly was the one in our household who was most often accused of "talking a blue streak." In our kitchen was a frequently used small white crockery porridge bowl decorated with a thin red band and a thinner blue one around the rim. A long lived family joke evolved from small Donnie's question to Mother, "Is that the blue streak that Milly talks?" Which goes to show that I was not the only perplexed one.

Sometimes when it rained we would be told to go out and "pull the string to make it stop." Milly remembers going out, at a very young age, to look for the string. All she could find was a length of ravelling hanging from the clothesline, so she pulled on it. Sure enough, as is frequent in Alberta, in a few minutes the rain stopped and the sun shone again. She was, therefore, puzzled and offended when her proud announcement was met with laughter from the adults. Milly also remembers an expression that I have never heard at all and she never heard before or since. One time, when she was an adolescent, Mother was very cross with her and told her, "If the devil carries you off in the dark, he'll bring you back at daylight!"

I understand now that many of these expressions, at least the ones that seemed unique to Mother, came from her mother's Pennsylvania Dutch background, probably originating with Benjamin Franklin in his *Poor Richard's Almanac*. Our parents seldom told us much about their own early years. I suppose they might have, had we asked, and I have often regretted that I was too timid to do that. As well, it simply did not occur to me. I liked it when Mother did sometimes tell us little stories from her childhood, but it was generally accepted by children that adults had the knowledge and if they wanted to tell you things they would. Questioning was not encouraged, not even in schools. We were taught strictly to be quiet and do what we were told.

Trying to sort out who was who in my mother's large family was confusing for me. I never knew most of them very well, even though her parents and some of her ten living brothers and sisters and their families lived less than fifty miles away, across the Red Deer River, in the region north of Drumheller. Some of these aunts and uncles I saw only once and some not ever, before they moved away to other areas. Because of uncertain weather and transportation, visits back and forth were limited to summer, if at all – the time of year when farmers were often too busy to make a day's journey. If there had been rain it was a very scary, slippery ride down the steep, muddy track to the small, hand operated ferry which would take us to the opposite river bank. Sometimes people had reliable vehicles, but more often they did not and, also often, no money for gas. If a car broke down on the way to the ferry or had a flat tire away out in the middle of nowhere, it usually meant a walk of many miles to find help.

Once we arrived at either our grandparents' farm, or one of the aunt's, other relatives in the area would soon arrive, and it took me a few years to sort out which of the many cousins belonged to which families. Since the adults were all busy visiting with each other, the women while preparing food and the men sitting around the porch, I don't believe I ever had any communication at all with my grandfather, and only once that I remember with my grandmother.

In the summer in which I was to turn twelve, one aunt and uncle came to our place for a Sunday visit, with a car full of cousins, all of whom persuaded Mother to let me go home with them, promising to bring me back in two weeks. It was an exciting idea. I had never been away alone before and I thought it would be fun, as well as a great holiday from farm chores and housework. Unhappily, it turned out to be the longest two weeks of my young life.

To my great surprise I quickly became dreadfully homesick,

feelings that were intensified by my aunt's unexpectedly severe and daily harshness with some of her children. Knowing the agreed upon date for my return home, and because I thought it would seem very ungrateful to tell anyone of my unhappiness, I felt quite trapped in an unsolvable situation, longing only to be back among the familiar. On my birthday my uncle drove all of us the few miles to the home of my grandparents, where various cousins reported the occasion.

My grandmother said to me, "Well, if it's your twelfth birthday, you should have a present," and went to her cupboard. When she came back she handed me my one gift that year, a small, pink glass dish – the free bonus from a package of cornflakes or puffed wheat – which I treasured as my one tangible connection to my Grandma Crocker until it got broken a few years later, while Mother was cleaning out the china cupboard.

For a few years when we were small, various of Mother's many single younger brothers, some close in age to their own nieces and nephews, came to stay for a time on our farm. Certainly our favourite and, I believe, our mother's, was our beloved Uncle Ronald, tall, slim and nice looking, with the characteristically dark hair and blue eyes of many of his family. He seemed to like children; he later had six of his own. Uncle Ronald always had time for us, played with us and told us jokes and stories. He was very good-natured and could always be persuaded to sing the many verses of *Strawberry Roan* for us while we clambered around his knee. I missed the visits of those young uncles as they gradually moved elsewhere and made lives of their own.

Another favourite was our Uncle Dell Price, husband of our mother's older sister, Etnie. This couple looked quite different from the rest of mother's family, both being rather short and stocky. Uncle Dell was a railroad engineer living in Kamloops, B.C., and he and his family were consequently entitled to a certain amount of free railroad travel. Most summers either our uncle and aunt or some or all of their four daughters would arrive for a few days visit.

Sometimes Uncle Dell arrived on his own, full of fun and jokes, always with new tricks to play on us; always cheering up the whole household just by his own smiling and cheerful friendliness and his innumerable "tall tales." We believed him when he told us that the train fireman, feeding the boiler with firewood, saved the crooked pieces for going around corners.

Our four attractive cousins, May, Nellie, Letty and Edith, many years older than we were and, therefore, always "adults" in our eyes, were kind and friendly to us. Letty in particular seemed to have inherited her father's generous, outgoing spirit and sense of fun, and willingly deserted the adults to join in our play and games, or to teach us new ones. Mother was obviously very fond of these nieces, and always cheerful during their visits, as well as a little less attentive to any misdemeanors of her children.

There was one particular story of Mother's that I loved and I always wished she would tell it again, or tell more, but I never said that, though I'm now sure that would have encouraged her. It was about her journey as a small child from the United States to Canada. She was born in Kansas, the third child of an eventual thirteen. Before she was two her family travelled by train to Kent, Oregon, and there they lived until small Letty was about nine years old. At that time they, along with some others, set out in covered wagons for the North Thompson River area of British Columbia, Canada, north of the town of Kamloops, settling finally on a mountainside near the tiny village of Little Fort.

It was then late 1906 or early 1907 and there were by then seven children, the youngest less than a year old. They brought a large herd of cattle with them and wintered over just south of the Canada-U.S. border below Osoyoos, B.C. The authorities there told them their cattle would never make it into the rough hills and mountains of the North Thompson region and advised them to sell the herd before crossing the border. This apparently my grandfather, Charles Deloss Crocker, did, before heading on early in the spring to his promised "free land." Born in the state of New York, orphaned and separated from his brothers and sisters when very young, all of his adult life he followed free land, led to wherever unbroken homestead land was offered by governments. He was still following it at the age of sixty-five, to the Peace River area of Alberta.

These were not details related by our mother, however. Her stories were of the beautiful green fields and hills of Oregon, the wild flowers, trees, grass and blue sky, seen through a child's eyes, so that I grew up thinking of Oregon as a very special and beautiful place. When I at last, as an adult, saw this little jewel of a state for the first time it was with a sense of recognition, as though I had lived there myself, and I knew why my mother had loved it.

She especially liked to tell of the time, as the children ran along behind the wagon – I'm sure some of them walked most of the way from Oregon to Little Fort – she found a braided rawhide whip, dropped by someone in a group of friendly Indians that often rode alongside the wagons. She was so excited to find it and, subsequently indignant, bitter still in her adult years that her friend, "Em," had taken it away from her. We used to hear quite a lot about Em, and I have assumed that her family was among those who also completed the long overland journey. As small girls, Mother said, she and Em used to sit for long periods of time, grinning at each other, with the points of pencils held tightly to their cheeks, hoping to make dimples.

Our mother must have been about sixteen when her father again uprooted his swelling family. There had been four births and an infant death in the years since Oregon. This time they went to live in one of the driest, most barren parts of central Alberta. This was in such stark contrast to the beautiful mountains, rivers and forests of British Columbia and the lush growth of Oregon that I can only imagine how the young girl must have felt about the move. There is no record of what her mother, our grandmother, Lydia Amelia Crocker, might have thought. Nearly all of Mother's stories to us of her growing years were about her life at Little Fort and Mount Olie, the mountainside on which they lived, and it was obviously one of the happiest periods of her life. I cannot recall a single story told by her about her life on the farms of Alberta. It was at Little Fort that she went to school, where she developed friendships with schoolmates and teachers, with some of whom she continued to correspond in adult years. We knew how special to her was the little china cream pitcher painted with violets that had been given to her by a teacher. Sometimes she showed us a letter carefully kept in her trunk, written by him in beautiful old fashioned calligraphy.

The story that thrilled and really scared me was about her father, "Papa," being followed by a cougar, more than once, I believe, as he came from barn to house with his lantern in the dark, after doing his evening chores. "Papa" could see the cougar's eyes glowing just outside the circle of lantern light, but he knew the animal would not come into the light and that as long as he, Papa, didn't run, it would not attack. With my active imagination I had no difficulty at all in seeing and feeling this whole situation, and this

98

created great problems for me for many years in going to the outhouse after dark, lantern or no lantern. It didn't matter at all that I had been told many times that there were no cougars where we lived. I *knew* there were at *least* wolves in the stand of maple and poplar trees that surrounded our farmyard, and the dim glow from the lantern was no comfort. I just felt like a more visible target. I took very seriously the fact that my grandfather was only saved from attack because he didn't run, so, every cell in my body swollen to bursting with adrenalin, eyes wide and heart thumping, I walked rapidly and rigidly to the house. It took all my strength to will my feet and legs not to break into a run, feeling intensely the hot breath, the leap, the sear of sharp fangs on my back, which I knew would come in the very next instant. If it had been five steps further I felt I would not have made it. Since admitting to fear was not possible, I had also to achieve, in the moment it took to open and close the kitchen door, a look of calm nonchalance which, if it didn't actually succeed in convincing anybody, at least allowed me to clutch my pride.

I have thought that Mother's life in the Little Fort – Mount Olie area of B.C. was probably the source of the many games she taught us. I very clearly remember my first game of Hide and Seek and the shock of discovering that another person could see me even though I could not see him, because my eyes were shut. I was about four and had "hidden" in full view on the bottom shelf of our library table, which was just long enough to hold me, and where my brother Howard found me one second later. I was very put out and it took some time to absorb the new and startling revelation that, with my eyes tight shut, I was the only one in the dark.

Occasionally one, or several of us would be called in from play to be told, "We're going to town (or "to Wagstaffs," "to Lindemans," etcetera). If you want to come, go wash your neck and ears." Not "your hands and face," always "your neck and ears." This now seems unusual though I had not thought about it nor even remembered the phrase until Howard reminded me of it recently. It didn't mean, of course, wash *just* your neck and ears. Roughly translated it meant, "Go clean yourself up, brush your hair and make yourself presentable," and that we knew without giving any thought to the actual words. It was just what our mother said.

I never saw my mother's abundant chestnut hair except in her wedding picture, piled high on her head, and in one lock, which she had saved when it was cut. Even before I was born it was cut short and waved, as old snapshots show, in the fashionable 1920's "bob." It had also darkened considerably, and that is how I remember it, contrasting attractively with her fair skin and blue eyes. Tall and slim, as we all were, she was the only one of us whose eyes remained blue all her life. Most of us had hazel or greenish-blue eyes, or brown like Dad's, and colors of hair ranging from Donnie's childhood blonde, through a few shades of brown, to

100

Harvey's black, again like our father's.

In my mind, two pictures of Mother stand out. In both she is standing at the sturdy, well used, oilcloth covered kitchen table. In the first, a straggle of dark hair falls out from under a white cloth tied round her head; there is flour on her forehead and her dark-rimmed glasses, where she has pushed the hair back. Her fists are in the large enamel breadpan and there is bread dough up to her elbows. In the other picture she is bent over the dishpan full of water, eyes squeezed shut, dress bodice down around her waist and corsets exposed, towel nearby and her hair in a soapy lather. In both cases it seems there was always a knock at the door. "Oh, good Lord!" she would exclaim. "Go see who that is!"

I have probably forgotten more of Mother's expressions than I have remembered. The one, however, that totally confounded me, that took me years to unravel and which, when I finally did, I thought the cleverest, most outrageous and most fun of all was the frequently heard command, "Go put your nose in your ear and blow your head off!"

Earthquake at the Seepy Are

How proud of my seven year old self I felt as I started out walking the mile to take my brother's lunch to him in the field. Because there were several of us, in our young years we were usually sent on errands in pairs, so I felt very grown-up and trusted when my mother asked me if I thought I could walk the isolated road, really only a dirt trail, alone. It seems quite possible that she knew the lunch would get there faster with one child than with two.

Harvey was thirteen and so, in my eyes, already grown-up. He was ploughing "The Seepy Are," a mile to the north of our home farm. We didn't know what that name meant, it was just what we called it. We had learned it as we learned the names for other things, "cow," "horse," "The Churn," "The Front Room." "The" was a very important word in our vocabulary. Having had little experience, in our younger years, outside our home, we only knew one churn, one front room, so "the" used in this way was really synonymous with "our." In other usages it came to symbolize a place and a whole range of experiences of that place, as in *"The* Little Trail," really a short path beyond the garden, but which we never saw in that way. "The Little Trail" was one of a kind, and the name denotes an aura. It was the place where we climbed a small rise through the bushes, only a few yards, to find Buffalo Bean flowers blooming in the springtime. It was the only place we ever found them, so the name came to mean a special kind of feeling, a mixture of secret anticipation and subsequent excitement or disappointment.

In the same way, "*The* Bottom Road" had no other meaning to me than the longest, most difficult mile of our journey to and from school – a road of heavy grey, deep-rutted clay, slippery and scary to drive the horse and cart through when wet, bone jolting when the ruts were dry. There were many such names for places, things, and people in our lives – "*The* Little Hill," "*The* Trees," "*The* Slough," "*The* Rawlyman," "*The* Gradge," "*The* Parcel, "Aunties," none of which, for us, had much to do with the dictionary meanings of the words, but all of which were understood in more or less the same ways by all of us, evoking then and still a whole rich range of feelings and experiences. It was very many years later that I learned what "The Seepy Are" really was.

In the early years of settlement, the Dominion of Canada surveyed the fertile belt of Western Canada into townships and sections. A section was one square mile, further divided into quarter sections, each containing one hundred and sixty acres. Large numbers of sections were reserved for grants to railway companies, resulting in the granting of over thirteen million acres in Alberta to the Canadian Pacific Railway (C.P.R.) and its subsidiary companies. The companies subsequently leased or sold some of the land to farmers.

The C.P.R., I am told, doesn't own much land now, but at that time they did own the west half of a section one mile north of our quarter section home farm, and our father had either a long term lease on it, or perhaps a lease-to-purchase agreement. At any rate, there it was, known to us only as "The Seepy Are," and never referred to in any other way. Since I did not ever have occasion to see it written, and since it was miles from any railroad, it never occurred to me in my growing years to make any connection.

I hiked along happily on the deserted road, my bare feet scuffling up the soft, sun-warm dust, watching for butterflies, wild flowers and birds. I passed the small stand of poplar trees whose round leaves we used for "pretend" money, and in whose rustling shade we searched for tiny, sweet wild strawberries. I came to the place by the neighbour's fence where they threw away broken or worn out farm and household equipment. How many treasures it contained for us to use in our playhouses among the trees! It was exciting to find beautiful pieces of broken dishes, with flowers and patterns on them such as we did not have in our house, probably part of the good china Mrs. Wagstaff had brought with her from Ontario. I walked on by, very conscious of the fact that I was being trusted not to dawdle on the way, and soon I came to the barbed wire fence enclosing "The Seepy Are."

I climbed through the fence and could see Harvey further out in the field. In a short while he drew the horses and plough up to where I waited. I liked our saddle horses and was not afraid of them, but these work horses were unfamiliar to me and seemed huge. Possibly they were Dad's two old Clydesdales, Dick and Jack, who I thought had the most enormous feet imaginable. Harvey told me they wouldn't hurt me, so I sat down beside him on a thick solid stretch of newly turned sod and watched him eat his lunch.

I had a question that had been bothering me for some days, and now it came to mind again. I loved going to school, learning excited me and I did my schoolwork with enthusiasm, so I was often finished exercises before the allotted time. Then there was nothing I liked so much, other than reading a book, as listening to the lessons of the children in the higher grades. In this way I had recently heard a new word, but listen as I did, I couldn't hear anything that gave me a clue as to its meaning. I decided that I would ask Harvey. I knew that he would know. Grown-ups knew everything. "What," I asked him, "is an earthquake?"

He replied, "An earthquake? Well, if you just wait a little while, I'll show you one." I waited. He ate his sandwiches. In a few minutes he leaned down, peering into the rich black dirt in the furrow at our feet. "Come here," he said, and I got down on hands and knees beside him, nose near the ground. "See that?" he asked,

106

pointing with his finger to the teeniest, tiniest little red spider, no bigger than a pinpoint, hurrying over the dirt.

"Yes," I said, holding my breath.

"That," said my all-wise, all-knowing, grown-up thirteen year old brother, his face and manner conveying nothing but kind and serious generosity in passing on his advanced and superior knowledge to his little sister, "is an earthquake."

He never enlightened me. I went around for a long time, at least until I told someone else, thinking I had seen an earthquake.

The Kitchen Cabinet

Two little brothers, early one Sunday morning, pulled the kitchen cabinet over on top of themselves. They were up before the rest of the family on this day that our parents traditionally slept in with no disturbance, a rule that was established early and firmly in our household routine. ("Sleeping in" would have meant rising at eight o'clock rather than at five or six.) Howard, the youngest of the two brothers, wanted something from the top of the cabinet, where a space of only a few inches from the sloped ceiling was stuffed with odds and ends of paper, bills, string and assorted small items which had no assigned location elsewhere.

Using a chair, Howard climbed onto the linoleum-covered countertop and, on his knees, hung onto the top ledge of the cabinet. Harvey, older by nearly four years, told him to get down and, finding himself ignored, began pulling on his little brother, who hung on determinedly.

Suddenly, whatever screws or nails which held the top section of the cupboards to the counter gave way, and forward it all came crashing onto the kitchen floor – crockery and dishes flying out of the two glass-paned side cupboards, rolled oats and sugar from the tin pull-out bins underneath, all the jumble of items which had been stuffed onto the cabinet top and, somewhere amidst it all, two little boys. Fortunately, they were not hurt – yet. Needless to say, *that* adventure got the rest of the household out of bed!

Given the disparity between what is considered "essential" in modern North American kitchens – gas or electric stoves, refrigerators, dishwashers, any number of small electric appliances and conveniences, as well as numerous storage cupboards stocked abundantly with dishes, cutlery, food and a large assortment of cooking utensils and equipment – and the contents of the majority of Depression Era kitchens, it is astonishing to realize the number and variety of meals that were put on tables in those years. In our home all cooking, baking, food preparation and dishwashing centred around the kitchen cabinet, known always as The Cabinet. This comparatively small piece of furniture contained *all* of the everyday dishes, cutlery, serving bowls and baking utensils for eight people, as well as many of our staple foods.

There was no set of "company dishes." There were, in a built-in, glass- doored china cupboard in the front room, a few pieces left of a china tea set, a platter, a glass berry bowl and a few other precious pieces, no doubt mostly wedding gifts to our parents, as had been the chest of Roger's silver plate cutlery.

The maplewood cabinet sat in a corner of the kitchen, adjacent to the big black cast iron coal and wood stove, with the door of a small bedroom – the "girl's room" – between. (The "boy's room" was at the end of a short hallway off the front room.) Similar in style to present day china cupboards or baker's racks, this utilitarian piece of furniture consisted of, in the lower section, four or five drawers down the centre, a cupboard door to the right and, on the left, a big tip-out hinged bin which held close to one hundred pounds of flour and a battered tin scoop. Originally the counter top had been tin or zinc covered, but when this became cracked and unsanitary Dad covered it with a piece of linoleum. A large, wooden, well used, pull-out baking board fitted under the counter. The top section of the cabinet had, as well as the two side cupboards, a shorter, mirrored centre cupboard with a small shelf or drawer beneath it. On these inner shelves, Mother kept the few spices and flavourings she used, as well as the small supply of salves and medications then available.

This cupboard was called The Medicine Cupboard. Sometimes medicine bottles were too large to fit on the crowded shelves, and would get poured into something smaller – a hazardous practice, as Milly found out when she once, at a young age, flavoured a cake with red liniment, from a vanilla bottle. The Medicine Cupboard had a little latch that had to be turned to open, which fortunately saved its contents in the Great Cabinet Tip-Over.

The curved tin bottoms of the rolled oat and sugar bins were quite battered and the mirror on the medicine cupboard foggy, with a crack across one corner. Since very little in the way of equipment

111

and furnishings that came into our home was new, the cabinet had quite probably also been bought at some auction sale. Each year many farm families across the depressed and drought-stricken prairies were forced to sell their meagre belongings for what little they could get, abandon their farms and try to start over in another part of the country.

When my sister, Bert, and I were very small we often crept out to The Cabinet in our nightgowns, while the older people sat with the coal-oil lamp in the front room, and in the darkness took a handful each of rolled oats and sugar from their bins. This mixture we put under our pillows and proceeded to eat. We inevitably got a good scolding the next day, and we could never figure out how our mother knew about our petty theft.

Except for Sundays, when the treat was either hotcakes or corn flakes, our standard breakfast was oatmeal porridge ("mush"), sprinkled with sugar and liberally flooded with whole milk or cream. I was fortunate in that I liked porridge. Those who did not had to eat some anyway, coaxed or prodded, and could otherwise fill up on toast, if there was time to make it before leaving for school. This was a slow process, two slices at a time, using an old, black wire, hand-held toasting rack, over the flame – or, if lucky, embers – of the firebox, with one round top lid removed. Leftover mush, cooled and congealed, was occasionally also our supper, if Dad was away or working late in the fields. It was sliced and

112

browned in butter in the big cast iron frying pan, served with more butter and homemade maple syrup – just boiled and flavoured sugar and water.

If there was ever a shortage of food in our home or a concern of our parents about that possibility, we didn't know that. There were shortages of certain foods at certain times, mostly coinciding with seasons, weather and World War II, so there was a certain predictability about meals. Sometimes the sternly enforced requirement to "clean up your plate!" became difficult, especially when it was the winter standby, stewed prunes. Bread crusts, avoided at times because of tender, cavity-ridden teeth, were fished out from under the edges of our plates, and dessert withheld until they were eaten.

Potatoes, heavily relied upon and served two, and sometimes three times a day – boiled, mashed, scalloped or fried – by early spring would be getting soft and wrinkled, and growing long sprouts in their cellar bins. These "eyes" and sprouts would be cut out and planted for that year's new crop, and it took much time to dig through the bins for enough firm potatoes to cook. Most of the other root vegetables in the cellar were used up or had rotted earlier, and meals for the remainder of the winter and spring relied upon those few items that had been successfully preserved – green beans, beets, peas, beef, plums and saskatoons. Most of the chickens had stopped laying and the few left were becoming old and tough, but they made tasty suppers, boiled with dumplings.

Only milk seemed plentiful year round and was, therefore, used in as many ways as Mother's imagination allowed. All gravies and sauces were made with milk; wonderful cream soups were served frequently – potato and onion, corn, tomato – as well as boiled onions in cream sauce. Desserts included many milk puddings, vanilla and chocolate thickened with cornstarch, rice pudding, bread pudding, big old-fashioned tapioca which had to be soaked overnight, and delicious egg-yellow baked custards, all of which were eaten with fresh, rich cream.

Mother baked bread two or three times a week, saving the water from boiled potatoes for this. Fast rising yeast was not then available, and the hard little square cakes of Royal yeast had to be crumbled and soaked, mixed with water, sugar and some flour and set in a runny "sponge" in a large kettle, to rise overnight on top of the warming oven – the cupboard-like compartment built as part of and above the cookstove, to hold pots and cooking equipment. The final stages of bread baking usually included buns or cinnamon rolls. If the bread bin was empty and the new batch not yet baked, there were often biscuits for supper. Sometimes Mother would cut some slices from the rising dough and fry it for us – delicious!

Dried white beans, cornmeal for porridge, or more often "johnnycake" (served warm with butter and syrup), and macaroni were all year round staples. Macaroni was most often used in a

114

casserole with canned tomatoes, dressed up with a sprinkling of breadcrumbs and butter, but a special treat was the occasional macaroni and cheese dish. I once watched Mother at her bake board, on the kitchen table as usual, efficiently rolling out noodle dough, yellow with eggs and whole milk. She cut the soft dough into long, thin strips with a knife and boiled them to serve with the chicken (old hen) stew. Everyone liked them and I assumed that the reason we had them so infrequently was because it took such a long time to make enough for our large family.

Homemade cake doughnuts took a long time as well, and always created some excitement for us. "She's making doughnuts!" someone would exclaim as we drove our school buggy into the yard, where our nostrils were assailed by the heavenly smell of boiling fat and warm, sweet, sugar coated doughnuts. We loved to watch them floating and bubbling in the big pot, sizzling brown at the edges, turned over by Mother at exactly the right moment, while she regulated the temperature of the fat only by the amount of wood she fed the stove, or the position of the kettle on the heat. Lifted out with a slotted spoon, the doughnuts were drained on saved pieces of brown paper before being rolled in sugar, cooled and stored.

We stood around, begging Mother to cook more of "the holes" – the little round centres left by her tin doughnut cutter, and she often did, but eventually ended our commotion with, "That's enough, now! Take one each and go get changed and do your chores." The doughnuts went into a mouse-proof covered crock in the front room lower cupboard, beside the big old copper boiler that held the loaves of bread; after one doughnut each for that evening's dessert, Mother doled out the remaining treats sparingly.

Sometimes it would be our mother's large, fat white cookies that were being rolled out on the baking board. When very young we would be supplied with thimbles and, noses at the table edge, allowed to cut out our own tiny cookies. Mother's rolling pin had one red handle broken off at some earlier time, but I didn't know that, and learned to use it as she did, fairly efficiently, if not as speedily. When I first saw, many years later, a two-handled rolling pin, I thought it had been incorrectly made, and continued, in my adult life to ignore one, to me, superfluous handle.

The long winters always ended, gardens were dug and planted and in early summer, tiny bits of green began to push through the soft soil. We were sent out to pick new little leaves of dandelions or pigweed for cooked greens, leaves which would turn tough and bitter in only a week or two. Finally, finally, one day upon the table would be placed a most delicious meal, often a once-yearly repast, and one I can still taste – tiny new, whole potatoes, tender two inch baby carrots and sweet little green peas, not yet filling the pods, all boiled gently and covered with a thin milk sauce. For the few weeks left of school, the monotonous winter diet of plum jam sandwiches was replaced by fillings of new spinach, nasturtium and lettuce leaves. Hens began laying eggs again and new chickens grew into fabulous fried chicken dinners.

After meals, The Cabinet became the scene of dishwashing in the big, chipped enamel dishpan, with water heated on the stove and a bar of yellow soap, which made no suds in the hard water. Pots, kettles and frying pans were scrubbed last and hung on their nails behind the stove. Morning and evening, after use, the cream separator was taken apart, all of its many metal parts rinsed and then washed thoroughly in clean water, scalded with boiling water, then left to air. The galvanized metal milk pails were treated in the same way and then hung in the anteroom. The clean cloth used for straining the milk as it was brought from the barn, had also to be rinsed and thoroughly washed after each use. The oilcloth covered table was wiped, the dirty dishwater emptied into the slop pail for the pigs, the dishpan and dishrag rinsed and hung on their nails. Coal pails and the large woodbox by the stove were filled, and kindling made for morning; the cat and dog were fed milk and scraps and the kitchen floor was swept. It was time for homework, reading or sewing, and bed.

Our kitchen cabinet was sold at the auction sale on the farm, just before we moved to British Columbia in November of 1943. It probably brought less than ten dollars. Today, if one could be found in some antique store, it would cost hundreds of dollars. The only identical one I have ever seen was years ago, in my cousin George's

Alberta farm basement, full of greasy tools.

I believe that most young children tend to notice more often the children who have *more* than themselves, rather than less. There were children whose clothes I envied, and some who had the kind of bought toys that we longed for. Brian Hanson, who sat behind me in school and whose father managed the Red and White grocery store, always had candy in his pockets, some of which he used to bribe me to do his spelling for him. Once, in grade five, he offered me a nickel to do his composition. I did the work for him but I was afraid to take the money; it seemed such a large sum and I thought that my mother would be mad at me for taking it.

Looking back, I see how very much less many other families had than we did in those difficult years. I realize how fortunate we were on the farm, in always having adequate (though not necessarily plentiful) clothing and food. There were hand-me-downs, plenty of patches and few choices; there were not many eggs and no fresh vegetables in the long winters, and little fresh fruit at any time. Nevertheless, even though it was occasionally only fried mush for supper, there was always food, which was certainly not the case for many families, and if I remember some hungry days at school, that is only because I could not choke down any more plum jam sandwiches.

White Sheep, White Sheep, on a Blue Hill - - -

The sheep of my childhood were not, in the beginning, cloud sheep, ("- - - When the wind stops, they all stand still - - - ") and the hill they stood upon was very green. A half mile up the dusty dirt road, through the barbed wire fence and another angled mile across the ploughed fields sat the picture book farm of the Wagstaff family. This farm looked very different from ours and from most of the ones I was used to seeing. The gabled house, the neat fences and gates around it were painted white and the barn, sheds and other outbuildings a deep, brick red. Our farm buildings and most of those in the community were not painted at all, but were a weathered silver-grey and this we, as children, considered normal.

I believe there grew in some of us Depression Era children an attitude that may still persist. In my mind, white houses came to mean "rich," and were seen more often in towns than on the farms. (In any case, we considered all the "town kids" rich!) There may have been a partially factual basis for this belief in the beginning. Painting one's house and barn certainly had to drop in priority for most Canadians in those years and only those with a little extra cash could do it. Though I became aware, as an adult, that I still tend to see white houses as "elegant" and a little superior, and though I had recognized the source of this attitude, I didn't know that others might have had similar feelings. That is until a visiting friend, also raised in Depression Alberta, and viewing for the first time some of our modern, weathered, West Coast cedar homes – a look that many people go to great expense and effort to achieve – remarked, "There are sure a lot of *old* houses here, aren't there?" I recognized immediately my own belief of early years.

John Wagstaff, with minimal farming experience, had come to Canada from England before 1905, homesteading through some difficult years with a team of oxen, living for at least one unusually bitter winter in a twelve by fourteen foot tent. He married a young woman, also of English heritage, raised in an Ontario city, with even less knowledge of western farm life than he had. Together, with hard work and the courage and determination that was necessary to all, they created a beautiful and prosperous farm and raised four children.

Farm neighbours relied upon one another in many ways. Doors were never locked in case someone needed refuge from a winter storm. No one, particularly in the early years, before cars became more common, would think of going to town without stopping to see if neighbours along the way needed anything. A half day trip to town and back because of broken machinery or horses' harness lost precious time in the fields. No less of a minor emergency sometimes was the day the bread needed to be baked and the yeast box was empty, or the butter not yet churned and sandwiches to be made for workers in the field. Then a child would be sent on a (hopefully) swift errand to the nearest neighbour with firm instructions not to dawdle.

I loved these little excursions to the Wagstaff farm when I became old enough or was judged responsible enough to go alone. Along the dusty path I walked, watching a bit warily for my first glimpse of sheep on the green hillside. If they happened to be in the nearest field I walked quickly and quakingly until I reached the far gate. I knew about horses, cows, pigs and poultry, but sheep were unfamiliar to me and I felt very nervous about them. Though they never bothered me at all, other than looking at me curiously from a distance ("- - - When the wind blows, they walk away slow - - - "), I had heard stories at home of rams chasing and butting people. I didn't ever let anyone at home know that I was afraid of the sheep, of course, because that might mean that someone else would get to run the errand, but it is unlikely that Mother ever knew why her cup of butter or sugar arrived as promptly as it did!

Having safely navigated the field of sheep, I looked forward with pleasure to the sight of the lovely white house nestled in the hollow near the grove of tall poplars, all the while hoping that the geese would be somewhere else that day. Geese were another rarity in my experience and they did often hiss at me as I trembled my way through them to the safety of the back door. There I was

121

always met with a glass of milk and a piece of cake or a cookie, and a nice little fuss made of me, walking so far alone. Somehow, after this, the sheep and geese were not so intimidating on the way home.

The social life of farming communities depended heavily at that time on visits with neighbours, sometimes for a meal, sometimes for a planned picnic gathering, or more often a Sunday afternoon drop-in visit with all the children crammed into the back of the current vehicle – buggy, truck or elderly car. For isolated farm women, opportunities for the company of other women, without families along, were rare. Mother and Mrs. Wagstaff partially achieved this through reciprocal visits on warm summer afternoons, walking through the ploughed fields to share a cup of tea and conversation in each others' homes, taking a chance that the hostess would be there. These visits always had a slight air of formality about them, and when they occurred in our house we children knew we were to keep out of the way and play outside, allowing the women the luxury of their short time together in peace. Since that was all that was expected of us, other than being called in briefly to say a polite, "hello," and be passed a cookie, we felt as though we had been given an afternoon off.

Few married women called each other by their given names, so it was always "Mrs. Nash" and "Mrs. Wagstaff", and an excuse to dress up a little. Most often Mother went on her visits alone, but sometimes one or another of us children were told we could get cleaned up ("go wash your neck and ears") and go with her. There were no children to play with, as the Wagstaff children, though probably in their adolescent years when I first knew them, were always "grown-ups" in my eyes, but I liked going anyway. I found the ladies' conversation somewhat boring, but I didn't often listen, as I was given beautiful picture books to look at and sometimes tea in pretty thin china cups. I must have behaved myself, as one day, in the summer I turned six, Mrs. Wagstaff came walking through the fields, her umbrella used as a walking stick in her usual manner, and presented Mother with a package wrapped in brown paper. It was a length of material for a dress for me to begin school that fall! The colour was a soft tan with a small white allover pattern that I thought looked like tiny rabbit tracks. I was really very surprised and pleased, but I'm sure I was not able to express anything other than a mumbled, "thank you," prodded by Mother. We were all, including Mother, a bit in awe of Mrs. Wagstaff. She was older than our parents, short and stout, and rather formal, though kindly, in manner.

Mrs. Wagstaff's umbrella was certainly a novelty to us, as no doubt it would have been to most prairie children. We had never seen one, and since we only saw it used as a walking stick or occasionally opened for the very hot sun, we didn't really understand its function. It also had a strange name and Bertie, unable at age two or three to pronounce or remember it, called it

123

"the cundercadella stick," which became its name in our household ever after.

I think Bert was also responsible for christening the brown dustmop that our mother acquired somewhere, possibly from a farm auction. Since Wagstaffs had a brown shaggy dog named Toby, and there were distinct similarities, the dustmop quickly became "the Toby" and was called that by the whole family, until I, for one, forgot until I was much older where the name had come from, and knew all dustmops only as "tobies."

When I was very small there were some winter visits, near Christmas, when we were all scrubbed, brushed, dressed in our best, bundled into the big bob-sleigh, with strict instructions to be on our best behaviour, and whisked through the fields of snow for dinner at Wagstaffs. And it *was* "dinner." That was the first difference. In our house and those few others we had visited, dinner was at noon and supper in the evening. "Dinner" in the evening certainly had a hint of formality and elegance about it. I think our mother was always a little nervous on these occasions, not surprisingly. Our parents were some years younger than Mr. and Mrs. Wagstaff and with six young children in a neighbour's home full of nice furniture, dishes and knick-knacks, some anxiety might be expected.

I don't think our mother's apprehension about our behaviour was particularly warranted, though Howard does recall the time on one of these visits when he, very small, backed up and accidentally fell into a pail of milk fresh from the barn. I can imagine the fuss and the cleanup that ensued, and Mother's embarrassment. Most of us, however, were too shy and too intimidated by adults and our rare visits to other homes, to do more than speak when spoken to, and often not then.

I was perhaps five or six years old when I woke one morning after "dinner at Wagstaffs" to find myself still in their home, in a strange bed, with sunshine gleaming off the dripping icicles outside the window. I didn't know why I was there or why my family had gone home and left me. Teenage Laura told me I had fallen asleep while the big people were playing cards. "Why didn't you wake me up?" I wanted to know.

"We tried, but we couldn't wake you," she said.

"Well," I insisted, "you should have pinched me." Even though she assured me they had, I never quite believed that! I didn't really mind, either. It was nice to be the only child for a few hours and to get all the attention usually shared with five brothers and sisters.

After I was dressed and fed some breakfast, Mrs. Wagstaff spread some large woollen blankets on the floor, I was placed in the middle and they were well wrapped round me. I was then lifted by Bill, probably about eighteen, carried out into the bright, frosty day to the team and sleigh at the door, and home we jingled through the sparkling drifts. I did feel very specially and kindly treated!

I was not yet six years old when Mr. Wagstaff died suddenly, but I have a shadowy remembrance of a gentle, rather quiet man on horseback, dressed in somewhat more refined clothing than was familiar to me. It must have been a terrible blow to the family with all three sons still under twenty, but they stayed on the farm, worked hard and more than managed; they made a very well recognized success of it.

(- - - "White sheep, white sheep, where do you go?") When I visited England as an adult, I was not surprised to find much of it as I had expected, looking like Wagstaffs' farm and the picture books, and full of kind and friendly people. And I found the sheep again, on the neat green hills of the beautiful Lake District, still staring at me in mild curiosity as I once again travelled through their territory, this time safe inside a car, staring curiously back at them.

Readin', Writin' and 'Rithmetic

In my early days of motherhood, I often listened to a small town radio station. One day the Manager, who was also the Program Director, News Announcer and Disc Jockey, played a rather lilting and attractive piece of music, announcing that it was the national anthem of the small country of Probenia, or Slakovitch, or somewhere remote like that. He went on, in his friendly and whimsical way, to wonder if there might be any visitors from that country driving around the Fraser Valley and listening to their car radio, and he hoped that if they heard their anthem it might make them feel welcome. It then occurred to him that if that had happened, the visitors might not understand English and would wonder why their national anthem was being played on the radio in this foreign country. Telling his audience that he had played the music only because he liked it, this Disc Jockey/Manager then asked us to imagine how we would react in a similar situation – if we were driving around in a foreign country and suddenly heard our national anthem on the radio. I had to agree with him that I, for one, would certainly have been startled, and might think that there had been some great national catastrophe at home; that our country had gone to war, or that at least the Prime Minister had died.

National anthems are strange when you think about it. It would make some interesting research, and maybe someone has already done it, to find out how the custom of having them got started in the first place. *Somebody* must have been first. Who chooses them, and when? What are the criteria? And who decides who is qualified to choose? I don't remember learning anything about any of that in school and, as deeply as our anthems, both music and words, were drilled into us, nobody ever talked about the composers, or when the songs were written, or why. I have been somewhat suspicious about the origin of *O Canada!* ever since I heard it played on a U.S. radio station as just an ordinary piece of music, not even titled – or at least the disc jockey seemed unaware that it had a title.

There is certainly one thing Americans are good at though, and that is promotion. They know how to make their citizens into national, sometimes international, heroes. I am willing to bet that more Canadians know about the author and the writing of *The Star Spangled Banner* than know the author or any history of *O Canada!* That is because the Americans get to the school children. There was a period of time when almost every child in the United States and Canada knew who Davey Crockett was, and large numbers of them went around wearing fake coonskin caps and singing, "Dave-y! Da-vey Crockett! Son - of - the -wild - fron - tier!" Most of those children are now adults and I bet they still know who Davey

Crockett was. If someone had caught Canadian children's imaginations with little Sir John A. MacDonald top hats and a catchy tune – let's see – "Sir John came – in – to – Ottawa town; he staggered into Parliament and – sat – him – down," I and a lot of others might have grown up knowing much more Canadian history than we did. And, surprise, we might have discovered that it contained a few colourful characters.

The only colourful character from Canadian history that was or is real for me from my elementary school days is Samuel de Champlain. That is because, in grade four, I had to do research and make a little book about him. I remember that little book well. It was about four by six inches and it had a light brown construction paper cover. While I have forgotten many of the details the book contained, I remember how hard I worked at it, how proud I was to complete it, and how much I came to admire Monsieur Samuel de Champlain. He became then a real person to me, as I travelled in imagination with him down the St. Lawrence River and shared his hardships. (I also remember my brother Howard's later irreverence in referring to him as Sam Champlain and being told by Mr. Ward that he didn't know Mr. Champlain well enough to call him by his first name.)

In any case, to get back to national anthems, if the authors of *O Canada!* and *The Maple Leaf Forever* are national heroes it has certainly been, down through the years, also a national secret. I

129

have never found anyone who knows anything about them. I think that is a serious national omission.

As I followed the formal education of my own children and grandchildren, however, and as I became involved in the education field myself, I became increasingly aware, often with surprise, of the benefits and the quality of my own early learning in the little two room, red brick prairie school. I do much thinking about what contributed to that. Certainly by today's standards we would have been considered deprived and in some ways we were. We had none of the equipment considered essential in schools now. The "library" consisted of three or four short shelves at the back of the classroom, and many of the books stood on them year after year, supplemented from time to time by donations from someone's attic or, I suspect, by some of our teachers, out of concern for our limited exposure to good literature.

The elementary classroom was the home of grades one through six, usually around thirty children, and one teacher was responsible for all. We sat in desks, in rows from front to back of the classroom, each grade to its own row, with the teachers' desk at the front, facing us. Eight children in a grade was a large class, so even though the teacher's load was heavy, with subjects taught at six different grade levels, it was hardly possible for any child to get lost in the system, as can and does happen now, with classes of thirty in one grade and a variety of teachers. Our teachers knew each of us, what our capabilities were in each subject, our handicaps and usually a good deal about our home lives and background, since teachers were always involved in the social life of the community, much of which revolved around the school.

Because of the age range in the classroom, most of the books on the shelves were more appropriate for grades four, five and six. I think it likely that story or picture books for the primary grades got worn out more quickly so there always seemed to be fewer of them. No limitations were ever put on our reading if we were finished our classwork and for me that was the best incentive possible. The one thing that, more than anything, intensified my desire to learn to read was that the teacher read aloud to us regularly. Again, because of the age range, she had to choose books that would hopefully hold the interest of all.

For a half hour each day after lunch we listened to the Greek myths, to *Peter Pan*, *Swiss Family Robinson*, *The Water Babies*, *Little Women*, *Treasure Island*, *Tom Sawyer*, *Gulliver's Travels* and many, many more. Often, caught by her own interest and our clamour for, "Please! Just one more chapter!" the half hour became quite extended. I was spellbound, and even in grade one felt a great secret excitement and awe at the slowly dawning realization of the world that learning to read was going to open up to me. In my six years in that classroom I read all the books in that small library over and over, whether I clearly understood the contents or not. Most of them, I have since realized, were good literature: *Oliver Twist*, *Wuthering Heights*, *Pride and Prejudice*, *What Katy Did*, *Girl of the Limberlost*. Because of the limitations of the times there was none of what is known today as "junk reading," at least in the school. Though some of the boys sometimes brought comic books to school, I seldom had a chance to see these and so never became very interested.

I believe our teachers had to be some kind of magicians to teach all subjects to six grade levels, but for many of us, learning was broadened and reinforced because of it. If you were in grade two and did not feel very secure about your numbers or your alphabet, there were the grade ones up at the front of the classroom, reinforcing them for you as they recited them aloud for the teacher. (I still have the tiny bird pin with green glass feathers that was my reward on the day I could count aloud to one hundred.) Then again, if you were in grade two or three and had finished your work (or maybe not) it was fascinating to listen to some of the lessons of the grades five and six. I liked it especially when they had to stand and recite poetry. I didn't always fully understand it but the rhythm was wonderful and so were the images it produced, and it provided, I believe, a foundation for my continued love of poetry. How proud and impressed I was, at age eight, to see my own big brother, Howard, two years older than I, called to the front of his class. I

132

still hear his boyish voice reciting the rhythmical lines of Canon F.G. Scott:

> Why hurry, little river,
>   Why hurry to the sea?
> There is nothing there to do
> But to sink into the blue
>   And all forgotten be.
> There is nothing on that shore
> But the tides for evermore,
> And the faint and far-off line
> Where the winds across the brine
> For ever, ever roam
> And never find a home.

How fascinating and mysterious I found those words. Perhaps they even seeded the curiosity and attraction that led this prairie child, many decades later, to a home by the sea!

Teachers had to be just as innovative then as they do now, possibly sometimes more so. Though many subjects were taught to classes individually, some of our teachers combined lessons when it seemed appropriate, so that the whole classroom might be working on different aspects of life in a tribal village in Africa, with each grade researching and contributing to a huge mural on the blackboard or, more often, to a lovely little three dimensional village of salt and flour clay in the sandbox. I thought it was so clever of the teacher to put in a piece of blue paper with a bit of glass over it for a lake!

Music was also explored or taught to us all together,

depending on the interest of the teacher and the scope of her musical ability. There was a piano in the classroom in some years and some of our teachers could play. Those who could not taught us songs and musical games – "Go In and Out the Window," "Drop the Handkerchief," "Musical Chairs."

My one taste of classical music in those years came in grade four when a teacher brought a small gramophone to school and played *The Peer Gynt Suite* for us, explaining the story and telling us what to listen for. I have never heard it since without seeing and hearing Peer Gynt running down the mountainside and jumping over the streams.

There were few "children's songs" as there are today, that is, songs and music written and intended to appeal especially to children, other than those nursery rhymes that had been put to music, so the songs we learned were classics and old favourites: *Drink to Me Only With Thine Eyes*, *Sweet and Low*, *Home on the Range*, *When Irish Eyes Are Smiling*, *Seeing Nellie Home*, *My Old Kentucky Home* along with the rest of Stephen Foster's, and many, many more. There are many wonderful songs sung and played for children now, but in our eagerness to give them all this variety we have sometimes neglected to also include the old ones, with the mistaken idea that they are "too adult" and that children would not be interested or could not understand. As a result we have, in the areas of art, music and literature, deprived several generations of

134

children of the right to be exposed to a rich heritage and a great deal of enjoyment.

Though there were drawbacks to the cross age groupings, I believe the benefits of learning in a broad age range of children did outweigh the disadvantages. It was much like being in a large family with a great variety of ages and temperaments. Most of us learned to support the needy ones and to watch out for the bullies!

"Spelling Bees" were of dubious benefit. On the one hand, everyone got an afternoon off from regular schoolwork and if you were good at spelling there was the bonus of being able to show off a little, with the knowledge that you would likely be able to hold out long enough to make your eventual humiliation at defeat seem minimal. On the other hand, I believe that Spelling Bees were pure torture for those who did not easily spell well. At best it was boring and at worst one's self-perception as "dumb" was reinforced swiftly, repeatedly and publicly. Particularly alarming were the occasional times when the School Inspector arrived just as we were beginning a Spelling Bee. These visits, always unannounced, created instant feelings of panic in the classroom, beginning with some of our teachers, whose anxieties were obviously transferred to us. We were terrified of "The Inspector," the closest thing we knew to God, though we didn't really know why we were so frightened. I and, I am sure, many of my classmates, did not at that time understand that the Inspector's job was to assess the work and classroom skills of the teacher, not her pupils.

There was little in the way of equipment for Science or Biology. The people in grades seven to eleven, taught by the Principal, Mr. Ward, in the "Big Room," sometimes did mysterious things in the "Science Lab," a walled off section of the girls' basement that doubled as a winter lunch room and a typing room. We in the "Little Room" always knew when they were down there by the incredibly terrible smells that came steaming up the heat register, and the occasional loud explosion when something hadn't worked – or perhaps had.

My earliest science and biology lessons were so wonderful and so eagerly anticipated that I didn't even know they were lessons. My teacher in grades one and two was Miss Marion Hodgson and though I have had, known and worked with many excellent teachers since, I venture to say, looking back with present knowledge through six and seven year old eyes, "They don't often make 'em like that anymore." First experiences of school can and usually do set for life our attitudes toward learning, so one's earliest teachers are of paramount importance. For me that meant grade one. Now, of course, it is nursery school, preschool, daycare and kindergarten. None of those were available to us, nor even heard of. Our preparation for school life consisted of a day at school sometime in the year before we were to begin grade one, taken there usually by an older brother or sister. I don't know what happened to the children who didn't have an older brother or sister. Probably most of them didn't even have a one-day preparation. I do remember some very sad little first graders .

I thoroughly recall my own initiation. One cold, fall day when I was five, I was awakened early and carefully dressed, washed and combed, bundled up with hat and scarf tied round my head and lifted by my father onto a horse behind Milly, then thirteen. I hung on tightly as Shorty galloped the four miles to school, and I waited while my tall, pretty sister put him in the school barn and unsaddled him, and the cold wind blew great clouds of prairie farm land through the town. Milly led me into the school, which I had never seen before, and to the girls' basement cloakroom, where she hung my outer clothes and wiped the dust from my face. There was no one around as classes had already begun.

Milly then led me upstairs to a door, knocked on it and as it opened, disappeared into an adjoining one, telling me she would come for me at lunchtime. Waiting for me in the open doorway stood the most beautiful lady I had ever seen, with wavy golden hair and blue eyes, wearing a lovely red silky dress, and welcoming me with a kind and generous smile. I could hardly believe that this beautiful princess, Miss Hodgson, was going to be my teacher, and I fell instantly in love. As I later learned, it was unusual for pupils *not* to fall in love with Miss Hodgson.

137

The room was full of children, all sitting in rows in little desks, at the moment all chattering, with many girls calling out, "Let her sit beside me! Let her sit beside me!" A little desk was pushed up beside that of one of the "big girls," Edith Goetz. I was provided with plasticene, crayons and paper, and I sat enchanted all morning, watching and listening to the beautiful lady at the front of the room. At noon, Milly collected me and we ate our lunches among her friends, after which I spent the afternoon beside her in "The Big Room," which was much quieter and quite boring. This was my total introduction to school.

Miss Hodgson genuinely liked children and I believe she genuinely liked teaching. She was thorough, she was disciplined, she had high standards and she expected all these qualities of her students. She was also generous and affectionate, and though she could and did mete out punishments for infractions, or – most dreaded possibility – send people to the Principal, she was never unfair and we knew that, so we continued to respect and love her. I was in some awe that she always knew exactly what was going on in the classroom behind her back when she was writing on the blackboard – who threw what, who was out of their desk, who passed a note – so I at first took her quite literally when she told us she had "eyes in the back of my head." I used to watch her hair carefully to see if I could catch a glimpse of them.

When the snow melted and the days grew warm in the

138

spring, our Nature Study classes began. For the last hour or two on Friday afternoons books would be put away, and the whole classroom of children would troop out into the countryside with Miss Hodgson. We would sit in a field, or under some trees by a stream and talk about the world around us. We brought her leaves and stones, bugs and beetles and flowers, everything we saw in the world we lived in so close to the ground, and each item was turned into a fascinating lesson, expanded upon by our innumerable questions. I had no idea that these were lessons or that they probably covered a required part of the curriculum. I do know that my love of and fascination with all things in nature, already seeded in my farm birth and environment, was nurtured and reinforced in ways that no textbooks could have done. Late in the day we all walked back to the school, the smallest children vying for a place beside "The Teacher" and a coveted hand to hold.

Though I thrived on reading, writing, spelling, poetry, music, or anything to do with words and rhythm, I became lost in the world of numbers. At that time, it was not recognized that a child might need different lengths of time to learn different types of material, so if one was quick at learning in some areas she was expected to be quick in all areas. Judgments were more definite, accepted and pronounced, so I quickly learned that I was "smart" in reading and writing but "dumb" in arithmetic. As often happens, I carried this belief well into adulthood when I surprised myself by

139

discovering that I was not "dumb" in mathematics; I just needed more time for it than I did for some other learnings. Even in grades three and four I had some recognition of that. Most of what we learned was by memory – the "times tables," decimals, fractions, square root and the basic laws of algebra and geometry. Every time I knew that I was just beginning to grasp something the whole class would move on to something else. When I'd nearly learned the eight times tables they would be halfway through the nines. When I was just getting a glimmer of fractions they would be onto percentages. I wanted to say, "Wait! Wait! I've nearly got it!" and I felt quite hopeless about ever catching up.

I could relate to and remember words because they either had an appealing rhythm or evoked vivid images, or both, but numbers related to very little for me. When, in adult years, I became acquainted with the marvellous methods and equipment used in Montessori and Waldorf schools, and saw how these were used by children to make mathematics visible, I couldn't help realizing how many tears would have been saved, how much despair, hopelessness and humiliation at being "kept in" after school to do arithmetic avoided, had that kind of teaching been available to me and others like me.

My lifelong interest and involvement in theatre and drama also began in grade one when Miss Hodgson cast me as Little Bo-Peep in the Christmas play. Another incredible world opened up!

This was reinforced throughout my school life, particularly by Mr. Ward, whose interest, skill and talent in casting, directing and producing plays immeasurably enriched our lives and our community. This, I think, offset in part a universal lack of attention to our social and emotional development.

The story of Mr. Ward's arrival in Huxley as a young teacher has no doubt been told many times, probably with various enhancements. I repeat here the one given me. Roland Ward came from Olds, a town thirty or so miles to the southwest of Huxley. He had either already been hired by letter, or was coming for an interview for the post of Principal in our little school. Having settled himself into Mrs. Myrvang's boarding house, he decided he should meet some of the members of the School Board.

He was told that Tom Paterson's farm was only a mile from town and so, lacking a vehicle, Mr. Ward walked out. He was stockily built, of average height, slow and deliberate in both speech and movement. With his thick black hair slicked back, and quite likely wearing his ever familiar navy pin striped three piece suit, he was met at the door by Mrs. Paterson, who pointed him the way to a field where her husband was ploughing.

Tom Paterson, a "dour Scot," had a reputation as strong willed, forthright and outspoken, and held a seat on the Huxley School Board for many years (as his son Bill often reminded us at school, once telling me in the schoolyard that I was not allowed to

141

"lean on that tree because my dad is on the School Board and you have to do what I say!"). Mr. Ward arrived in the hot, dusty field and, when Tom Paterson pulled up his horses and plough, introduced himself. Tom Paterson, covered in sweat and soil, looked him over, and in his heavy Scotch brogue greeted him, "Yeerrr an ugly buggerrr, arrren't ye?"

Mr. Ward, never one to be intimidated, drawled evenly, "Well, you don't look so hot yourself." The story is that they got along fine ever after.

Mr. Ward became a great asset to the Huxley community, promoting and organizing many programs for both youths and adults. Each year that he taught in our school he produced, as well as the Christmas concert, an ambitious three act play with his senior pupils in grades ten and eleven. These dramatic productions were presented in the spring, and most years there was also an evening of one act plays at some point.

From my very first introduction in grade one to the world of theatre, when Miss Hodgson cast me as Little Bo-Peep, I was hooked. Happy among my school memories is the spring I was in grade eight and the Seniors' play was being cast. I knew I would not get a part, but oh, how I silently dreamed of one! Because classes were very small – about thirty pupils in grades seven to eleven – sometimes the lower grades had to be drawn on to fill minor roles. I had read the play; I had the temerity to secretly covet

142

the lead role, that of a bride in her wedding day finery in a great and humorous battle with her groom-to-be. The play was cast. A pretty, delicate looking grade ten girl, Margaret Andersen, was to be the bride. There was no minor part for me. I was glad I had not made my hopes public.

That year I had taken, as an elective, a class called "Journalism." We hadn't done much with it, but I liked it. It gave me a legitimate reason to write more, my second love. One day, several weeks into the play rehearsals, which were not a part of our grade eight lives, Mr. Ward came to speak to me at noon hour. Margaret Andersen was sick. She could not continue in the play. If I would consent to take over her role at this late date, he would release me from Journalism classes and give me an "A" grade. An A! I could not believe what I was hearing. Didn't he know that I would have happily taken a *zero* in Journalism, or anything else, for what he was offering me? I could hardly credit that he was acting as though I were doing *him* a favour!

Somehow, strong objections at home were overcome (my parents did not encourage either my acting or my writing), and I played the bride, in a beautiful borrowed wedding dress, opposite talented, intelligent Harry Andreassen. My gratitude still goes out to the Goddess of Compensation for Adolescent Miseries.

Mr. Ward was teacher and Principal of Huxley School for more than twelve years. Many of his former pupils kept in touch

143

with him as he progressed from teaching to an administrative position at the University of Alberta in Edmonton.

"School days, school days! Dear old Golden Rule days! Readin' and writin' and 'rithmetic - - -." Though our lessons weren't exactly "taught to the tune of a hick'ry stick," the importance of our education was taken seriously, by teachers, by parents, and therefore by us. Because teachers were looked up to and highly respected by the adults of the community, because our parents taught us to believe that the teacher was always right, I know that I was very fortunate to have had teachers who were always worthy of respect and who, though there was no such expression then, provided good role models for the children in their care. Our teachers came mostly from small towns or farming communities like our own, and had gone on to larger centres for their teacher training, usually only a year, after High School. The present very broad and detailed study, research, and information on child development had barely begun in those years, and I am sure had neither been heard of nor thought of in the Huxley, or any, farming community.

Whatever the limitations, whatever may look like, or were, the handicaps and deprivations, whatever other joys and tears it held for us, many ideals and life goals were conceived, many worthwhile attributes nurtured, and many values that later provided clear, strong and positive guidelines for our lives, were instilled along with the lessons in the little red brick schoolhouse.

A Bottle of Pop

There was a young woman in our town who never knew how a kind and sensitive act of hers touched a child and has been remembered for more than sixty years. Her name was Verna Murray. I only ever spoke to her once. She was one of the "big girls," all of fourteen or fifteen, and I was a mere seven. She seemed far removed from me in other ways, too. She was small, slim and neat, with large dark eyes in a pale heart-shaped face, short dark hair, and a quick, precise, self-assured manner about her. Her clothes fitted perfectly, as though they had been made on her, and though I didn't feel either envy or adulation, I did often feel clumsy and awkward in her presence, self-consciously aware of unidentified but vaguely perceived differences between "farm child'" and "town child."

In our two room school on the edge of town, the younger children were customarily dismissed a half hour or so earlier in the afternoon than students in the higher grades. This meant that those of us who travelled from farms had to wait around somewhere for our older brothers and sisters to collect us for the journey home. When I first began school the four mile ride was on horses, but when I was seven my younger sister, Bertie, started school and there

147

were then five of us attending. Our father could not spare so many horses from the farm work, even when we rode double, so that year saw the first of many weird and wonderful one horse carts, buggies, sleighs and contraptions that he either built, adapted or bought at farm auctions for our transportation to and from school.

In the summertime we younger ones often started walking home, usually with classmates, and our horse and buggy would catch up to us on the road. In winter, however, it was not only much too cold, but also almost impossible to walk at all, with the weight of clothing we needed to wear.

Our clothes were mostly of cotton fleece or flannelette, with heavy coats and overshoes. The only way to achieve some warmth was to pile on layer after layer, with wool toques, two or three pair of mitts, and a scarf wrapped around face, neck and head. We could barely see, let alone move. Our habit, in cold weather, was to walk from the school a block or so to the Red and White grocery store, and there wait inside in the warmth for our buggy or sleigh.

One cold day in the fall of the year that I was in grade two, I was the only child in the Red and White Store, waiting alone at the window for what seemed like a long time for the horse and cart. Mr. Hanson, the storekeeper, stood further back in the store behind the counter, visiting with two other men, one of whom I knew was Mr. Murray, the operator of one of the five grain elevators that stood by the railroad tracks. In a little while Verna Murray came in from

148

school and joined her father. There was much friendly talk and laughter, and I was aware, as I watched out the window, of an easy warmth and affection between father and daughter, which made me feel vaguely lonely. I also began to feel awkward and a bit like an intruder, acutely conscious of my bundled up look, with stockings wrinkling down that I couldn't reach to pull up, and I wished the school cart would come.

Then I heard Mr. Murray say, "Let's all have a bottle of pop! Sure! I'll buy everybody a bottle of pop! What kind do you want? Eh?" There was more friendly banter about letting him pay, and what each would have. I continued to gaze out the window, my back to the rest of the store.

I heard the clink of the bottles on the counter, the caps being popped off, and then I heard Verna Murray say, "Daddy, you've forgotten somebody." I knew she meant me, and I became confused with a mixture of gratitude, self-consciousness, shyness and embarrassment.

"Eh? What?" asked her father.

"You've forgotten somebody," followed by whispers. Then Verna Murray came over to me, knelt down, and asked me what kind of pop I would like.

I didn't know much about pop. I had tasted it a few times. Occasionally, on an infrequent trip to town, our mother bought a bottle of orange crush, which she shared with us. Once I had a bottle of Pepsi Cola, our free treat at the annual school picnic. I thought it tasted terrible, and gave it away, very disappointed. But Verna Murray was waiting, and though I didn't look up, I felt the eyes of the three kindly men. Overwhelmed by my feelings, I wanted to cry, but I managed to mumble, "Lemon," then, immediately aware that I didn't know whether there was even such a thing as lemon pop, became suddenly afraid of further embarrassment. I doubt that I even added, "please." But off went Verna Murray in her crisp, light way and came back with a bottle of lemon pop with a straw in it. I am sure that I was also much too overcome to say, "thank you," to anyone.

Many, many years later and far from the old Red and White store, I related this story to groups of students training to work with young children, as my first memorable example of an adult's awareness and sensitivity to the feelings of a young child. Verna Murray, wherever you are, a very belated thank you!

Picnics and Politics

"Get the washrag and scrub your face," ordered Mother. And they *were* rags, not manufactured face cloths, but pieces cut or torn from any soft cloth item no longer useable in any other way – flannelette nightgowns, sheets, shirts, cotton fleece underwear, thin terry toweling – all saved, washed and used for washrags, dishrags, floor rags and all cleaning purposes.

We were going on a picnic. I wonder if anyone, anywhere, still has picnics like the old-fashioned kind we grew up with. They were not frequent, at most one or two in a summer, and they seemed to peter out as the Depression years stretched and we began to enter our adolescent years, but in the earlier days they were elaborate affairs. They were also a very great deal of work, especially for women, who baked and cooked for several days in preparation. Only the best was taken for picnics, particularly when the outing was planned with neighbours or relatives, just as today no one takes their poorest casserole to a pot-luck dinner. Casseroles, at that time usually put together with leftovers – and, therefore, with a much more humble status than they have today, would never have been taken to a picnic. That would have been an embarrassment not only for the cook, but also the whole family.

151

Bags and baskets and boxes were packed with the best dishes and cutlery the household contained. These were carefully wrapped in the newest or least stained dishtowels, sheets, and even pillowcases. No proud homemaker was going to let a neighbour see her old, everyday worn ones. Out came Mother's big white damask tablecloth and serviettes. Blankets and perhaps a few pillows were taken to sit on. Children ran back and forth as directed, fetching, carrying and eventually helping to load the vehicles – buggies or wagons in early days, later replaced by old trucks or cars.

The food was always wonderful! I can't imagine that I will ever again eat potato salad that will taste like that, which is not surprising. The potatoes were dug on the farm; the eggs with their big orange yolks were laid that morning in our henhouse. Today these are called "free range" eggs and considered special (and consequently, are expensive). To us, they were just what eggs were supposed to be like, and what everybody else had. "Run out to the garden and pull up six green onions," instructed Mother, and in those went. All cooks made their own salad dressing from fresh farm cream, fresh farm eggs – how could it not taste good? Everything was homemade and homegrown and everything must have been "organic" in those days before sprays, preservatives and pesticides. (With little sticks, we sometimes spent hours knocking potato bugs off the plants into an inch of coal oil in our tin cans.) All of this was ordinary, and there really were no other choices.

152

Always there were mounds of fried chicken. Several innocents, having made the ultimate sacrifice the day before, had been plucked, prepared, cooked in large pans on the stove, cooled overnight and then packed in layers in the large turkey-roasting pan, with bits of brown paper between to soak up the fat. While the chickens were frying, buns and cinnamon rolls, pies and cookies were baking in the oven, and someone, often me, had to churn the butter.

To this day I do not understand the composer of the song my mother used to sing:

> Churn-ing, churn-ing,
> Making butter's the best of fun!
> Oh, we're sorry when summer's done!
> Mary, Molly and I.

I also felt quite resentful. Did the composer think it was fun? Did Mother? I definitely did not. I decided the song writer had never had to churn butter. That had to be one of the most boring of all farm chores and one that seemed to take the longest to show results. I sat on a stool outside the kitchen door with the tall crockery butter churn on the doorstep in front of me. It had a thick round lid with a hole in the middle for the wooden handle, like a broom handle, to fit through. Attached to the end of this was the paddle, really just two small rectangular boards crossed at right angles, with the stick in the middle.

The churn was half filled with cream, paddle placed in churn, lid over paddle handle, child placed on stool, handle placed in child's hands. Thump! Thump! Thump! Up and down, up and down went my arms and the paddle in the cream until, what seemed many hours later, my arms ready to fall off, the cream was finally splashed into butter, too thick to paddle anymore. Each time I stopped to rest my arms, out came Mother to look in the churn, monitoring progress. If the cream was very fresh it took much longer to turn to butter. The original crockery lid, broken at some earlier time, had been replaced by a round wooden one made by Dad.

One warm summer afternoon, while I was doggedly churning away and wishing I was off playing with the others, the bottom suddenly broke out of the stoneware churn and all the half-churned cream flowed out into the dirt yard. Horrified, I yelled for Mother, scared that she would think I had done it on purpose. Though she *was* upset about the loss of the cream and churn, and so did a bit of yelling herself, I could tell that she didn't really blame *me*. I think that the bottom of the churn was probably already cracked, and she would have known that from washing it. After that, churning was done in a metal cream can, a shorter version of the old milk cans that one still sees around.

Buttermilk was drained off the butter and stored in jars in the cellar for drinking and baking. The soft butter was placed in a large

154

bowl and washed by covering it with fresh cold water and kneading it with a wooden paddle, draining off the milky water (saved for the pigs) and repeating this process until the water remained clear. The butter was then salted, kneaded well, and packed into clean crocks with cloths and lids over them to keep out mice and insects, then stored in the cool dugout cellar. Waxed paper, foil and plastic wrap being far in the future, butter for picnics was put into some nice dish with a cover.

Picnic desserts were phenomenal. Pies were prevalent – raisin, saskatoon and my favorite, rhubarb; "Go pick me enough rhubarb for three pies, and don't take all day about it!" And soon, mouth-watering aromas from the oven filled the house as the sweet, red juice seeped through the flaky crust in the tin or enamel pie pans.

Traditions that we grow up with, even those we don't like, seem to provide some feeling of security, so that we never feel a particular event is quite right if these are changed. I am reminded of the year when, with my own growing children, I decided not to cook brussels sprouts for Christmas dinner, as it seemed that few people ever ate them. My twelve year old daughter, Chris, came into the kitchen and began looking into the pots. "Aren't we having brussels sprouts?" she asked.

In great surprise I answered, "But you don't *like* brussels sprouts!"

155

"But we *always* have them for *Christmas!*" said Chris.

Just as Christmas would not have been Christmas without a stuffed turkey, so a picnic was not complete without THE CAKE. It was the pièce de résistance and, days before the picnic, we began pestering Mother. Even Dad, life-long lover of sweets, showed his anticipation. "What kind of cake are we going to have?"

Mother, perhaps enjoying this little fragment of power, would usually say, "I haven't decided yet!"

It might be a big layer cake, chocolate, white, lemon, coconut, spice or marble, or sometimes real angel food, made with the traditional twelve egg whites, anxiety and much tip-toeing. Icings were usually the delicious boiled kind, a touchy process that I never mastered. Mother, a superb cook, was justifiably proud of her creations.

Even jelly was sometimes taken on a picnic. It *was* jelly, not Jell-O, as that brand name had not yet been invented. It came in powders as it does today, though not in so many flavours, and it had to be made the day before as, with no refrigeration, it took a long time to set. It was a popular special occasion dessert, and looked really beautiful, as most cooks had large, fancy tin or aluminum moulds for it. When it was turned out successfully onto a big plate or platter, a tricky process requiring great skill and timing, it looked like a shimmering ruby red castle. It was usually decorated with whipped cream and – can you believe it? – I can remember Mother

156

one time actually taking along on a picnic the jar of cream, bowl, eggbeater, sugar and vanilla, and making the whipped cream for the jelly while sitting on a blanket in a field, in her good dress.

Ice-cream was one dessert that was seldom, if ever, taken on picnics. There was always a problem in the hot prairie summers with keeping food cold enough, even at home. Dugout cellars were cool, but not cold. Most foods had to be used up quickly; bacteria grew fast in unpasteurized milk and foods made with milk. Meat rotted or became fly-blown. Day-old food was always suspect. Fortunately for the Depression's enforced frugality, the pigs and chickens didn't seem to mind eating any of this.

In the pasture to the east of the farm ran a creek, north to south, crossing our land and that of several neighbours. In the winter this usually flooded and then froze solid, making great, albeit bumpy, skating rinks for Harvey and Howard, who often crossed fences to skate with the Jensen boys, Edward and Arnold. Before the ice began to melt in early spring, Dad would hitch a team to a hayrack and haul large loads of straw to cover an extensive area of the ice, which then stayed frozen for most of the summer.

Making ice-cream on a summer Sunday was nearly an all-day activity, with most of the family taking part. First, someone had to saddle a horse and, with axe and gunnysack in hand, ride the mile to the straw-covered ice, hack off a few large chunks and carefully replace the straw. Meanwhile, the big old-fashioned ice-cream

157

maker was brought from its winter storage spot, Mother removed from the wooden bucket the lidded metal canister containing the wooden dasher, washed all parts, and began mixing the rich cream, egg, sugar and vanilla filling. With the canister placed in the bucket and the turning mechanism fitted over the top, smashed up ice was placed in layers with rock salt in the space between canister and bucket wall, and the handle turning process began. The canister rotated in the ice; the dasher inside swung back and forth. As various child-sized arms became tired, others took their place, until the ice-cream began to freeze and thicken, when only the strongest arms were able to continue turning.

The melting ice flowed out a little hole in the lower side of the bucket, and more ice and salt were added as needed. Eventually it was time to take the lid off to see if the ice-cream was firm enough to eat. Sometimes this was felt to be needed several times, with a spoon nearby for testing, and we would hear from Mother, inside the house but obviously monitoring by ear the activity on the front porch step. "You kids stop taking that lid off so much, or it will never be ready!" But eventually it was indeed ready, and around the kitchen table we crowded, bowls and spoons in hand, arguing about whose turn it was to "lick the dasher," while Dad spooned out this infrequent treat. I have never understood why that ice-cream seemed so much colder than any since, but I was greatly teased for stirring mine till it had partly melted. We had a peculiar little competition in trying not to be the first one to cough as the cold food hit warm esophaguses. Obviously, ice-cream for picnics would have been difficult and impractical.

Many kinds of homemade pickles were included at those outings, and sometimes sandwiches and cookies or doughnuts, if the day was going to be so long that we might need a later snack. Our drinks were big jars of lemonade, involving the squeezing of many lemons. We had no type of thermos containers, but on a picnic with our neighbours, I once watched Mrs. Wagstaff unwrap a beautiful bone china teapot. I was very young, and I have no idea whether or not she served tea from it, and if so, how it would have been kept hot. Maybe she used it to pour the lemonade.

We dressed in our best for picnics, even when the outing was a long wagon ride to a grassy field. This may sound odd now, and impractical, but picnics were one of our few social events, a chance for friends and neighbours to meet and visit. People regarded them in much the same way as they would dinner with friends today in a nice restaurant.

Every summer when my sister, Bert, and I were small, our mother made us each a pretty flowered voile dress for good, often with a big floppy sun-hat of the same material, with paper sewn into the wide brim and ties for a bow under our chins. Our brothers had one pair each of nice pants, white shirts and neckties from Eaton's catalogue.

"Take the shoe polish," said Mother, "and go clean up your shoes." I was nine or ten years old, relatives were visiting, a picnic to Pine Lake, a resort beach an hour north by motor vehicle, had been planned and prepared, vehicles were nearly packed, children were scrubbed, dressed and almost ready to go. I suppose if I had thought of it or been told, I would have taken my shoes off, but I had been told to hurry. The shoe polish was thin liquid in a bottle, very black and smelly, with a little fuzzy cloth sponge on the end of a small wire attached to the inside of the screw-on lid. One cousin and I went into our small bedroom where I set the bottle of polish on the dresser, then knelt down in the narrow space between bed and dresser, sponge in hand, applying the watery polish to my scuffed and worn school shoes. Suddenly, with a great shock, I felt a large swoosh of liquid splashing from above onto the back of my head, neck and shoulders. I have never asked, but later assumed that my cousin was about to hand me the bottle and knocked it over. What an utter mess! And what a great uproar ensued. People were upset and cross. People yelled and scolded. The picnic was delayed. Men found things to do outside and children quietly faded into invisibility. Except me.

Mother, still scolding, stripped me and tried to rinse the shoe polish from my dress and underwear. My aunt took me, weeping profusely, outside with a basin of warm soapy water and tried as kindly as she could to remove the stains from my hair and skin. I don't remember any of the results of all this or what I wore to the picnic, nor do I remember any of the rest of that day. I did wonder then, as I have wondered since, how it never seemed to occur to otherwise intelligent adults, to question how I could spill a whole bottle of shoe polish over the *back* of my own head and neck.

Each summer the Huxley Community as a whole held a Picnic and Sports Day in town, in the large, open grassy field above the main part of the village, between the community hall and the school. It was a day long affair, with many sports events and races planned for both adults and children – ball games, horseshoes, relay races, three-legged races, sack races – and a free ice-cream cone and bottle of pop for each child. The town picnic provided an anticipated, rare day off for farm families, an infrequent opportunity to visit with scattered friends and neighbours. Many stayed on for the grand dance in the hall that evening. Most years we attended the picnic, as did families for many miles around, driving in with all children, except those left at home to do chores, carrying picnic lunches and blankets, later to be spread on the ground between vehicles. Every kind of transportation was to be seen, wagons, buggies, democrats or whatever old motor vehicles were still operable or whose owners could afford the necessary fuel and license plates.

Our family never owned a manufactured buggy or democrat, but Dad usually had some old car or truck around. A buggy was

161

pulled by one horse and seated two people, with possibly a small child or two squashed in among adult feet. A democrat (in spite of inquiries, I have been unable to find out the origin of the name), drawn by two horses, looked somewhat like a buggy, but was larger and sturdier. It would have one, two or even three upholstered, full-width seats. It compared to a buggy as a modern family van might compare to a sportscar. Another vehicle seen more frequently as the Depression deepened was the "Bennett Buggy." Pierre Berton, in his book *The Great Depression 1929-1939* (McLelland & Stewart Inc. 1990) describes it as " - - - the broken-down, horse-drawn automobile that more than any artifact symbolizes the drought-ravaged years of the Great Depression." R.B. Bennett was Prime Minister of Canada from 1930 to 1935, beginning his term just as the hungry thirties began and, therefore, got the blame (not all of it unwarranted) for the Depression from many people who, through no fault of their own, were suddenly suffering joblessness, foreclosure on homes, businesses and farms, and ending up on relief (severely inadequate welfare).

"Many, if not most people on the prairies, as elsewhere, could no longer afford to operate their automobiles – Model T and Model A Fords, 4-90 Chevrolets, Essexes, Stars, Studebakers and others. With their usual stubborn ingenuity, these people thought of a way to make the best of a bad situation and, since the population was largely rural, nearly everyone had horses. Motors were removed from cars and wagon tongues attached to the front ends, with teams of horses hitched thereto. Windshields usually opened by tilting outward at the bottom, so a driver could sit in the cab, steering with the wheel, while driving the horses with the reins through the windshield. Sometimes a Bennett Buggy was not much more than a low wagon built on a car frame to take advantage of the springs and the easy running, rubber-tired wheels. Naming the contraption after the Prime Minister was just a classic example of the dry Depression humor that helped see these people through those extreme times."[1] People began also to refer to abandoned prairie farms as "Bennett Barnyards" and to city shacktowns filling with the growing numbers of jobless, as "Bennett Boroughs."

The most vividly memorable summer picnic of my childhood took place in 1935, when the Depression was well into its sixth year and the word that best described the situation and state of mind of the great majority of Canadians was "desperation." Pierre Berton goes on to say, "The times were ripe for a Messiah, and Alberta found one in the person of - - - William Aberhart, without doubt the most electrifying political figure the country has ever produced."[2] This high school teacher, evangelical lay preacher and reluctant politician swept to power in Alberta through his personal

[1] Howard Nash, 1994.
[2] *The Great Depression 1929-1939*, McLelland & Stewart Inc., 1990.

magnetism and oratorical skills, his weekly radio Bible broadcasts, and his promise of twenty-five dollars credit per month for every family in the province – "Social Credit" – though he did not explain where that money was going to come from and, indeed, he did not know. That promise was never fulfilled, though Aberhart and his successor, Ernest Manning (father of Preston Manning, Canadian Reform Party founder), governed Alberta for the next thirty-six years.

Again, according to Pierre Berton, "There has never been anything in Canada remotely like the Alberta election campaign of 1935. - - - "Bible Bill" Aberhart's march to victory, accompanied as it was by the kind of hi-jinks associated with old-fashioned medicine shows, has had no counterpart."[3] His political rallies were " - - - part picnic, part religious rally, part political kick-off and part vaudeville show."[4]

I, at age seven, knew none of these things, had probably never heard the work "politics." I knew only that we were going to a town picnic and, until I was adult, had assumed it was the annual one we usually attended. It *was* different; there were many more people than usual, great squashing crowds, and high excitement in the air. Though children were pushed into line for our free ice-

---

[3] *The Great Depression 1929-1939*, McLelland & Stewart Inc., 1990
[4] Ibid.

cream cone and lemonade, and vaguely encouraged to participate in the various races and sports events, adults' attention seemed to be focussed elsewhere that day, as they talked animatedly among themselves.

We were at an Aberhart, Social Credit political rally. Suddenly the crowd compressed, surged forward. Squeezed to my mother's side, I held on to her as the mass of people pressed around and above me, with many arms and elbows in my face. Between the stifling, shifting, excited bodies, many exclaiming, "He's coming! He's coming!" I caught a glimpse of shiny black cars. "Make room! Make room!" called the organizers; the crowd opened slightly and there, not four feet in front of me, from the lead car emerged the most gigantic person I had ever seen. At the time I only thought, "fat." I had seldom seen a fat person, a rarity in Depression years, but Bible Bill Aberhart was not only fat, he was mountainous in every part, more or less in proportion. His mostly bald head was large and oval, his cheeks, his jowls, his overhanging brows, his chins were fat, his nose and lips thick. I gazed in awe, wondering if this was a real person.

My mother was pushing and urging me, "Shake his hand! Shake his hand!" I was so close to him that his great paunch, on a level with my head, obscured his face. I didn't know why I was to shake his hand and I felt an aversion to doing so but, used to obeying, I stuck out my scrawny little brown hand which

165

immediately disappeared into Mr. Aberhart's great, pink pudgy one, much as my mother's fists disappeared into bread dough. The crowd closed in and we moved to find air.

The next scene was in the stifling hot Community Hall. Somehow, our parents had found seats less than halfway from the front in the standing-room-only crowd. Outside doors were opened and scores of people milled outside each one to hear and see what they could. The colossal man shouted and ranted from the stage. The audience shouted, sweated and applauded. I was tired, hot, restless and bored. Then, wonder of wonders, a magician appeared! I had never seen such a thing. He pulled reams of colorful silk scarves from everything. I hoped he would throw some into the audience. After that a family of acrobats performed, again, a totally new experience for us. A beautiful young daughter, dressed in shining satin tights, climbed to the top of a high pedestal, positioned herself, seated, on a tiny perch, and proceeded to slowly and carefully entwine each of her legs over her shoulders and cross her ankles at the back of her neck. I was mesmerized. The adults talked about that for days and weeks.

"They soak themselves in vinegar, you know," someone told my mother, who passed on the information to the rest of the family. "That is how they make their bones soft enough to twist themselves into those shapes."

I have in my possession a small book called *The Edinburgh*

166

Book of Plain Cookery Recipes, from the Edinburgh School of Cookery and Domestic Economy, Ltd., founded October 1875 (with "Special Curriculum for the Housewife's Diploma"). Among the many recipes for simple, old-fashioned cakes, puddings, meat and vegetable dishes, are a few surprisingly "modern" ones – baked, stuffed cod, grilled steaks, potato chips, pea soup. The most intriguing recipes, however, are in the *Sick-Room Cookery* section, and include *Treacle Posset* (one tablespoonful of treacle, one gill of milk, boiled, curdled and strained) *Port Wine Lozenges*, which contain one quarter ounce of isinglass, *Toast Water* and *Restorative Soup*.

The authors conclude the *Preliminary* (Preface) with, "- - - whether the income be large or small, the food costly or simple, there should be equal care and attention exercised, so that waste may be avoided, and that the best result for the amount of money expended may be obtained." In my imagination, I read this out to my mother, my aunt, and all the prairie farm women who struggled to feed their families through the long years of the Great Depression. Clearly and firmly I hear their voices down the years replying, "Well, I sure don't need a book to tell me *that!*"

The *Parcel*

Green stockings! How could we wear *green* stockings to school? And to make matters worse, they were really scratchy and made our legs itch, even through our long fleece-lined underwear. They weren't a nice dark green either, but a kind of yellowy olive colour, and they were knit of very thick wool in a wide ribbed pattern. My sister and I thought they were about the ugliest things we had ever seen. Today they would be considered quite special, as hand knitted pure wool stockings. They were special then, too, I'm sure, just as I'm sure they must have been very much warmer than the thin cotton stockings we usually wore, but in our limited world stockings were supposed to be brown. They were actually a tan color and if you were a girl that's what you wore – long tan cotton stockings, held up by a cotton vest with four long garters on it when we were little, later by pieces of sewing elastic stitched in a ring for garters and often by rubber canning jar rings when there was no elastic in the house. How those rubber jar rings hurt! – unless we managed to get a couple that were quite old and soft.

In the spring, after we were allowed to wear short summer underwear, our stockings were rolled to just below the knee, or to the ankle, at least while at school, and rolled up if deemed prudent

169

on the way home. Grownup ladies wore tan stockings made of something called "lisle," (pronounced "lile") a mixture of cotton and rayon. "Rich" ladies had silk stockings. If you were a man or boy you wore grey wool or cotton socks for everyday, and thinner black or brown ones for good. *Nobody* wore *green* stockings!

Our mother had got Mrs. Bock, who lived on the neighbouring farm to the west, to knit the stockings for us. I think Mother was impressed that Mrs. Bock could knit. Mother sewed all our clothes, beautifully, often without patterns, did lovely embroidery and crochet work, made quilts, curtains, tablecloths, rag rugs and everything else that was needed in a large farm family, but she didn't knit. One time later on, she acquired a knitting machine and tried it out. I don't remember it ever producing anything useable and it eventually disappeared. I'm sure that Mrs. Bock knit all her family's sweaters, socks, scarves, toques and mitts. I don't know where the green wool came from, probably a mail order house, as did a large part of everyone's supplies. Probably also there was not a wide choice of colours and materials, and this was so with many things. Whatever one wanted to buy, there were at most four or five choices. Cloth was made of wool, cotton, linen, rayon or silk, or blends of those. In larger centres like Calgary or Edmonton, there possibly were more choices, but even there it would have been nothing like today, with the infinite variety of materials, patterns and colours. In any case, city goods were not generally available to farmers or their wives and children. Calgary was one hundred miles away on a gravel road and getting there was a major event. Even later, when Dad had a car or truck, it only happened twice for me, in my fifteen years of farm life. For many farm children it didn't happen at all.

I think now that our mother may have secretly been a little surprised herself at the colour of the stockings, but she would never have let us know that. It was so uncharacteristic of her conventional good taste in colours and materials to have chosen that for her children. I had some vague intuition about that at the time, too, in my first total disbelief that she actually did expect us to wear them. Her insistence that it was a "nice" colour was a little too assertive, and we not only didn't think so, we couldn't really believe that *she* thought so. Her other argument, "Mrs. Bock was a nice lady to knit them for you and you should be grateful," pricked our guilt and we knew it was true, but our anticipation of complete disgrace if we had to wear these stockings to school totally overshadowed any of Mother's attempts at reason. In the end, we wore them because they were what we had, and because we were told to, which is what we would have expected to do in the first place with no argument, if Mother hadn't betrayed her own doubts by trying to talk us into liking them.

In every large family at any time, clothing must obviously be a major item, not only of expense, but of thought, planning and care.

The Depression years and farm life itself brought their own particular challenges to this facet of living. Our family, as most others that we knew, depended heavily on Eaton's mail order catalogue. How many hours of looking and planning, scheming and dreaming, and literal counting of pennies, choosing, rejecting and juggling – and sometimes arguing – went on in the evenings over the catalogue! Multiply that by many thousands of people over many years and Mr. Timothy Eaton would be in awe at the enormity of what he had started.

As far as our clothing was concerned, the big event of the year was the arrival of The Parcel. Though smaller mail order parcels came from time to time throughout the year, sometimes from the Army and Navy catalogue, there was only one that really excited us, because it held all the materials for our winter clothing. What a great deal of work and planning our parents must have done to accomplish this. No doubt the order coincided purposely with the end of fall harvest, the only time of year when farmers received cash for their work. But what about the years when there was no cash, when the crop had been poor, or hailed out? I know that happened to my parents, as to many others, but I don't remember there ever *not* being a fall parcel from Eaton's. Whatever the farm had or had not produced, children still had to have shoes and warm clothing to go to school, and so somehow miracles were produced.

The Parcel, to my young eyes, was always *huge*. Often we

brought the box home from the Post Office after school in our buggy or cart. We always knew it was expected and our mother, too, kept looking for it every day, so our excitement would build, and by the time it actually arrived the event would be second to only one other in the year – the Christmas Concert.

The box would not be opened until after chores, supper and homework were done, and we couldn't get through those fast enough. Milking cows, feeding calves, pigs and horses, washing dishes were all done in record time, although I don't venture guesses as to how thoroughly. Even Mother's anticipation showed as she cooked supper and supervised her household. Finally, finally Dad cut the strings, the box was opened, and we were allowed to see, feel and smell the newness of whatever had been ordered for each of us. There ensued a lot of trying on, and discussion, with, "does that pinch?" and, "wiggle your toes," "turn around," orders to get our hands out of the box, stand back, quit crowding, and so forth. Sometimes there was further excitement, sometimes disappointment, but since we were never told ahead of time what had been ordered there was always the hope of something special, and there was always the feel and smell of newness. Even the inevitable big royal blue cotton fleece-lined bloomers were all right at first!

There was also the fun of seeing what the others had got. The boys clothing was so different from ours and that was always such a mystery to me when I was very small. I really envied them their nice new bib overalls with the brass buttons! My sister and I got to wear those around the farm in the summer, cut off at the knees, when they were nearly worn out, but even though we loved the freedom of bare feet and no shirts in the hot sunshine and dust, it wasn't the same as what I thought it must be like to get a brand new pair of overalls. In those years, it was still not acceptable for women and girls to wear men's style pants, even for farm work and riding horses, though some did. World War II, with women working in munitions factories, began to change all that, but it was not until the mid 1940s that we girls even had pyjamas, and it was years later that pants on women were considered "respectable" in school or office.

One year my brothers got some lovely pale grey leather moccasins in The Parcel. I thought they were beautiful and I really wanted some, and I must have asked because Mother told me definitely, "No. They are boys' shoes." They looked soft and cozy but my brother has since told me that they were cold to wear.

Starting from the skin out, there was first, for everyone except our mother, long, one-piece white cotton fleece-lined underwear. We couldn't get very excited at the thought of again being cocooned in this for several long months, but while new anything was nice. There were buttons down the front and a trap door in the back, and the first thing that usually happened was that

174

the button burst off the trap door and got lost, and we had to pin it and then sit on the pin all day in school.

The other thing about cotton long johns was that they stretched sideways and shrunk lengthwise, and the fleece wore off the inside very quickly. Then we had to fold the leg over at the ankle to get our stockings on, which made a big lump inside our boot, which hurt all day. By late spring of the following year they were worn and stretched and shapeless, and when Mother decided the weather was warm enough she would cut the legs and arms off for us (not too short) and we wore them like that until the hot summer weather. What a tremendous sense of freedom for us, when the day finally came that our mother cut off our underwear! By early spring we were all really tired of it, and so we four youngest would begin our begging campaign, planning it out on the long drive home from school, taking turns to ask, hoping to wear her down. How thoroughly sick and tired *she* must have got of our annual refrain, "The Andreassen kids have *their* underwear cut off!" I have wondered since if our campaigns did any good, and if Mother did ever cut off our underwear any earlier, if only to shut us up. To us the waiting seemed interminable, and the begging campaigns absolutely essential or, we really believed, she would never cut them off at all.

What I suspect now is that she knew all along exactly when she would do it and that's what she did, and her standard yearly answer to us was always the same. "I don't care *what* the Andreassen kids have. You'll get yours cut off when I say so. Now go and do your chores." For many of our growing years our summer underclothes were sewn by Mother from bleached cotton flour and sugar sacks. I don't recall ever wearing any outer garments made from these, but I know that children in other families did. These cotton sacks were also made into a variety of household linens – dishtowels, embroidered pillowcases, doilies, dresser scarves and tablecloths.

Our mother never wore the ugly underwear that the rest of us wore. In The Parcel would be soft, thin, feminine looking wool vests and drawers, which she didn't show to us, but we saw them later in the washing. They had lacy edges around the neck and the short sleeves, and I couldn't wait to grow up so I could wear underwear like that. (When the time came, I was living in a different climate so I never did.)

Also in The Parcel for our mother, and what she didn't seem to mind us seeing, was a heavy brocade, complicated looking, boned contraption with many laces back and front, which was called a corset. Most mature women wore them. They must have been hard to put on and terribly uncomfortable to wear. When I was a very thin thirteen, Mother decided I was becoming a woman, so she bought me a "corselette," a less laced version of her corsets, but with bones, garters and about a thousand hooks and eyes up the side, one of which centred right on my skinny hip bone and kept it rubbed raw. I didn't know why my mother bought me that. Maybe her imagination saw some budding figure where there was as yet none. I had mixed feelings, pleased that I was singled out for her attention and that she saw me as somewhat "grown up," but resistant to wearing what felt like a suit of armour for reasons that totally eluded me. I wore it a few times, more to please my mother than anything, and then gradually stopped. Eventually it disappeared from my dresser drawer, gone possibly to some luckless cousin. I gather my mother decided it was a mistake as my sister, a year younger, was never presented with a similar garment.

The other thing that stands out about the corsets in The Parcel is how often Eaton's seemed to send the wrong thing, and how Mother seemed to get more upset about that than about other substitutions. She would hold them up, all the laces dangling, and inspect them, while we looked on, waiting to get past this boring piece of harness and into the "good stuff," meaning ours, of course. "Aw, they've sent me the wrong one! The fools!" she would exclaim, and there would ensue an examination of the bills and maybe the catalogue, and more exasperated remarks about T. Eaton's, "the blamed fools!" Dad made comments and suggestions, while we shuffled our feet and kept quiet until things simmered down, lest we get sent to bed before the rest of The Parcel contents had been examined.

177

After the long underwear came the big bloomers, all fleecy on the inside, dying our underwear blue, and after that yards of soft dark grey flannelette for making our petticoats (known today as "slips"). There would be doeskin, a heavy flannelette, in pretty colours and patterns for our Christmas dresses. It was always the same pattern for my sister and me, hers usually in pink or red, mine in blue. One time when we were about twelve and thirteen we decided we were tired of always having the same colours and we asked Mother if we could trade, so that time she made my dress pink and my sister's blue. Neither of us liked them and felt like the other had on her dress. There was also doeskin for shirts for the boys, usually plaid or checked. Everyone had to have something new to wear for the Christmas Concert and afterward to school.

When we were very young my sister and I wore little black boots, leather around the foot with felt above, and laced above the ankle. They were very pretty and we loved them, but they were cold to wear and they wore out quickly. Most years we also had one pair of patent leather shoes for good, and the boys had a pair of oxfords.

Then came the outer wear. For the snow we had high topped rubbery overshoes. They had stiff metal buckles that froze together in the snow, hurt our fingers, broke off, got rusty and were generally miserable. I don't know what those overshoes were really made of, but they felt like the inside of tires. They kept out the snow, but not the cold or wet. I was always sure that they made my feet colder. We all wore them except our mother, who had pretty, velvety black overshoes, which I loved to see and touch. They had laces hidden by soft black fur from the toe up the front and around the ankle. She wore variations of this boot all her life, though in later years they were made to go right on the foot, rather than over the shoe.

There were shirts, boots and work pants for Dad, who never wore the denim pants or bib overalls worn by many farmers at that time. Blue denim, contrary to its present status, was a very humble material then, considered by most children and adults to be appropriate for farm work, but sometimes an embarrassment to wear in public. Even in elementary school, where most farm boys wore denim bib overalls, it was understood that they wore them because that was all they had. The Parcel often yielded as well an assortment of necessary items for the farm, a piece of horse's harness, or a needed tool, possibly a blanket or yards of grey flannelette for Mother to sew into bedsheets, and almost always a length of thin striped terrycloth to make roller towels.

Nearly every farm home had a roller towel in the kitchen. It was an earlier, simpler version of the roller towels now used in some public washrooms. It consisted of pieces of wooden dowelling placed between brackets that were mounted on the wall. A length of towelling was sewn together to make a continuous circular towel and this was hung on the rollers. The towel was three or four feet long, depending on the height of the shortest person who needed to reach it, and it was usually placed near the enamel washbasin and the water pail. When you washed your hands or face you pulled the towel around to the next clean spot, if you could find one. Otherwise you did what every other kid did, wiped your hands on your clothes. The dowelling made a great rattling noise as it turned around in the brackets, so if you were supposed to be washing up, and if no one else was in the kitchen to watch you – or tattle on you – you could try to fake it by making a great clatter with the roller towel. The usual reason for wanting to do this was that there was no water left in the pail, which meant that you had to go outside and get some from the water barrels, or from the large galvanized horse trough that stood behind the house to catch rainwater off the roof. This trick only ever worked for a few minutes, because the next person to come along to wash would know immediately what had happened. And it was no use saying you'd used the last of the water and thrown it out. They knew you hadn't. In a family of eight there is always someone who knows where any given person is at any given time! Anyway, you were still supposed to fill the pail.

Instead of the usual thin leather helmets lined with cotton that the boys wore in winter, they and Dad sometimes got in The Parcel, wonderful brown fur caps, with flaps that would turn down over ears and forehead. That was another thing I wished was made

180

for girls. Helmets or toques did not keep the snow out of our necks, even with a scarf around them. There were wool mittens and cold stiff cowhide mitts to go over them. Hands inside these plaster casts instantly froze, until after the mitts had got quite worn and soft, at which time they were no longer waterproof. When I was around twelve, snowpants, the forerunners of today's wonderful snow and ski suits, were invented. They were made of a heavy wool Melton cloth, and Mother bought my sister and me each a pair. That is the first time I ever remember being close to warm enough in the winter.

Coats and jackets were a large important item, and must have often been a problem for our mother, with so many children to dress. The boys and Dad wore mackinaws in the winter, heavy wool jackets with big collars that could be turned up, lined with sheepskin or other warm material. I always thought Mother's coats were really pretty, even when they had been worn for several years. The winter ones were of wool, or wool and cotton mix, and were often black, grey or brown, but sometimes pretty colours, a rich blue or green or dark red, with usually some black imitation fur around the collar. If they were not too worn when she was finished with them, she could sometimes make a coat or jacket for one of us, otherwise they went into the hooked rag rugs, and we spent long hours on winter evenings cutting them into strips which were rolled

181

into balls and put away until there were enough.

Sometimes one of us got a new coat in The Parcel and that was a Big Event. I got one once when I was eleven or twelve, a beautiful blue "princess style" coat. I loved it and wore it until it was much too small. At twelve I also got my first "bought dress" and that indeed was a Big Event! It was not in the winter parcel, but a summer one, and what a great thrill of surprise it was when Mother came to me with a catalogue, pointed out two dresses and told me to choose one of them. I could not believe this special thing was happening to me! Never before had we had choices of our clothing. I suppose the older ones may have, perhaps as they got to a certain age, but I wasn't aware of it.

The choice was not difficult. One dress did not appeal at all and the other one was beautiful! It cost two dollars and ninety-eight cents. Then, oh, the exciting torture of waiting! What if they substituted something else? What if it didn't fit and Mother would send it back? Finally it arrived and to my eyes it was all that I could have dreamed and more. It was made of a lightweight gauzy cotton with short sleeves, a wide set-in waistband with ties at the back and a gathered skirt. It was white with large deep pink flowers and green leaves scattered here and there. It fit perfectly! Never do I remember feeling so special, both in receiving and wearing that dress, but as the old song goes, "It wore, and it wore, and it wore, 'til it went, and it wasn't no more."[1]

At times our coats, as well as other clothing, were given to Mother by people whose children had outgrown them. I seldom knew who they were. I was often heir to my older sister's clothes, which Mother would cut down for me, and I liked that. Milly was eight years older than I, and I thought her clothes quite beautiful.

Two winter coats stand out in my memory, one because I liked it and one because I didn't. The first (oh, great joy!) came out of The Parcel when I was about ten and there was one for my younger sister, too. They were a deep, rich tan colour and were made of some kind of short fake fur. They were warm and soft and we thought very pretty. We wore them until they wore out, at which time Mother cut out the good pieces, which she sewed together into a small blanket. We used this to huddle under in the sleigh and it lasted for many years, until most of the fur rubbed off.

The other coat was given to Mother by a neighbour. I was the one it fit, and who needed a coat. I was a very thin ("skinny" was the word usually applied) thirteen at the time and becoming even more self-conscious about clothing than I had always been. This coat was shiny black, made of a stiff, unyielding, hairy, scratchy fabric that looked and felt like horsehide. Maybe it was. It

---

[1] Alice Blue Gown. 1919. Music, Harry Tierney; Lyrics, Joseph McCartney.

had large black buttons that were hard to fasten, long, tight sleeves and a large shawl collar of the same material that covered my shoulders and half my back. It weighed a ton. When I took it off I could stand it on the floor and it stood up by itself. When I had it on I could hardly walk for the weight of it, and it was so ungiving that I had to be helped in and out of the sleigh. I couldn't do anything else, either, because I couldn't bend my arms. If my toque fell off, if I dropped my mitts, if I itched, if my nose ran – a chronic condition in the winter for most of us, I was helpless. It also did not keep me warm, and other kids made fun of it. The best that could be said for it was that it kept out the wind. It was a veritable fortress. I think my mother must have noticed some of its negative aspects, as she didn't make me wear it more than one year, and my sister didn't have to wear it the next. It just quietly disappeared, probably in a box of clothing to some of our "poor relations."

To me, The Parcel was always bottomless. That perception, I think, was because it was perennial. No matter what came out of it in any given year, or what didn't come out of it, there was always going to be another one next year. And whatever our secret hopes and disappointments, there was always something new in it for everyone, even if it was only a pair of long fleece-lined underwear.

As for the outrageous green knitted stockings, all our protests were in vain. Mother had paid or traded something for them, they were warm, and we had to wear them. When they got

184

holes in them they were mended and we continued to wear them, and scratch, until they were beyond redemption, at which time they were cut into strips and hooked into a rug.

Weird and Wonderful One-Hoss Shays

or

Gittup, Darky

Have you heard of the wonderful one-hoss shay,
That was built in such a logical way
It ran a hundred years to a day, - - - ?[1]

Only in our memories, and perhaps those of some of our teachers and fellow students, will any of our father's amazing vehicular contraptions for getting us to and from school live on. Built in logical ways though they may have been, most of them shook, rattled and rocked themselves apart on the rutted gumbo roads after one or two years, but necessity plus Dad's inventiveness always produced another.

One warm spring day, when I was six, I walked the four miles home from school by myself. I started my first school year riding behind my big sister, Milly, on a horse, with our two brothers on another one. I don't know where they all were that day; possibly they had to stay at school longer for some reason, but I had walked on ahead, expecting them to catch up to me. As I walked through

---

[1] *The Deacon's Masterpiece*, or, *The Wonderful One-Hoss Shay*, by Oliver Wendell Holmes, 1809-1894.

the gateway of poplar and maple trees into our farmyard I saw Dad busy hammering at something. He called me over, told me to climb into a large wooden box he was building, and to sit on a low bench. He then, to my mystification, measured with a stick from the floor to the top of my head. He was building our first school cart, a large shingled wooden box with a flat roof, two rubber tired wheels, a door at the back, a peephole at the front, and a pair of shafts with which one horse could pull it. Inside were the little wooden benches, one along each side. It was crowded, as it jolted over the rough roads in summer. It was often very cold in winter and the benches were hard, but it got first four, then five and sometimes six of us to school and back in all kinds of prairie weather.

In the winter, like most of its successors, the box was "lifted off the wheels and set on the front bobs of a sleigh. A bob-sleigh has two sets of sleighs under it, similar to a wheeled vehicle that has one pair of front wheels and a pair of rear wheels. On a bob-sleigh the rear set of runners is stationary while the front ones swivel, allowing the driver to steer it around corners. A sleigh that is not a bob-sleigh would have two long runners, one on each side all the way from front to back. Most children's sleighs are of this variety. When our carts were put on the sleighs we were able to use two horses instead of just one. The horses were still used in the fields at that time, so in summer we only got the old pokey leftovers, but in the winter the horses were idle so we got to use the better ones and we could go a lot faster and pile on a lot more kids!"[2]

The bottom of the cart or sleigh would be filled with clean straw in winter to keep us off the cold floor. In this straw would be placed a large rock which Mother had heated in the oven. This, plus whatever old blankets we had, kept us warm on the way to school in below freezing weather. Things were not quite so nice on the way home. We had not just come out of a warm kitchen with stomachs full of hot oatmeal porridge. Sometimes we had to run the blockade of snow forts and snowball battles in the schoolyard, so we often started out cold, with snow inside our clothing. The cart and blanket also sometimes had snow in them and the rock was cold. Even the poor horse was cold and often, by the time we reached home, had a long icicle hanging from her nose. Temperatures of twenty and thirty below (F.) were not unusual, were indeed expected, and if there was, as often, a wind or a blizzard, they would drop to much lower than that.

The clothing available then was not very efficient in keeping heat in small bodies, or large ones either, for that matter. With us, then, as with many others, there were occasionally some frostbitten cheeks, noses, fingers, toes or ears. Our mother would anxiously rub the frozen parts with snow, the accepted painful remedy. I'm

---

[2] Howard Nash, 1992.

not sure if the snow or our tears thawed our cheeks, but I well remember the misery for days of swollen, hurting, itching chilblained toes.

Oliver Wendell Holmes goes on to say, "Now in building of chaises, I tell you what, there is always somewhere a weakest spot, - - - And that's the reason, beyond a doubt, that a chaise *breaks down* but doesn't *wear out.*"[3] Well, that first poor old cart literally squeaked, rocked and shook itself to pieces. Its successor was short lived, to all its occupants' and probably the horse's relief. Dad may have used the same basic low box and wheels, but this time the top was a large sheet of galvanized tin curved across from wheel to wheel to look just like a small tin Covered Wagon. There was a flap of canvas at the back and another at the front. Because of the curved top it was impossible to sit up straight in this cart unless we sat on the floor. I'm sure the only thing that saved us from scoliosis was the habit of some of our teachers of going round the classroom with a ruler and the command, "Sit up straight!" often accompanied by a sharp poke in the back. A lot of "corrective" attention was given by adults to children's posture at that time.

The worst thing about that cart was the noise. It banged and clanged over the stones and the ruts, scaring our horse, Darky, and letting everyone within a mile know that we were on our way.

---

[3] *The Deacon's Masterpiece.*

There was no slipping quietly into the schoolyard hoping no one would notice, if we happened to be late. Our arrival was announced with a din and a tinny clash of cymbals, as we clattered over the railway tracks into town, and I'm sure that our noisy departure in the afternoon, usually by way of the one main street, occasioned a collective sigh of relief from the village as it settled back into its usual tranquillity.

When rain fell on the tin roof the noise was deafening, and when it hailed it sounded like machine guns in our ears. Hailstones were BIG in Alberta! The horse would bolt, we would all be bouncing and shouting at Harvey to hold the horse; he would be shouting at the horse, and nobody was listening to anybody.

One cool fall day on our way home, poor old Darky, her nerves already nearly shot, shied at a passing car, a rarity then, and dumped us, inside the cart, upside down into the ditch, with a tremendous clanging finale rivalled in volume only by Beethoven's *Ninth*. We crawled out, unhurt, and listened to the wonderful silence! My brothers got Darky unhitched and out of the ditch and some of us got to ride home, trailing harness, while the rest walked. We left the covered wagon in its final shallow resting place from which, I assume, Dad later collected the last remains. There were no mourners.

The thing I liked best about our four-wheeled buggy was the feeling of stability, after the unsteadiness of the two-wheeled carts.

191

I think Dad meant this one to last, and it did. At first it looked like a small, square, old-fashioned wooden car, painted bright red. The wheels were large and thin with many spokes, which gave the buggy a light look and feel. Because it was so much higher from the ground than the previous ones and, because the cab was narrow, making me feel somewhat claustrophobic, I was at first a bit nervous in it, thinking that it might tip over. At least I got to sit upright on the seat with Howard, two years older. Our younger sister and brother had to squash on the floor in the front, with their heads bumping under the hood.

After the winter, Dad sawed the top off it and it became a reasonably roomy open buggy, with no battered heads. I liked riding in it then and I liked driving it, as I sometimes did alone, particularly during harvest time when Mother needed supplies from town, or food to be taken to the men in the fields. Most of us learned early to saddle and bridle a horse, or to harness it and hitch up to the buggy. I liked that part of farm work, and curry-combing the horse afterward, but Dad had a very heavy saddle and getting it onto the horse took me a long time. Sometimes I would try to get the horse to stand sideways in the stall, while I stood on the top rail of the manger and tried to manoeuvre the saddle onto its back. This often resulted in the horse deciding to move at the crucial moment, landing me backwards in the manger with the saddle on top of me.

Most frustrating and aggravating was when the horse

192

decided he didn't *want* a saddle, so he would distend his belly, making it impossible for me to fasten the cinch tightly enough to keep the saddle on. I always took this personally, and thought the horse was really just letting me know that he was the boss. That actually may have been the message intended. I would back myself up to the barn wall, get first one bare foot and then the other up onto the side of his belly, push with my feet and pull with all my inadequate strength on the cinch. My child sized feet made little impression and the horse let me cinch and fasten the belly-band when he was good and ready. I was always a little nervous, too, when there was one of Dad's big workhorses in the same stall, afraid that it might step on my bare feet with one of its huge hooves.

Best of all I liked the warm, rich autumn days on which we arrived home from school to be told to leave the horse hitched up and to change into our work clothes. It was time to bring in the garden produce, before the first frost. Directed by Mother, we would lead the horse and buggy down the long garden rows, where mounds of pumpkins, squash, cucumbers, marrows, turnips, parsnips, cabbages and carrots waited. We piled them high in the buggy and I thought they looked beautiful, though I wasn't always so fond of eating them. They were all unloaded then at the house in preparation for the great surge of canning, pickling and pie making, or for storage in the dug-out cellar under the house.

One member of our family probably has a different memory

193

of that buggy, if he hasn't managed to block it out. Our horse, along with those of other farm children, stood all day in the school barn, where there were stalls and mangers with feed boxes. "We usually carried a greenfeed bundle (sheaf) to give the horse at noon; if not that, a little bag of oats or chop. The horses were to get a drink on the way home if possible, at Paterson's spring or in a slough along the road. Often in winter there was no open water along the way. Then someone had to water them at the pump or ride down to the creek and chop a hole in the ice. That had to be done each day anyway for the cattle. It seems this chore was always done in the dark."[4]

A half mile from home there was a fair sized slough in the ditch and field beside the road. We often went there in the spring to collect jars full of muddy water and pollywogs. When the water was high this was a good place to water our horse. To do that we had to drive into the shallow ditch and through the edge of the water. On one particular day Howard, who was driving, happened to go in at a rather steep angle, and the buggy tipped sharply. Donnie, then about six or seven, panicked and began yelling that we were going to tip over. The rest of us told him that we were not, but he was standing up, starting to climb out over the side. He got onto the large back wheel, on the bottom rim between the spokes, arms

[4] Howard Nash, 1992.

clinging to the top, while yelling, "Stop! Stop!" not hearing all of us yelling at him to get back into the buggy.

I then became very afraid that he would drown, but Howard, his hands full trying to manoeuvre horse and buggy, said, "He won't drown. He'll jump off." Darky, intent on getting her long overdue drink of water, was not about to stop and I guess that Don was afraid to let go, so down he went on the wheel, coming up awash with water, mud and tears.

I'm afraid the rest of us thought it was hilarious and I don't think we let him back into the buggy, in spite of dire threats of, "- - - going to tell Mamma on you!" I don't remember any particular consequences of dumping our poor little brother into the slough, but maybe *I* have blocked *that* out.

Much of what we had on the farm – furniture, dishes, machinery, livestock – was bought at farm auctions, when people were selling off their farms and possessions and moving elsewhere. An auctioneer was hired and it was his job to organize the sale and get the best prices he could for everything. One time Dad came home from an auction with a "cutter," a small sleigh made to be pulled by a team of horses, for which he had paid fifty cents. All of his life he loved a bargain. The cutter was made from the hood of an old car, complete with windshield, with a box seat for two attached. It was very small, but fast and fun to ride in. At least it was fun for me.

195

By some only partially correct logic, "younger" was often equated with "smaller." My sister Bertie (short for "Alberta Rose") and I were only a year apart in age, and by the time we were seven or eight were much the same size. Our parents didn't seem to notice this, however, and in the case of seating arrangements for school carts I certainly wasn't about to point it out. So there were Bertie and Donnie again, squashed under the hood of the cutter, with Howard's and my feet in their faces. A few times they clung onto the sleigh runners or the very tiny ledge behind the seat, but this was very chancy, as the cutter was light and swift and tended to take some pretty sharp corners. "Yogi Yorgesson" (Harry Stewart) in his Swedish parody of "Jingle Bells," used to sing in the 1950's:

> Dashing t'rough da snow,
> Vit da cold vind in our face,
> Ay can't hold da horse,
> He t'inks he's in ay race.
> Ay can't hear my vife yell,
> Ay can't see her face,
> Ay guess ay must have lost her ven
> Ve turned at Yohnson's place - - -

Whenever I heard that song, I always thought of that cutter with one or another child falling off the back into a snowdrift as we flew around a corner.

School was not the only thing for which the sleighs, cutters and buggies were used. In summer, transportation was mostly by

196

horseback or in whatever old truck Dad had around at the time, with all of us kids piled in the back. In the winter, for major trips to town, or on the infrequent occasions when all or several of us were going somewhere, Dad hitched the team to the big bob-sleigh with the large wagon box on it. It would be partly filled with straw and warm blankets and that's where we children rode, warm and protected from the wind, while Dad sat on the high seat at the front to guide the horses. Mother usually sat beside him, wrapped well in a buffalo robe and blankets, but in very cold weather she sometimes joined us in the box at the back, in her good coat and hat and little black fur-trimmed overshoes. Other times our parents would set off by themselves to visit a neighbour or go to town, bundled into the cutter, which barely held the two of them, looking, in retrospect, for all the world like a living Currier and Ives print.

The only times I was ever really afraid on our journeys to and from school were when there were electrical storms. These are always very loud and dramatic on the prairies and we heard often of barns, houses and animals being struck by lightning. It was sometimes exciting, from the safety of our home, to watch the bright sheets of lightning flooding the sky, or see the sky crack open with a great zig-zag arrow of fire while ear-splitting thunder shook the house. It was a different matter, though, travelling along in this, a lonely little cart and horse on a long country road with almost never any other traffic, and I felt very exposed and vulnerable.

197

Somewhere I thought I had heard that dry wood was not a good conductor of electricity, so I would secretly hold onto the side of the buggy for protection. It never occurred to me to question how houses, barns and trees got struck by lightning, if that were true.

If it was raining, or had been, one road in particular became a thick mass of gumbo, heavy, slippery, waxy grey clay, that clung in ever increasing layers to the buggy wheels and the horse's hooves, so that soon Darky could barely lift her laden feet. The two tracks in the road became deep ruts in which the buggy slipped and slithered, while the horse slid and strained with all her strength to move the buggy through the greasy mud. I was always very frightened that, even if we didn't get struck by lightning, we would get totally stuck in the mud, or slide into the deep ditch. We didn't *tell* each other that we were scared, of course, but I suspect that I was not the only one.

The most beautiful, sensational vehicle we ever had arrived one sunny day in early winter when I was thirteen. Sadly, as with so many beautiful and fragile things, its life was to be short. Dad had bought it somewhere, probably at an auction sale, and we all trooped excitedly out into the yard to see it, not believing our eyes or our good fortune. There it sat against the snow in its shiny red and black glory, a real, honest-to-goodness Santa Claus sleigh! It was made from the body of a good make of car, possibly a Buick, with a wonderful curved and padded shiny black leather seat like a

198

big comfortable sofa. The metal at the front of the sleigh had been brought up and curved outward, exactly like the Santa Claus sleighs we saw in pictures.

The whole thing was mounted on thin, open metal runners, curved high at the front in a half circle. On either side were the original car doors, which fastened firmly with little spring catches, and there was a running board as a step up, to get in elegantly. No more clambering ungracefully in cumbersome winter clothes over the wheel or the back of a box! The sleigh had obviously been recently painted, the outside shiny black and the inside, the runners and even the tongue, the long pole by which the team of horses pulled it, a beautiful, shiny, Christmas red.

What a joy it was to ride in that sleigh! It is probably just as well that picture taking at that time was not very advanced, was expensive and rare. I'm sure that no picture could do justice to my memory of that sleigh. I am sure also that there must have been days that winter when we drove through storms and bad weather, but I don't remember any of them. In my memory, *every* day that we drove THE SLEIGH was beautiful and bright, with snow and hoarfrost glittering in the sun, like trees and fields full of sparkling, coloured diamonds as we sped through them, with harness jingling and a powder of brilliant crystals flashing in our wake. I felt like the Snow Queen, or at least as though I was riding in a Christmas card. I'm sure that's what we looked like, too, the four of us bundled under blankets in our usual places, Howard and I on the seat, Bertie and Donnie on the straw covered floor in front, facing us, finally with their heads in the sunshine.

Everybody liked our sleigh. Even the teachers came out to look at it, and Miss Oak once accepted a ride to the store in it, giggling all the way. The "town kids" hitched rides on the back or on the runners as we proudly showed it off. It felt good, for a change, to be a little envied. We had been, so often in our lives, on the opposite side of that. Even the horrid, stiff, black horsehair coat I had to wear that winter could not mar nor detract from my pleasure in our own "wonderful two-hoss shay!"

That winter, Mr. Vik, our neighbour across the fields towards town, had made arrangements with Dad for us to give his daughter a ride to and from school. This was fun for us. Blanche was just a bit younger than my sister and I and it was novel for us to have a classmate ride with us. Their house was a half mile off the road we took, so in winter we always drove in to get her and this made a welcome diversion in our routine.

One sparkling cold morning of deep, firm drifts, in late winter, as we were literally dashing through the snow on the stretch of road to Blanche's house, our sleigh suddenly and gently sank into the snow and the horses came to an abrupt full stop. Howard got out to look. ("What do you think the parson found, when he got up

and stared around? The poor old chaise in a heap or mound - - -. ")[5]
The pretty, fragile runners had collapsed. Mr. Vik hitched our team
to his bob-sleigh and we continued on to school. I was completely
sure that Dad could fix our sleigh, but it was not to be. Though
Howard patiently explained all the reasons why it was impractical
and maybe impossible to fix it, and why all my naively proposed
solutions would not work, I had a hard time accepting that nothing
could be done. I don't know what became of the sleigh. Possibly it
took its place among the many relics in the "machinery cemetery"
that dominated our large farmyard, from which Dad drew his supply
of parts for repairs to farm implements.

  I don't know either, how we got to school the rest of that
winter. It was as though the miracle of that sleigh, for me the peak
of our school cart experiences, became enshrined in my memory,
completely overshadowing and excluding any possible replacement.
I mourned privately, and life moved on, as it always does, but,

- - - I tell you, I rather guess
She was a wonder, and nothing less- - -![6]

The wonderful two-hoss shay.

---

[5] *The Deacon's Masterpiece.*
[6] Ibid.

And Don't *Go Through Jensen's Yard*

As I watched a replay on television of the very stirring opening ceremonies of the 1994 Olympic Winter Games in Lillehammer, Norway, I was reminded of how firmly attitudes toward other people and countries are set in childhood. Many times in my adult years I have felt very fortunate to have grown up in a home free of racial prejudice, and if there was any in the community I was not aware of it. Oh, when the war came along in 1939, we heard some mild gossip that a few German families had suddenly become Russian or Rumanian, but there didn't seem to be a lot of animosity about that. And furthermore, who could blame them? Many people in that large and scattered farming community were fairly new Canadians. It is unlikely that anyone wanted to be connected in any way with Adolf Hitler or Fascism. It must have been painful enough to hear about what was happening in their birth countries, where no doubt there were friends and relatives to worry about.

I'm not sure why, as children, we were so conscious of the various nationalities and ethnic groups that formed our community. I always assumed that everyone was, but recently I have wondered if it was mostly just our household. Our father, all his life, was keenly interested in the backgrounds of other people, where they had come from and how, what work they had done there and what precipitated their move. Probably very few of us were more than second or third generation Canadians. People from the same countries or cultures gravitated naturally toward familiar and shared languages, memories and customs. In such a sparsely populated community, all these things were noticed.

We learned about ethnic differences in quite natural ways, sometimes from the way our schoolmates were dressed, sometimes from their speech or from what we told each other about the customs and expectations in our homes, and very often from food. Some children had very oniony things in their lunchpails, or thick sausages such as we never saw at our house. I, for instance, had never heard of garlic. The Norwegian Andreassen kids always had the most wonderful looking, wonderful smelling food in their lard tin pails, thin, rolled up pancakes with icing sugar on them that they called "Lefsa," very different from our good, thick Sunday morning "hotcakes." They had waffles long before we'd heard of them and many other mysterious, delicious looking treats. We had no hesitation in trading our mother's excellent bread, cookies, cake and doughnuts for any of this, if we could persuade the Andreassen kids, which wasn't often.

Emil Jensen was one of a number of people in the community who had come to Canada from Norway in the early

1900's. He later went back to his homeland, married and brought his wife and children to Alberta to begin homesteading. How very difficult it must have been for those young farm wives! Far from their native homes and families, unable, in many cases, to yet speak English, with no near neighbours, the dry and barren prairie must often have seemed very harsh. How glad they would be to find a few other families with whom they could at least converse.

After the death of their mother in Prince Rupert, B.C., Ruby, Harry and Bertha Andreassen, as young children, came to live with their aunt and uncle, Mr. and Mrs. Jensen, and their five older cousins, in a three room farmhouse, in a low creek ravine a mile and a half from our farm home. They were always called "the Andreassen kids" and they were among our earliest friends. Their teenage cousins, Inga, Huldis and Bertha, friends of my "big sister," brought them to our house to play when I was about four or five years old. Thereafter we visited and played at each other's homes, not frequently, but enough to broaden not only our meagre social life, but also our awareness of customs and ways of living that were different from our own. We had a couch in our front room; Jensens had a "davenport." I thought that was a very elegant and impressive word! Our mother wore tan colored lisle stockings and Eaton's catalogue oxford shoes as she went about her energetic , endless days, cooking, sewing, ironing, baking bread, churning butter, gardening, preserving food, and scrubbing clothes, windows and the brown kitchen linoleum. (I thought linoleum was *supposed* to be brown. It wasn't until I was a bit older and we got a new linoleum that I understood that it was brown only because the pattern had all worn off. It took me some time to get over my disappointment. I *liked* the old warm, brown linoleum.)

Mrs. Jensen, of course, did all this varied work, too, but I never saw that. My indelible memory is of her back, as she stood cooking at her kitchen stove on her spotlessly scrubbed wood floor, in her bare feet. We had never seen *anyone's* bare feet, except our own, and the occasional classmate's, on Sports Day. I'm sure the reason I remember Mrs. Jensen in this way is because that is the way I most often saw her, on our way home from school.

In good weather, Howard, Bertie and I often started walking home from school with Ruby, Harry and Bertha, while waiting for Milly and Harvey to catch up to us with our horse and cart. Going through Jensen's farmyard cut a good mile or so off our walk, and we were always invited to do that, though we had strict and repeated orders from home that we were NOT to go through Jensen's yard. It was very hard to obey this rule. We knew that our mother didn't want us standing around looking hungry until Mrs. Jensen felt that she had to feed us, but we also knew that wasn't the way it was at all. I can't say we exactly *hurried* through their yard; I can't say we didn't each secretly wonder what good things were coming out of that oven, but we didn't have to stand around looking hungry. Mrs.

206

Jensen had a heart as big and as warm as her magical wood stove, and we seldom got very far past her door without someone running after us with big warm cookies or slices of warm homemade bread and syrup. So, more than occasionally, we broke the rule and took a chance on not having anyone go home and tattle on us. This meant that we had to eat our cookies and get back out onto the road before our horse and buggy came along.

When we visited each other in the summer we usually played in our playhouses. The Andreassens were allowed the use of an empty granary and we considered them very lucky to have real walls and a roof! Our playhouse walls were outlined with binder twine among the grove of trees surrounding our farmyard. What *really* impressed us, though, was that Ruby and Bertha had little containers with real bits of food, flour, rolled oats, sugar and milk and sometimes a real egg, which they mixed into little cakes. These were then baked in Magic Baking Powder tin lid cake pans in Mrs. Jensen's oven and brought back to the playhouse for us to eat. While we got to stand by the table at home and cut out little cookies with a thimble when our mother was baking, in our playhouses the food was mostly "pretend," except for the sometimes pilfered garden carrots, peas, radishes and turnips. Our cakes, pies and doughnuts were made from leaves and straw and dirt, or just our imaginations, until Ruby, on one visit, showed us how to make real mud pie cookies with water and soil, patting and shaping them and

207

setting them in the sun to "bake." I have not forgotten her insistence, as we served them for tea, that we could not just *pretend* to take a bite, we had to take a *real* bite! I can still feel the mud grating across my teeth.

Bertha and Ruby had different kinds of dolls than we did, too, with strange names that we'd never heard of. They had one named Gary Cooper and one named Clark Gable, who seemed to "speak" in a grown-up manner. They had a daily newspaper in their house and knew about "movies," which we did not. Though I didn't think about it then, I now realize that the Andreassen kids didn't have binder twine playhouses among the trees as we did because, as near as I can recall, there were no trees in their farmyard. It was creekbed land of heavy clay and difficult to grow anything in, except in the fields, which were on higher ground.

As a child my unconscious assumption was that if adults wanted something they would have it, and I think this is so with most young children. It never occurred to me to wonder why Jensens had no trees and few or no flower gardens. If I had wondered I would have just thought they didn't want any. Our mother had wonderful, prolific flower beds in the rich, black loam of our gardens, great frothy masses of Cosmos and Baby's Breath, tall, vibrant stalks of deep blue Delphiniums and many-colored Larkspur, silky Godetia, Clarkia and Poppies, Sunflowers taller than our father, spicy Sweet Williams, purple Pansies with their little

208

velvet faces, heavenly smelling Roses and Sweetpeas, blue and pink Bachelor's Buttons, sunny Marigolds and innumerable others – seeded among the tilled rows of the huge vegetable gardens and in the caragana enclosed front yard off the long porch. Mother's flowers were her recreation and her personal and justifiable pride, and probably also her one luxury in an often harsh and exhausting life.

Long after I was grown I returned for a Hometown Reunion in the community where I was born. There I re-met many early schoolmates, among them, Bertha Andreassen, and we had a brief visit. She told me then that they could never have flowers at their house because nothing would grow in the heavy clay. As a small child she knew she was not "supposed to" ask for or expect gifts, so she never told anyone, but every time her cousins brought the children for a visit to our house, all the long walk this little blonde girl would be secretly anticipating and wondering what kind of flowers our mother would give them this time, because she always knew they would be given *something*. I'm sure many people share the memory of Mother in her garden, scissors in hand, cutting armloads of flowers for her guests. I felt, and still feel, very grateful to Bertha for telling me this little story. I cannot think of a higher or more fitting tribute and memorial to my mother.

I have never been to Norway but I have, from childhood, an unshakeable image in my mind of a clean, proud country full of generous Norwegians, all with hands held out to the rest of us, offering Lefsa and big, warm cookies.

Of Hippies and Hoboes

Go to sleep, you weary hobo,
  Let the towns drift slowly by.
Can't you hear the steel rails humming?
  That's a hobo's lullaby.

Don't you worry 'bout tomorrow,
  Let tomorrow come and go,
Tonight you're in a nice warm boxcar,
  Safe from all that cold and snow.

Pete Seeger

In a place where I once lived, there were many people whom other people called "hippies." Sometimes this name seemed to denote a lifestyle and sometimes it seemed to denote a style of dress. Both of these varied so widely that it is now hard to discover what anyone's definition of "hippie" is. In the 1960's, it used to denote a philosophy, a way of thinking that was reflected in dress and lifestyle. It is difficult also to know if any of these people regarded *themselves* as "hippies." Some of them may have, in fact, been left over from the nineteen sixties. Others obviously were not. Some are now well established in homes and some kind of work, often creative, often independent, that supports themselves and sometimes families. Others move in and out with the weather,

211

living in old converted buses, plastic and plywood shacks or with friends, and many of these have no visible means of support. Many seem politically and socially conscious and work hard to preserve and improve the community in which they live. Some act resentful of the community, seeming to feel that it ought to share everything with them, whether or not they are willing to contribute.

When I was a child in the Depression years of the 1930's, people called those who fit some of these general descriptions "hoboes," and they were perhaps a little easier to define. No people who lived in houses, even if they moved frequently, no matter what their lifestyle or how odd their thinking might be considered, were ever called hoboes. They might be called a lot of other things and I'm sure often were, but a hobo was someone who was on the move. Hoboes arrived on freight trains or on foot and they left the same way. As with "hippie," it is difficult to separate out the various definitions – hoboes, bums or tramps. The appellations were used interchangeably in those years, if not always accurately, for any male who either rode a freight train, looked ragged or a bit seedy, or who knocked on doors asking for work or food.

Hoboes were around, of course, long before the Great Depression of the 1930's, just as hippies were around long before the 1960's. They were just called different things. One origin of the slang word "hip," meaning to be aware, "cool," informed, was the older term, "hep" of the early 1900's. Even as late as the 1930's one still heard about "hep-cats," young people who were supposedly more "with it" than others. In some places and times people who rejected the conventional were tolerated and in some they were not. Socrates is probably a good example of an early hippie, and from what I have read it seems likely that his wife, Xanthippe, thought he was a good example of a bum. In other parts of the world, at various times, free-thinking "hippies" and "hoboes" were sometimes burned as witches.

The difference between the "genuine" hobo or hippie and the thousands of men who rode back and forth across Canada on the top of freight trains during the Depression, is that the "genuine" or chronic hobo or hippie has usually chosen his or her way of life. Another difference is that the "professional" hobo and hippie knows how to get money and the necessities of life when he or she wants or needs to do that.

Most of the endless stream of men who "rode the rails" in the 1930's did not do so from choice. Left with no work and no prospects of work in the cities and larger towns, they set out on a desperate search for jobs in other parts of the country, leaving home and families behind. Social assistance was mostly unheard of, was only just coming into existence at that time and in any case, where it was available, was hardly enough to keep body and spirit together. Also, "going on relief," as it was then called, was considered very degrading and shameful, was only discussed in whispers, and those

213

who were forced to resort to it went to great lengths to hide that humiliating fact from friends and neighbours.

Most of the men who rode the freights did not find work or, if lucky, were given a few hours here and there, at best only enough to get their needed food. Most of them subsisted on handouts from stores or from the back doors of homes, and they usually asked for work before they asked for food. Probably many of them learned "tricks of the trade" from the "professional" hoboes they inevitably met in their travels. These "professionals" often only asked for food.

Men did not come to our door as often as they did to many other homes, because our farm was so far from town and from the railway tracks, but occasionally one would come, perhaps just for that reason, thinking that there would be more chance of work or food where there was less competition. Our father seldom had work for any of them, but each one always got a meal, was treated with respect, recognized for what he was, a person more than willing to work for his living and that of his family, and having a very hard time keeping enough food in his belly through no choice or fault of his own. Dad was also always interested in where the man had come from, what things were like in his home town, and what he used to work at. In this way we had first hand news of other parts of the country not available to us in other ways.

Intrigued by the rare presence of a stranger, we children

would stand around quietly and listen, as our mother cooked up eggs and potatoes, until we were sent off to finish whatever chores we were supposed to be doing, or perhaps down the cellar for a jar of canned plums or saskatoon berries for the meal. Sometimes the man would speak to us, possibly missing his own children, but we were usually too shy to answer, and having then had attention drawn to our presence, would get sent about our business. ("Have you fed the chickens yet? Well, get on out and do it.")

My only direct experience with a man coming to the door to ask for work came on a Sunday morning in the late summer when I was ten. At that time it was my chore to make breakfast for the family on Sunday, while Howard and Harvey, twelve and sixteen, milked the cows and our parents got an extra hour of needed sleep. I had got the fire going in the big cook stove and was mixing batter for the hotcakes, when there was a knock on the door. It startled me as it was only about eight o'clock in the morning and none of our neighbours ever came that early. Visitors of any kind were rare. I didn't know whether I should answer it or not. With my younger sister and brother urging me on, however, we all went to the screen door and I saw my first black person. He was very tall and broad shouldered and after I had said, "Hello," through the screen he asked me to ask my father if there was any work for him in exchange for some food. I said I would and left him on the doorstep.

215

I was then thrown into a terrible dilemma. I knew that on no account was I to wake my parents, but what was I going to do with the waiting man? After hanging around a few minutes in the front room, desperation got the best of me, and I hesitantly tapped on my parents' bedroom door. "Whattya want?" in a sleepy voice from my father.

"There's a man at the door who wants to know if you've got some work for him," I mumbled.

"What? Speak up!" I repeated it, slightly louder. "Oh, I ain't got any work for him," said my father, sounding cross.

Now what to do? Again I dithered in the front room. I was old enough to know that the man was probably hungry. He had likely slept in our barn or haystack. I didn't want to tell him that there was no work for him and to go away. I was a little scared and wished my parents would come out. Finally I had to go out. He'd been standing on the step in the hot sun for what seemed like a long time. I went to the door.

"My dad says he doesn't have any work," I said, looking at my bare feet.

The man then asked politely, "Do you have a piece of bread or a sandwich I can take with me?" I immediately felt relief that I could take some action and said I would get him something. He walked across the yard then, and sat in Dad's old truck, waiting.

I went to the breadbox and discovered that there was only

one crust end of bread left, not enough with which to make a sandwich. Mother was planning to bake bread that day and the dough, which had been "set" the night before, was already rising in the large enamel dishpan on top of the warming oven above the stove. Now I was in a worse dilemma than before. I looked at the bread end and tried to think of something I could do with it. I didn't know what to put in a sandwich anyway. We didn't have things like peanut butter or cheese. Jam sandwiches were the big staple of our school lunches, supplemented by garden vegetables in the summer. I gave up on the bread. I searched around and got an apple from the box in the cellar, though I knew I was not supposed to help myself. Apples were usually just bought in harvest time, to make pies for the threshing crews. Of course, there was the big chocolate layer cake, made for Sunday dinner. I'd made it myself, my Saturday morning chore, and one I liked because then I didn't have to wash the breakfast dishes. I cut a large piece of that. O.K., an apple and a piece of chocolate cake – I knew it wasn't a proper breakfast and I felt awful, inadequate and resourceless. My brothers came in with the pails of milk and one or both of them confirmed that I was doing the wrong thing. Besides that, I didn't have breakfast ready.

I was just rather hopelessly looking for a paper bag to put the apple and cake in when my parents came out and took over. Dad went out and invited the stranger in for a big breakfast and I got on with making the hotcakes. Mother looked at the cake and apple and

217

asked what they were for. "I was making him a lunch," I mumbled.

"That's not a proper lunch," she said. I knew that, but I was so relieved to be out of the whole situation that I didn't say anything. I still thought they could have given him the cake and apple to take with him, though.

In 1939 Hitler invaded Europe, England declared war on Germany, Canada soon followed and everything changed. Almost all of the men disappeared from the freight trains, gone to war or to work to support the war. Suddenly there were more jobs than there were people to fill them. A few chronic hoboes, vagrants, bums or tramps still rode the rails, still came into town once or twice a year on their never-ending journeys, and got handouts from The Red and White or from Robertson's grocery stores. The "depression songs" were replaced by the "war songs," songs of heroism and patriotism, but I still clearly hear my mother's voice singing as she went about her endless work in those most difficult years of "the dirty thirties:"

> I went to a house, and I knocked at the door,
> And the lady said, "Bum, Bum, you've been here before!"
> Hallelujah, I'm a bum! Hallelujah, bum again!
> Hallelujah, give us a handout to revive us again!
>
> "Oh, why don't you work, like other men do?"
> Oh, how can I work when there's no work to do?
> Hallelujah, I'm a bum! Hallelujah, bum again!
> Hallelujah, give us a handout to revive us again!

In the 1950's and '60's I lived with my young family in a Fraser Valley town, across the highway about a half mile from the railroad tracks. A few times in those years, different men came to our back door to ask for work or food. If I was not alone, I invited the man in and cooked him a meal. If I was alone I asked him to wait outside and I made him a lunch to take with him, with lots of sandwiches.

Aunties Are Coming!

An exception to our "Pigpen Roof Watch" for company, written about in another story, was when our Aunt Kathreen and Uncle Jack and our cousins came to visit, which probably doesn't count as a genuine Pigpen Roof Event because, of course, we knew they were coming. We were watching for them, all degrees of excitement permissible!

How we all looked forward to our visits with these relatives! Along with the annual Christmas concert they were the highlights of our year. This was our very special aunt, our father's younger and only surviving sister who, as a vivacious young schoolteacher, had followed her brother from their Fraser Valley home to Alberta, stayed, married and raised a farming family. We often heard the story of how "Auntie" and Uncle Jack were married in our parents' home, six months before my birth, her own parents far away on the coast of British Columbia. In their later years, Dad and Auntie used to sometimes argue about the date of her wedding. Dad, trying to figure it out "logically," insisted that they must have been married on Saturday, January 1st, as no preacher was likely to have time to come out to the farm on a Sunday. Auntie, however, continued to tell him firmly that she was married on Sunday, January 2nd, 1928, and we, the "children," listening as middle-aged adults, marvelled that he could think that any woman, and especially this intelligent, energetic matriarch, would be wrong about her own wedding date.

Though we had a number of other aunts, our mother's sisters, whom we saw infrequently, this was "Auntie," the special one, dark-eyed and loving, and the family of uncle and cousins became a collective "Aunties" by extension, as in our running wild shouts and breathless whoops of, "Aunties are coming! Aunties are coming! We saw their car from the pigpen roof!" We never said, "The Flecks are coming!" I, for one, hardly knew for a number of years, that they *had* a surname. Often, of course, we didn't have a chance to go to the pigpen roof, busy as we were in the bustle of getting the household ready for a visit of several days, and last but by no means considered least, getting ourselves cleaned up. There was sometimes then a few minutes to sneak off to the pigpen roof or even just to climb up on a hayrack or wagon box in the barnyard for a quick inspection of the highway across the fields. One had better not be caught climbing around on greasy things after getting cleaned up, nor be out of earshot, either, in case some chore had not been completed satisfactorily.

"Aunties" lived what was then nearly a day's journey by car to the north of us, so we seldom saw each other more than once a year, either at our house or theirs, and this was a good deal dependent on whether anyone had a motor vehicle at the time and

222

what condition it was in. They once arrived in what I thought was a really elegant car, with a canvas top, shiny leather seats and isinglass windows. It must have taken a great amount of planning and arranging for farm families to get away, with horses, cows, pigs, calves, chickens and other poultry to feed and water each day, the cows to be milked twice a day, the milk to be separated and stored, and all the other necessary daily chores. The timing would have to be just right, maybe somewhere between the young chickens, small animals and gardens having grown to a stage of less required care and the beginning of fall harvest.

We liked our cousins and had fun with them. The three oldest, Alice, Joyce and Jackie, were close in age to us, the three youngest, and one great thing about their visits was that suddenly all the rules changed. It was like a holiday. The adults were so busy talking (all at once, as they always did) and visiting with each other, that they didn't bother much about all us kids, except to call us to meals or to get cleaned up to go somewhere, or line up to have our pictures taken, a BIG production, in those days. Snapshots were always taken, for reasons which still elude me, in the same spot.

"Hurry up! Go comb your hair and go out and line up in front of the caraganas," ordered Mother or Auntie. The caraganas formed a tall, neglected hedge around a flower garden which opened off the long front porch running along one side of our house. We never stood *inside* the caraganas, among Mother's beautiful roses

223

and delphiniums, or in front of the house itself. Consequently, there are no surviving pictures of these.

There ensued much fiddling by adults with the old cameras, black boxes with long accordion-fold front pieces to pull out. There were also many instructions, with Dad and Auntie usually as cameramen.

"Move closer together!"

"Quit shoving!"

"Look at your dad!"

"DON'T MOVE!"

"Smile, now!" and Dad's inevitable, "Stand still or I'll cut your head off!" He said this loudly every single time he took our picture and I, having no knowledge of cameras or picture-taking until I got my first big Brownie box camera at age eighteen, made no connection. I took his words literally, visualizing the many saws and axes around the farm. After the initial fright, however, I eventually realized that he was not really going to cut my head off, and decided that he was just threatening a dire punishment if we did not stand still. I didn't think it was a very nice thing to say to one's children.

Nobody nagged us about chores when Aunties were visiting, though *somebody* must have done them. There were crowds of people to do dishes, bring in wood and gather eggs, so then it didn't seem like chores anymore.

224

Going to bed became fun. Our house was not very big and I never knew where everyone slept, but with only three small bedrooms and a Winnipeg couch in the front room, it had to accommodate up to thirteen people. I think our two older brothers must have slept in the hayloft – a privilege I often begged to share, but that was not considered appropriate for girls. Alice and Joyce and my sister Bertie and I were assigned a double bed in one bedroom, two of us at the head of the old iron bedstead and two at the foot. In another corner of the room, our little brother, Donnie, and their little brother, Jackie, slept head and foot in a cot.

Then the "wild rumpus" began! We bounced around and jumped on the bed and played and traded places and tickled Joyce and pulled the covers off each other and generally had a great noisy time, and only once in a long while came an unexpectedly cheerful adult voice from the front room. "You kids go to sleep!" But they were having such a good time themselves, talking loudly, laughing, playing cards and drinking coffee, making so much noise that they either couldn't hear us or didn't care.

There is a longstanding tradition, perhaps it is a characteristic (or both) in this family which, as far as I can tell, seems to be passed along from generation to generation. I have been unable to decide whether it is an inherited gene or a learned behaviour. I remember when I first became consciously aware of it. I had always known, as we all did, that our father had a loud voice.

225

I'm sure we knew that at birth, or before. When we lived later on the chicken farm at Aldergrove we had a neighbour who always called him "Big Nash." In my teens then, I thought this was in reference to the six inch high, thick, black letters he had painted freehand on our rural mailbox – B. NASH. I later realized that it was an allusion to, first of all, his voice, and second, his presence. He was not an exceptionally big man, a bit over six feet tall, with a proportionate frame, but he did have a big and self-assured presence, to match his voice. I imagine that in his own cowboy days, before any of us were born, his presence might have somewhat resembled that of John Wayne in the old cowboy movies, though our father, with his dark hair and eyes, was better looking than John Wayne. At any rate, our Aldergrove neighbour, Joe Hardy, could always hear him from his own farmyard, the equivalent of a block down the road, giving us our daily instructions about chores, chickens and what not.

My revelation about the family trait occurred when, as an adult, I was once again visiting Aunties on their Alberta farm. Present also, as well as Auntie and Uncle Jack, were Dad, some of my brothers and sisters, most of our cousins with their husbands and wives, and many children. Having just three hours earlier consumed a large farm supper of roast beef, potatoes and gravy, many garden vegetables, homemade bread, butter, pickles, and apple or saskatoon pie with ice cream, it was now time for evening coffee. Around the big kitchen table, laden with fresh buns, cold meats, cheese, pickles, jams and jellies and four or five kinds of cake and cookies, sat about fifteen adults. Playing around the kitchen floor and in various other parts of the house were the children, many of them.

Suddenly I saw something very strange about the whole picture. Traditionally, adults believe that adults are mostly quiet and children are mostly noisy and much of what we read reinforces that idea. Now here were all these adults, all talking animatedly at the tops of their voices, all at the same time (except for Uncle Jack, who always came in with a comment two or three topics late – he was a little bit deaf, so that several people would yell at him, "We're not talking about that anymore!") And there were my cousin Alice's eight little children, along with their many young cousins, all playing and talking very sweetly and quietly among themselves for all those hours. But they must have been watching and learning, or maybe just subconsciously absorbing the adult customs, because now they are all grown up with families of their own, and at a recent family reunion I noticed that it was still the adults who were all talking loudly (all at once) and the children who were all quiet, but I knew they were also secretly watching and learning.

I have thought quite a bit about how they all came to talk so loudly in the first place and, while I have seen a few possibilities, no one answer seems to fit. Our father had seven brothers and sisters, and one could assume that in any large family, getting the desired

227

share of attention might require some loudness. Then there was my discovery, while researching the family history, that our Uncle Ted's partial deafness began with a childhood illness, so perhaps, he being the youngest, the rest of the family were required to speak loudly. However, not *all* the uncles had loud voices; a couple of them were very gentle and quiet indeed. And as for the attention-getting theory, our mother had eleven brothers and sisters, none of whom had loud voices. So suspicion falls on inherited genes, reinforced by the occasional surprise of a loud voice, very reminiscent of Dad's or Auntie's, popping up here and there in a young descendant. With voices, I can only go as far back as our grandparents, our father's parents, neither of whom had loud voices. Therefore, the mystery of which great-great-great ancestor passed on this inheritance must remain. No matter; he or she is still being heard!

There was usually some special outing planned for us all by Mother and Auntie when they came to visit. One very unusual and exciting adventure was the year we all drove the hundred miles to see the Calgary Stampede Parade. This took much letter writing, discussion and organization on the part of the adults and certainly some concern about outlay of cash, at least for car fuel. Aunties had a car or truck that would get them there and back, but Dad needed to borrow a vehicle, as our current one was his old red International truck. He thought it perfectly adequate to pile his brood in for the

228

excursion, but Mother did not, so for once her idea of what was appropriate prevailed, no doubt with support from Auntie.

The big day arrived and we were scrubbed, brushed and told to put on our "good clothes," easily done, no need to stand around deciding which outfit to wear. We each had, girls, one good dress, socks and shoes; boys, one dress shirt, shoes, pair of pants and tie. Eaton's catalogue school shoes had worn out long ago or were too small, or were being worn around the barn and chicken yards for chores with scraps of cardboard stuffed inside to cover the holes in the soles. We mostly ran around barefoot in the summer. Dad left early in the truck and arrived back a few hours later with Billy Donor's car, accompanied by elderly Mrs. Donor, who was to go with us to see the parade – part of the car/truck trade deal, I'm sure.

Think how it would be if you were from some far, far star totally unlike Earth, and then you came down for a look. That is how I was. I did not know what the Stampede was, I did not know what a parade was, and I had almost no conception of a city. Adults said things like, "There will be Indians riding in the parade. There will be floats." *Floats?* There was a small round metal float in our cream separator. Just about the time your arm was ready to fall off from turning the handle the little attached bell stopped ringing, because you were now turning fast enough, so you opened the spigot at the bottom of the large metal separator bowl. The fresh, warm milk came gushing out, the little float bobbed up and down, while the skim milk ran out one spout into a bucket for the calves and the rich yellow cream ran out of the other into a crock for us, to be made into butter and poured onto our porridge and almost every dessert we ate! (Cholesterol was not yet invented.)

Mostly those who could explain were too busy. Mostly they said, "Oh, just wait and you'll see," or "You will like the floats." That mystifying word again. I could have asked Howard but he was riding in the other vehicle. They finally said, "This is Calgary!" I saw houses close together with squares of green in front of them, and I asked what they were. "Lawns." I was told.

"What is a "lawn"? What is it for?"

"It's grass." I thought of the green grass I knew – soft and three feet tall behind our house, wonderful to lie in and watch white animal cloud shapes float in the high blue prairie sky, or in which to hide in a game of Hide-and-Seek and not care ever to be found. In *our* back dooryard, besides black soil hard packed from many feet, grew each summer, a few patches of an obviously hardy green plant about five inches high, which eventually produced very tiny yellow cone-shaped flowers. These we children watched for, bit off and ate. (I was quite surprised several decades later to recognize the plant as Chamomile.) I quit asking questions. We were shy of Mrs. Donor, who had no children and was perhaps shy of us as she didn't speak to us, and Dad was busy trying to make polite conversation, not his usual style.

230

We stopped in a very dusty field, very full of cars and trucks, and then we walked a long, long way. It was extremely hot. We came to a place of stifling crowds of people, not moving, and pushed our way through to the other end, blindly following Dad's moving back and long strides. We were on a sidewalk made of cement, which I, of course, had never seen before either, and we children were sat upon the hard edge of it, to stare across a paved street at all the people on the other side and wait interminably for I knew not what.

Mrs. Donor became uncomfortable, so Dad went back to the car to find something for her to sit on. We were fed some sandwiches. The heat and the wait grew. After what seemed a long time, there was a stirring in the crowd behind us and we heard people saying, "The parade is coming!" We leaned out and what should we see but our father, the big, red Hudson's Bay blanket around his shoulders, prancing down the middle of the street, waving and making faces at the crowds. Mother, shy as her children among strangers, did not think it was very funny.

The parade finally began, with lots of people waving from cars, very boring, but then came the promised Indians on their horses, beautiful and majestic in white and tan buckskin and feather headdresses. The heat shimmered; I fainted. I was revived and Harvey was sent to take me back to lie in the car. A short time later, Auntie also became faint and was brought back to rest in the other vehicle. Howard later tried to explain floats to me, and also the midway with Ferris wheels and rides, where he and Harvey had been allowed to go for a few hours while the rest of us went to see our Uncle Ted, ill in a Calgary hospital, that visit probably an initial reason for the trip. Several years would pass before I actually saw a float or a merry-go-round and had some idea of what a parade was all about.

I was twelve or thirteen when Auntie and Mother decided, for reasons unexplained to us, that they ought to have some of their children baptized. To that end, Mother sent to Eaton's catalogue for pretty summer straw hats for Bert and me, our first. When Aunties arrived a week or so later, we discovered that Alice and Joyce had also acquired new hats.

I had never heard the word "baptism" and when I asked Howard about it, he told me, "It's when they give you a name in the church." Since I had always had what seemed to be a perfectly useable name, I was not enlightened and began to feel that perhaps my name was not quite legitimate. As well, we were all uncomfortable with the unavoidable awareness of voluble disagreement among the adults. The men, I believe, thought it all unnecessary – a bothersome whim. The women, dependent on the men for transportation, were no doubt frustrated and unwilling to give up their plans without argument. In the end nothing came of it, and we heard snatches of conversation about the Preacher, who lived in another town, being unable to schedule a suitable time.

I felt great relief. It all sounded like an exercise I would have found much too public and embarrassing. Mother was annoyed that she had spent some of her inadequate funds on our hats, and insisted that we wear them on every possible occasion. Otherwise, she said, "They were just a waste of money!" I didn't much like my "Dusty Rose" hat. It was a little too snug, and hurt my head, so *I* thought it was a waste of money anyway, but I didn't say so. ✓

Our trips to Aunties, though they seemed less frequent than theirs to us, were just as exciting. For a few years, Dad had a little old truck with a wooden box and we were packed in the back of it, with a blanket or two and all the bags and suitcases. Here we could sing and make as much noise as we wanted, as was certainly not possible inside a car.

Our excitement, at first sustained by anticipation and the "foreignness" of lands ten miles beyond our own, gradually diminished as the hours dragged on and we grew tired in the jolting truck box. The long miles of farmland began to look all alike and we roused ourselves mostly then to read from the grain elevators and call out the names of the small towns as we went by: Lousana, Delburne, mysterious Alix, where we knew our farm cream was sent to be made into butter. Sometimes there was a toilet stop in Bashaw and once or twice in memory the incredible treat of an ice cream cone!

Revived, we were alert for our yearly ritual. "Here it comes! Ready!" Howard would yell, peering around the truck cab at the road ahead. Then, all together as we rattled over the Red Deer River, looking up at the open metal above our heads, we would sing out, "CON - TENT BRIDGE!" It was the only "real" bridge we knew, which, over the years, has shrunk so much that now, on my occasional trip back, I can hardly find it.

A few more towns, a few more distant elevators and we were into the noisy, happy welcome of Aunties' yard, glad to get our stiff bones out of the truck and be swooped off to the barn to see the new baby pigs or kittens. (Though it was behind *our* outhouse once that Jackie, all of eight or nine, tried to teach us to smoke – not tobacco, but whatever was then the elementary school substitute, probably weeds.)

Two younger cousins, Edward and Anna, grew up after we had left Alberta, in 1943, and Auntie and Uncle Jack had many years to enjoy their new farmhouse after the old one was torn down long years ago. Wild tiger lilies still bloom in their coulee and the farm, expanded and operated now by a grandson, stands as a monument to them, as all present day prairie farms stand as monuments to our parents and all those others, including children, who lived, worked and played on them in that very different century.

Headcheese, Lye Soap and Sauerkraut

Oh, no! Oh, no! Now I had done it! I hastily righted the bottle but the dark blue ink spread over the hand embroidered white dresser scarf in a large, incriminating stain. I knew Mother would be very angry; what was I doing with the bottle of ink in the bedroom anyway? It belonged in Dad's tall desk, which we were not to open without permission. Ink was used by children only on the oilcloth covered kitchen table for school homework or the occasional letter writing. If I had been off in Fantasyland writing poems I could be in even more trouble, particularly if my chores were not finished.

Quaking lest I be found out before I could clean up the mess, I removed the cloth, replaced it with another and put the ink back where it belonged. I can't imagine what guardian angel of nine year old girls was around that day or week. It is still amazing to me that in that small house of eight active people, with water available only in the kitchen in full public view, I was somehow able to rinse out the cloth and dispose of the bright blue water without anyone noticing. Alas, this was not washable ink. Some came out but not much. Still quaking and not knowing what else to do, I rolled up the wet cloth and buried it deep in the dirty clothes barrel – the thin wood crate-type barrel that stood behind the hall door and had probably come into some store full of apples or other produce. To us it was only The Clothes Barrel, hauled out early Monday mornings to have its contents sorted into large soiled piles on the kitchen floor, ready for the huge chore of the weekly wash.

What a great deal of work it all was! The fire in the big kitchen stove had to be built to a high heat, the large, oblong copper boiler brought in, placed on the stove and then filled with water by buckets from the old horse trough and the barrels that stood outside under the eaves to catch rainwater. This was the water that was used for everything – all cleaning, bathing, dishwashing, and every other household use of water, except drinking and cooking. In the days before flake and powdered soap Mother would shave slivers from the big yellow bar of Fels Naptha into the water as it was heating. When boiled, the water had to be transferred to the tub of the washing machine, standing by then in the middle of the kitchen, with the round galvanized bathtub full of cool water placed on the floor or a bench under the wringer, ready for rinsing the clothes. Into the rinse water went some of "Mrs. Stewart's Bag Blueing." These were little round blocks of dry blueing (for making clothes whiter), about an inch in diameter, tied in a small piece of cloth. They came several to a box and were soaked in a small pan of water, which could then be used sparingly in the tub of rinse water. They were probably more economical than the liquid blueing, especially if children were pouring it in.

The first washing machine I remember had a gas motor. It filled the house with gas and oil fumes and also with noise. It was so loud that, even standing next to each other, we would have to shout to be heard. Each article of laundry had to be hand fed through the rubber wringers, rinsed by hand and then put through the wringers again. In winter especially, when no doors and windows could be open, the house became full of steam. If it was a very large wash, with many sheets and blankets, as it seemed always to be, a second boiler of water would be heating while the first loads were washing. Water was always scarce in winter and we were often sent out on washdays or bath nights to collect buckets of clean snow to fill the boiler and tub. This was a discouraging process. Even though it was not usually difficult to get large solid chunks from firm snowbanks and fill the boiler quickly, by the time we got back in the house with a second load, the first had melted down to about an inch of water in the bottom of the container.

There was a spigot at the bottom of the washing machine tub to drain out the dirty water, which had also to be carried outside in buckets and emptied. If it was summer most of it went on gardens. There was never enough room on the clotheslines for everything; therefore, the long chickenyard and barnyard fences were utilized for the many pairs of denim overalls, heavy socks, shirts and outerwear. This was often my chore in summer, made very slow, to my mother's exasperation, by my complicated organization of certain colours together, or all shirts together, all socks in pairs, and so forth. Bleachables were spread on the long grass behind the house and the sun did that job for us, while smaller items were hung on chairs or small lines in the house.

Whatever the temperature, often far below freezing, if the sun was shining Mother hung the washing outside. We would be sent to bring in the clothes after school and carry in frozen flannelette bedsheets and suits of long underwear, which would be propped around the steamy kitchen until they had collapsed enough to be hung over a chair. As one who has hung countless items on many clotheslines I have to say I have never again found that wonderful winter scent of fresh windblown prairie laundry. Where does it come from? Perhaps straight off the tops of the Rocky Mountains.

When our home eventually contained an old floor model radio, and when there was twenty-five or fifty cents for batteries, which was not always, Mother began to listen, while doing the laundry, to the very first "soap operas." These were no doubt named thus because of their soap product sponsors. Throughout the warm summer holidays, each Monday I would get almost as caught up as Mother in *Pepper Young's Family, The Guiding Light* and *Ma Perkins,* her favourites, all beginning with sonorous music and a brief recap of last week's intriguing complications. These were all

238

broadcast from mid-morning until just after lunchtime, and each ended with a hushed baritone voice intoning such confidentialities as, "*Will* Great-Aunt Columbine learn of Murgatroyd's treachery before too late? *Will* young Belladonna survive the mysterious illness and find true happiness? - - - Tune in next week - - -." The clever sponsors and broadcasters undoubtedly knew that washday was the only time that overburdened, isolated housewives could be in one place long enough to listen. The result was that, in our home, a few new products were tried out from time to time – Lux Flakes, Ivory Snow, some harsh and evil smelling red bars of Lifebuoy soap and a biting red toothpaste which sent me back to baking soda.

At school we learned, with actions, "This is the way we wash our clothes, wash our clothes, wash our clothes, all on a Monday mor-ning! - - -This is the way we iron our clothes, all on a Tuesday mor-ning!" So far, so good. At that time I believed all songs, poems and stories to be the literal truth and here was a song telling us the rules for housework. Our family seemed to go off the tracks a bit after Tuesday, though. My mother *never* got all her mending done on Wednesday; it looked to be a non-stop everyday (and evening) process, as did Thursday's, "This is the way we bake the bread." As for, "This is the way we go to church," at our house we milked the cows, fed the cows, watered the cows, put the cows out in the pasture, fed and watered the horses, the pigs, the calves, the chickens, the cats, the dogs, the people, put the milk through the

239

separator, washed the separator, the dishes, the milk pails, our faces, made our beds and swept the floor, "all on a Sunday mor-ning!" The song left out a lot.

Ironing, also with its great fresh, clean smell, was done (on Tuesdays) with "flatirons" on the kitchen table, covered with layers of worn flannelette sheets. Our three irons were heated on the kitchen stove; a bit of spit on a finger applied quickly to the iron told us when they were hot enough to get the wrinkles out of the pre-dampened and rolled clothing. Misjudgment usually meant a great scorch or burn mark and it became a fine art to learn, without gauges of any kind, what heat was appropriate for which types of fabric. An iron hot enough to get the wrinkles out of cotton would shrivel or melt holes in rayon at the first touch.

The irons were very heavy and tiring for small arms and backs and, I'm sure, for big ones as well. It was a whole new revelation to me when, at age seven, I was told by Mother, who apparently just noticed what I was doing, that it was necessary for me to iron the *backs* of my dresses as well as the fronts. It was a startling thought and at first I didn't believe her, when she told me that even though I couldn't see my back, other people could.

Mother tried everything and absolutely nothing we had was wasted or thrown away. There was always a use or a future use for whatever might seem ready for discard. People of later generations sometimes mistake the saving ways of their grandparents and great-grandparents for miserliness, perhaps not understanding that this was, for most of my parent's generation, a *learned* response to a very scary situation which had come into their lives. It had not always been so, and it was not their choice.

In my childhood there were remnants around of a few nice "bought" toys, of our older brother and sister. We were told that there used to be a telephone in our home. Our parents' generation had every reason to expect, in the early 1920's, that if they worked hard, their lives would continue to improve. That did not happen. For most of them, life got very much worse, causing great anxiety about their futures and the futures of their children. We, after all, know when the Depression ended. They were in the middle of it and could not see an end at all. If they carried their saving ways with them into their old age, even though to others, by then it may have seemed unnecessary, it is because they learned first hand and harshly, how rapidly and unexpectedly economies and worlds can change, and what devastation that can cause to those who have not learned methods of survival.

> Do you remember - - - Grandma's lyesoap?
> Good for ev'rything in the home,
> And the secret - - - was in the scrubbing,
> It wouldn't suds - - - and couldn't foam - - - [1]

Someone, perhaps a neighbour, told Mother how to make

---

[1] *It's In The Book*, by Johnny Standley and Art Thorsen.

her own soap. This must have been done right after a pig was butchered, in order to have the necessary fat. Great pans of it were "rendered" out in the hot oven and, I seem to remember, mixed in some way with wood ashes and lye. Mother sat out in the yard to do most of this and we were kept well away, warned that we could be seriously burned. It seemed to be very long, hot work for whatever it produced. I remember only some hard, unpleasant smelling soap that burned my face. I gather that Mother did not feel it was worthwhile, as she only made it once or twice. A few times she saved the scrap ends of the Palmolive bar soap and melted them down in a little water on the back of the stove to make a rather slimy shampoo that slithered through our fingers and did not lather well in the hard water. Hair washing was done weekly at the kitchen table, each in turn bent over the big chipped enamel dishpan, with someone standing by to pour a jug of rinsewater over the wet, soapy head. It always seemed to be a noisy affair, with yells of, "too hot!" and, "too cold!" and, "you made me get soap in my eyes!"

I'm sure the boys' hair washing was much simpler; they did not have to endure the torture of having tangles brushed out, though there were always more yells when Mother trimmed our hair, clipping our necks with an old, dull pair of hand clippers with teeth missing. She was the proficient (if impatient) barber for the whole family, including Dad. For special occasions, if there was time, we sometimes had our hair curled with curling tongs, which seem to

242

have changed very little in appearance over the years, except for the long electrical cord attached to today's models. Ours were heated by propping them down the glass chimney of a lit coal oil lamp. This sometimes resulted in a bit of sooty hair, singed hair, or singed necks or ears. There was also a waving iron, which made strange, bumpy "waves" in our hair. They must have been quite fashionable in the early nineteen thirties as I notice in pictures from that period of Queen Elizabeth, the late Queen Mother, that she has the exact same bumpy waves in her hair.

There were few cleaning aids; no Windex, Mr. Clean or Vim. There was lemon oil for dusting, vinegar and Bon Ami for windows, Old Dutch Cleanser with her strange hood and fascinating wooden clogs, and there was bar soap and "elbow grease," as we were often told. On Saturdays the house got cleaned, bedsheets were changed, floors were scrubbed, furniture was dusted and polished, often by me, dawdling over the lovely, curly golden wood of the piano and having a peek inside Dad's desk, at the small photo of the young girl with the long dark braid of hair that I so admired. I never knew who she was and I never asked. (I couldn't. I wasn't supposed to be looking in my father's desk.) Years later the picture disappeared and I realized that it was of Dad's younger sister, Charlotte, who died at twenty six, before I was born. We were never told much about her.

Large numbers of flies in summer were an ordinary part of

farm life. There were screens on some doors and windows, but there were also some holes in them, as well as six children running in and out of the doors frequently. After the house was swept and food covered and put away, Mother would shoo us all outside while she "fly-toxed" the rooms with a small pump spray can full of the poisonous liquid. Doors and windows remained shut for a half hour or so, after which we were allowed in to help sweep up and burn the zillions of fly carcasses and wash off all the exposed surfaces. Then it was time to thumbtack a few sticky "fly coils" to the kitchen ceiling, where they dangled, eventually buzzing with many stuck flies, and were subsequently dropped into the fire. Once in a while someone, not paying attention, would get hair entangled in one of these coils and that produced a very great mess, with often some necessary hair snipping.

There was always a big cake baked on Saturday for Sunday dinner and usually a few pies. We never knew when company might come. Saturday was also bath night for all children, in the round galvanized tin tub set on the kitchen floor in front of the open oven door, with those judged cleanest scrubbed first in the few inches of water. In summer it was always necessary to prewash feet.

I have heard so many people over the years mention the fun they had berry-picking, as children. I always wonder what it was they liked about it. Even had it been a voluntary activity, I can't

244

think I would have called it "fun." First there was, toward the end of summer when the wild saskatoon berries ripened, the long, jolting ride in the back of a wagon box, later a truck, with many pails and containers, to where adults thought the most productive bushes might be found. It seemed always a long, hot day, with many flies, ants and mosquitoes, scratchy bushes and cranky people. Our mother was quick at picking and because her (now understandable) goal was to get as many jars of fruit as possible into the cellar for the long winter ahead, tended to be impatient with those of us whose efforts were a lot less contributory.

Farm life must have been always a race against time – get the berries picked and canned before all the garden produce was ready, get children's clothes made or mended for school before September, repair machinery, get hay cut and stacked before the major preparation for and work of fall harvest in the fields, get in the wood and coal and make or mend the quilts and coats before the snow came. Seasons, weather and growing things do not wait until people are ready.

Food preserving methods and equipment were not nearly as perfected as they are today, so every year there were a few jars that did not seal properly and would spoil. It seemed that this happened most often with peas, and we all knew when a jar had burst in the cellar by the terrible sulphurous smell as we opened the big trap door in our entryway (known by us as "the Anteroom."). Mother

245

canned or made pickles of everything she could from the gardens – green, yellow and broad beans, beets, peas, rhubarb, cauliflower, tomatoes, pumpkins, cucumbers and, almost always, a case of blue plums from the grocery store, even occasionally a case of peaches. She did not make a lot of jam, probably because it took so much more sugar. It may have been cheaper to just buy the big cans of plum jam from the store. A few times there were chokecherries, the tiny, dark, tart bush berries that like the dry country. I think we had to go a long way to find these, and the pit in them is so big that the edible yield is small. Mother made a bottled juice from them which tasted wonderful! A few of us, at least once, swiped a bottle from the cellar and drank it out behind the trees. Our enjoyment was significantly enhanced by the fact that the juice had begun to ferment. Mother, as innocent as we were of any knowledge of alcohol, didn't know that she was sometimes serving her guests a delicious, sweet wine-in-process. ✓

Occasionally we were able to gather enough gooseberries from the low, prickly bushes in the coulee, for Mother to make a pie. Dad always got very excited about this. (Actually, he got excited about *most* pies or desserts, all his life.) Mother learned from our European neighbours to make sauerkraut, very foreign to our taste, but a way to use up all the cabbages before they spoiled. This was put into large crocks in the cellar with all the other canned and fresh food stores. There were bins for root vegetables – carrots,

246

beets, potatoes, turnips, rutabagas, as well as vegetable marrows, pumpkins and squash. Most of these vegetables did not keep through the entire winter, and some that did were rather soft and had long root beards by early spring.

The cellar was dug out of hard packed clay, with open wooden steps leading downward into the dark. The only light came through the large trap door above and we were not allowed to waste coal oil by taking the lantern in the daytime. The week's supply of butter was also stored there in crocks, and usually cream, milk and buttermilk, so children were sent down to fetch things fairly frequently each day. We were nearly always in bare feet. Though I would never have said so, I was determined that there was no way I was going to touch that dark, damp, cold dirt floor with my bare feet! Howard had reported seeing a "lizard," really a tiny salamander, in the cellar and that finalized my resolution. I don't now know whether I ever really did see one, or whether I imagined it, but it didn't matter. The effect was the same.

Slowly I crept down the steps, eyes wide for any slight movement in the dirt behind them or the big rocks at the bottom. By standing on the bottom step and holding onto the doorframe, eyes still fixed on the rocks, I could get one leg and foot around the corner of the open doorway and onto the edge of a potato bin, built from the floor to about three feet high. I worked my way, in the dim light, along the thin edge of board, holding onto the shelves above until I came to the one that contained what I had been sent for. I then had to do it all in reverse, carefully, so as not to drop the glass jar of fruit or meat, and now doing it one-handed. I also had to, at intervals, answer Mother, who was calling out very crossly by then, "What are you *doing* down there? Do *you hear me*? Hurry up and get up here with that jar of meat, RIGHT NOW!" Never in her life, I'm sure, was she able to understand how it could possibly take me so long.

The big copper boiler was again in use at butchering time, as it was for all food preserving. Our major source of meat was home canned. Neighbouring farmers usually got together for butchering, sometimes sharing the meat, sometimes just taking turns to help at each other's farms. It was not work that could be easily done alone. The animal had to be killed, disembowelled, skinned, cut up and the meat and remains taken care of, all very quickly, because of flies and the difficulty of keeping things cold. Though I never had to be directly involved, other than sometimes helping Mother with the canning, this was by far the most disliked of my farm experiences. The whole procedure took place directly outside our kitchen window, as our tall wooden swing frame was used as a scaffolding from which to hang the carcass, ready for quartering. I did have to stay in the kitchen; there was the everyday work to be done that Mother, busy cutting up the meat as it was brought to her, and canning it, could not attend to. I tried hard not to look out the

248

window; not to know when the animal was being killed, but that was difficult to achieve.

There was a lot of noise, both from the men and the animals. Pigs squeal and cattle bellow. Worst of all, my little brother sat on the kitchen table and "entertained" us by giving an eloquent and detailed description of the slaughter as it was taking place. The smell of the warm, raw meat was nauseating. I couldn't understand why my mother didn't mind. I now realize that she was far too busy to think about whether she minded or not. She cut the beef quickly into stew sized chunks, packed it in clean, hot quart jars, sprinkled a little salt in each, sealed them with the glass lids and red rubber jar rings, plus the metal cap, screwed on tightly, and stood them in the boiling water in the copper boiler. Small boards had been placed in the bottom to keep the jars from direct contact with the heat of the metal. Even so, sometimes one would break. The lid was put on the boiler, water brought back to a boil and kept boiling for several hours. The fire in the stove, therefore, could not be allowed to drop in intensity, making the whole house very hot.

Heart and liver were not canned, but cooked and eaten fresh, or sometimes, when there was more than could be used immediately, sent with a child across the fields as a gift for neighbours. Fresh roast beef or pork for a day or two was a rare treat. Bones were boiled for soup, or soup stock that could also be canned for future use, and children stood at the table turning the old

249

metal meat grinder, mincing meat for sausage. Our dad went around all the first day saying things like, "Oh, boy! Beefsteak for supper!" I never understood his enthusiasm. Our mother was a marvellous cook, but the steak was *very* fresh, fried like many things in the big, black cast iron frying pan, until well done. Dad raved about it, but it hurt my teeth. They had too many holes in them, and this meat took much chewing. Dentists were still in the future for our family.

When all the meat had been canned and cooled it was stored on the cellar shelves and, though varied from time to time by chicken, turkey, duck, or the occasional partridge or prairie chicken Dad shot, was the basic item in our meals throughout the year. This meat I loved! It was a rich, tender, flavourful stew, very easy on sensitive teeth.

When pigs were butchered some people smoked hams and bacon, but that was not done in our household. One year Mother, determined to make use of all possible parts, learned how to make headcheese. She stuffed it into little cotton bags that she sewed and it hung in the anteroom, looking like long, fat sausages. To my great surprise, in spite of what the name suggested to me, when I was prodded into trying some I found it delicious. On a shelf near the headcheese was something else Mother made one year that no amount of prodding would ever get me to try! Inside a large glass jar, in an all too transparent jellied substance, were stuffed the whole, visible, cloven dead feet of pigs. Pickled pig's feet. Howard urged me to try them, saying he was sure I would like them, and had they been ground, or otherwise disguised I might have. I stared at them in somewhat morbid fascination every time I walked by, trying to understand why anyone would want to eat them but, even though I knew it wasn't so, the only thing that my mind could ever envision was several pink pigs, running around the pigyard on the stumps of their legs.

Spring Cleaning was a major yearly event of suddenly unpredictable daily routines, much energetic bustle and a house turned inside out and upside down. Getting it done before one's neighbours also became a mild mark of status, "Have you done your Spring Cleaning yet?"

"Oh yes, I finished last week!" I liked neither the upset of it, nor the insecurity of the unfamiliar disorder. It was years after I had a home of my own that I realized there had been an original valid reason for annual Spring Cleaning that no longer existed. Almost all homes at that time were heated with coal, in a large kitchen cook stove and a "heater," a parlour stove in the living room, such as at our house or, for homes with basements, sometimes a furnace with large heat registers in the floors of some of the rooms. In winter, stoves were "banked" at night with coal, drafts closed, to keep some minimal warmth in poorly or mostly noninsulated houses. Even so, people often arose to ice in the wash basin or water pail. There was little wood available and it was used mostly in summer when heat was not needed at night. Hauling coal from the mines by horses and wagons or sleighs was a long day's journey. It was shoveled through an outside opening into a bin at the end of our anteroom, and carried into the house in buckets each day. Coal is very black and very dirty. Coal dust got into everything, so ceilings and walls became unavoidably smoky.

In our house, as with many, there was not a full mortar and brick chimney. There were tin stovepipes connected from both kitchen and front room stoves to openings in a short brick chimney, encased high in a floor to ceiling cupboard in a corner of the kitchen. These pipes filled with soot over the winter and each spring had to be taken down and cleaned, always with a great clatter and mess, it seemed! At the same time Dad took the heater out of the front room for the summer, storing it until it was time to put it up again in the late fall.

Mother, head tied in a cloth, energetically swept and scrubbed, polished and directed. Cupboards and drawers were emptied out and washed, windows, curtains and blankets were washed, wool quilts aired, bed ticks (large cloth cases like present day duvet covers, used to make mattresses) were emptied out, washed and filled with fresh straw, and floors were scrubbed and waxed. Walls and ceilings were washed and sometimes painted with kalsomine, a powder that came in large boxes, in lovely pastel

252

colours, and was mixed with water to make a thin wash. Furniture was moved to new positions, and the washing machine was hauled out of the kitchen onto the shaded front porch, that ran the length of one side of the house, where the laundry was done each week throughout the long, warm summer and fall.

Ah yes, the blue ink stain on the dresser scarf. I quaked all week, but instead of thinking of some way of dealing with it or telling someone, I tried, unsuccessfully, not to think about it at all. If Mother had not been so busy that washday she might have noticed how uncharacteristically quickly I dragged out and emptied the clothes barrel and began sorting the dirty clothes. I searched, unobtrusively I hoped, for the evidence that was soon, I knew, to convict me. I think I had some faint hope that I might throw it into the washing machine unnoticed, but I had no hope at all that the stain would come out.

I found it. For one tenth of one second I thought that someone else had found it first. But no, it was still where I had stuffed it in the bottom of the barrel, still wet and still scrunched up as I had scrunched it. I looked – and I looked again. There was not even the faintest trace of blue; not a mark, just a white, damp cloth. To say that I was relieved and amazed would be an understatement. I was confounded. I have never, in the many years since, found a plausible explanation. No miracle has ever been more gratefully accepted.

The Season to be Jolly

The possibility of missing the Christmas Concert was totally outside the realm of our thought or imagination. That idea was not one that ever occurred to us, even for consideration, in the same way that it would never have occurred to us to think of the possibility of the sun, moon and stars suddenly disappearing forever. Though I am now aware that the adults must have given this alternative some very serious emergency contemplation, perhaps even discussed it in our presence, I don't remember hearing that. If I had, I would certainly have immediately rejected and erased from my mind both the idea and the words that voiced it, voided them, obliterated them completely, and gone on knowing that no matter what difficulties were presenting themselves at the moment, we *were* on our way to the Christmas Concert. So absolute and unshakeable was this knowledge that no other eventuality could ever find its way to consciousness.

There we were, the whole family, parents and six children, on a snowless, windy, frozen late December evening, half a mile from home on the dark, deserted dirt road, on our way to the event that, in importance, overshadowed and outweighed in monumental measure any other in our limited lives, and our vehicle had broken

255

down. "It was most unusual to be able to set off for THE CONCERT in a motor vehicle, and that evening must have been one of the few times that it happened. There was no snow at all for the traditional bob-sleigh ride, and so our father had heated water for the radiator and got the car[1] started, then covered the front end with a heavy horse blanket and his big buffalo fur coat until we were all scrubbed and dressed in our only good clothes."[2]

Though my memories reveal gaps, the feelings and perceptions are still vivid. I was in school, not more than seven years old. I remember how dark it was, how terribly cold it was, how four of us huddled together in the back seat of the old car, trying to keep warm, as our "Mamma" held the two youngest with her in front. I have glimpses of our father's tall figure, dressed in his one suit under a heavy overcoat and tweed cap, collar up around his ears, moving in the icy wind and blackness as he tinkered at the front end of the car.

At some point a decision must have been made and discussed, instructions given. In the next scene we are all out of the car, and I am straining against the freezing, blizzard strength wind

---

[1] Memories of make of vehicle vary, but according to Mildred (Nash) Michie (whose memory is even *older* than ours), it was a bright blue Overland Whippet, which was always breaking down, so Dad did not keep it long.
[2] Howard Nash, 1997.

to keep putting one foot in front of the other, but barely able to remain upright in heavy winter clothing. With each painfully cold breath my lungs felt as though they might burst. Mother, struggling herself with the weight of a three year old, urged us all along the half mile incline toward home, through choking clouds of dust blowing from fields unprotected by their usual drifts of snow. Finally, exhausted, we staggered into the shelter of the grove of trees surrounding the farmyard and then the warmth of the kitchen.

There was no time to collapse. The coal oil lamp was lit. We were hurriedly unwrapped and warmed; the prairie soil was washed from our faces and out of our ears, and brushed as well as could be done from our new "Christmas Concert" clothes and shoes, until Mother was satisfied that the six of us looked, if not quite as "brand new" as originally, at least presentable enough to cause her no embarrassment in public. Finally there was time for some anxiety to manifest. All of us, except Donnie, not yet in school, had roles to play in the concert.

Would they start without us? How would they know where we were and if we were coming? We had no phone, nor did our neighbours and, in any case, anyone we might have phoned would already be at the hall. Disappointment threatened as anxiety spilled over into irritability. It seemed a very long and uncertain wait, in our heavy coats and hats. Suddenly there was our dad, this tall man with the big voice who was always in charge, appearing from

257

somewhere, rushing us loudly out the door and into the luxury of our neighbour's warm, borrowed car, and speeding us off to the town hall four miles away!

Into the bright lights of the magically transformed hall we were hustled, where the whole dazzling audience, the monumental and awesomely glittering Christmas tree, the formerly cold, bare stage on which we had rehearsed for the past two months, now breathtakingly unrecognizable in the warmth and glow surrounding a manger and the First Holy Night, and all our schoolmates and teachers anxiously waited for us. They had waited for us! Amid our jumbled explanations many hands rushed us backstage and into our costumes; the night of wonders finally began. I breathed out.

Then we were on the bright magic stage in our cheesecloth angel dresses, tinsel in our hair and on our wings, and the hot stage lights in our eyes; our small male classmates in shepherd and wise men robes, their faces scrubbed, unrecognizably subdued – their mothers were out there somewhere! Soft blue light surrounded Mary and Joseph, centre stage in the dimly lit stable, with the baby in the straw. Soft light glowed from their faces and Mary's blue veil. We knew that Mary was really our big sister but, like all of our classmates and teachers, she too had undergone transformation.

I never knew where it all came from, the stage sets, the lights, the music, the costumes, the decorations. The concert had been weeks in the planning with, I now realize, many community adults helping but, because our only assignment was to thoroughly memorize our roles in the plays and skits, to practice the songs, carols and dances we were being taught, and to trudge daily from mid-October onward the few hundred yards across the field to the hall for onstage rehearsals, the culmination of it all in a wonderful concert seemed to me like sudden magic.

As I grew older, I began to recognize School Principal Mr. Ward's talent for theatre, his special abilities with staging and directing, and the superb effects he achieved with lighting. He could not have had much to work with, but his concerts and plays became widely known for their high quality, so that people came in severe winter weather from many miles outside our own community to attend them. In spite of his sometimes short temper, he had a way of pulling the best from his actors, actresses and stage crews, and probably also from the school's one other teacher, as well as adults in the community. He had high expectations of us and, inexperienced as we were, we achieved things we did not know we were capable of because someone had faith that we could.

Christmas concerts, as with almost all school or public functions, always began with everyone standing to sing *O Canada!* and ended with the singing of *God Save the King*. The stage curtains were barely closed before the stampede and the tumultuous, noisy scramble in the tiny backstage dressing rooms began. We knew what came next – Santa Claus! Costumes were pulled off

259

hurriedly, usually not particularly carefully, in spite of the efforts of teachers and a few selected mothers to create some kind of order. The release in many small bodies of adrenalin after onstage tension, plus barely containable anticipation, produced NOISE. Socks were lost, shoes were lost, buttons were left undone, costumes trampled underfoot in our anxiety to get out into the audience before Santa Claus arrived, and to bask in our well deserved accolades from parents and teachers.

The students were not the only actors. Some male adult always got onstage and did a big build-up to Santa's arrival, fueling our excitement more. Soon we'd hear a jingling of sleigh bells that seemed to come from the roof of the building, and just as we were about to *burst,* in leapt Santa Claus through the ceiling! (Or so it seemed to me. I think there was a projection booth up there for the stage lights.)

Santa Claus, as I found out when I was older, was always played by our young neighbouring farmer, Shirley Fawcett. He bounded all over the hall, "Ho-Ho"-ing and sitting on laps, embarrassing his female neighbours and kissing some of the lady schoolteachers, which put us in even more awe of him. Onto the stage he jumped, and with high school and community helpers, began to give out the presents stacked under the great tree.

Each child in the school and each child under school age was to get a gift, as well as a bag of nuts, candy and an orange. Earlier,

260

in school, we had each picked a classmate's name from a hat and this was the person we were to provide with a gift at the Christmas concert. This was all supposed to be very secret and democratic. We were *not* to tell whose name we got, and were given very strict and serious instructions to take the slip of paper home to our parents, who then took over the gift procuring and wrapping. Often we didn't even know what we had given. Our only part, really, was to pick the slip of paper from the hat. In theory, this was a fair method, but in practice it didn't always work so well. Many of us couldn't keep secrets very well, and could be cajoled or bullied into telling whose name we had. Some people didn't like the person whose name they had and would try to trade for someone else, sometimes with bribes. None of this remained very "secret" and so there were often some hurt feelings, some temporary animosity, and an occasional very unhappy time when a child got no present at all, because someone had traded a name and then one or other of the "tradees" had a change of heart. More likely both had already told their mothers the same name and neither would dare admit to trading names, knowing, as we all did, that it was a serious and punishable offence.

Parents provided small gifts for their own preschoolers and the School Board provided the treats. Of course, there were the usual few joke gifts for certain adults, Santa Claus not excluded. Most of this went over my head, as by this time I was usually sucking on a ribbon candy, saving my favorites, the pastel sugary ones, for last. Eventually Santa Claus went roaring out the back door and we heard him jingle away. Adults visited with friends and neighbours and children ran around, comparing presents with each other and trading candies. For present day younger generations to understand the specialness of our treats, it perhaps needs to be said that, for many of us, this was often the only candy, nuts or oranges that we had in the whole year; it was definitely the only time we each had a whole bag to ourselves, with no pressure or expectation to share.

Soon, fathers were at the door with the horses and the big bob-sleighs. Children were all bedded down in the straw in the deep box, blankets piled over us, and home we jingled through the frosty night, warm and cozy, clutching our goody bags in our mittened hands and watching the millions of stars in the black velvet sky far above.

This was the traditional scene. A few times unexpected circumstances dictated something different. There was the year of "Measles for Christmas." The whole community had them. Schools were closed, the Christmas Concert was cancelled. People were very, very sick for many weeks. Whole families had the measles, including ours, one after another, until most of us were in bed. There was no medication of any kind, and a doctor was far away. Finally our mother and oldest sister, after nursing the rest of us, became so seriously ill that the doctor had to be fetched. Those were the days before antibiotics or sulfa drugs; people who got pneumonia often died. People died from influenza, and from blood poisoning, often started from an infected scratch. Dad, who should have still been in bed himself, got out to the barn each day in the freezing, deep drifts of snow to care for the animals. A neighbour came in a few times and prepared food for those of us who could eat. Our fourteen year old brother, Harvey, helping out on a farm in a neighbouring community, where measles had not yet struck, was told by adults not to come home for Christmas, to avoid exposure.

Our whole family was, by then, very ill. Bertie and I, seven and eight respectively, had been put to bed on the couch in the front room to allow Milly, sixteen, the bed that the three of us usually shared. One night, feverish and full of nightmares, we managed to terrorize ourselves by imagining that a small red reflection, glowing on the ceiling from a chink in the heater, banked for the night with coal, was the eye of a pirate standing above us with his long knife, about to murder us. We lay rigid lest he hear us breathe. Each time we inched the blanket down from our covered heads the eye was still there. (What had our teacher been reading to us? *Treasure Island*?) Finally, not yet murdered, but still shaking and holding on to each other, we crept over the top end of the couch and three steps into our mother's bedroom. "Mamma!" in a hoarse whisper , hoping she was awake. She was. "Our bed is all messed up." She

263

told us, weakly, to get the coal oil lamp from her dresser and fix it. We lit the lamp, all that was needed to vanquish the pirate, and went back to sleep. Christmas was bleak and unremembered.

The year of "Calamity Averted," also known as "Remember the Year We Almost Had No Christmas Tree?" ended more happily. Evergreen trees (known to us only as "Christmas trees" until our great enlightenment upon moving, in our adolescent years, to evergreen British Columbia) did not grow where we lived. Each Christmas season, Dad would drive with horses and sleigh twenty or more miles to the banks of the Red Deer River to bring home a tree. One year the blizzards were too persistent, the snowdrifts too deep. Roads were not passable. We waited silently, day by day, our faces growing longer, for the weather to break. Finally it was almost Christmas Eve. Time had run out. There would be no Christmas tree. It was unimaginable; disappointment flooded us into deeper silence.

Mother, hatted, coated and overshoed, disappeared outside, possibly with some help, I never knew. Into the kitchen she brought a young, leafless maple tree, cut from the windbreak that surrounded the farmyard. It was dried off by the stove, and we spent the day and evening wrapping every branch and twig with strips of long-saved green crepe paper, and then hanging from its branches our carefully preserved and mostly homemade decorations. I thought it was a miracle. It is the only tree I really remember.

264

Christmas Day, though always anticipated and usually pleasant, sometimes seemed a bit anti-climactic after the long preparation and the excitement of the school concert. Mother began making her Christmas cakes many weeks ahead and, though I never liked fruitcake, there was a festive aura about the house as we helped with the cutting up of glazed fruit, the cracking of nuts and the mixing of ingredients. The house was filled with the delicious aroma of baking cakes, as well as a few cries of, "Don't slam the door! My cakes will fall!" When cool, the cakes were wrapped in clean cloths and stored in covered crocks in the cellar for several weeks, allowing them to age or "ripen," as they became moist and flavourful. I was very fond of mincemeat pie, though, and again we children were involved in the chopping of suet and apples, the mixing of raisins, currants and spices. The traditional Christmas pudding, also heavy with dried fruit, could not be steamed in its cloth bag until Christmas morning, when the pot bubbled away for hours on the back of the big stove, while the stuffed turkey, or occasional goose, browned with mouth-watering aromas in the oven below.

The Christmas tree and front room had been decorated days before, when Mother brought out her box of carefully saved decorations from an earlier, more prosperous era. Dad stood on a ladder to stretch the paper streamers diagonally from corner to corner of the ceiling, and last, to hang the big, fold-out, red paper bell, a little more tattered each year, from the centre, above the dining table.

The hanging of stockings was not a   part of our traditions. On Christmas morning we found one present each from "Santa Claus" under the tree, as well as a small gift, usually homemade, from the parcel sent by our beloved Auntie, our father's younger sister. A parcel had gone from our house to our cousins as well, but Mother was in charge of all this, probably making the gifts while we were in school, so I seldom knew what was sent. In our younger years there was usually also a parcel from our grandmother, Dad's mother in faraway British Columbia, with a little gift for each, and always a few sprigs of red-berried holly from her tree, something quite unknown to us and, therefore, exotic and special. After I had learned to read, my eagerly awaited gift from Auntie, a former school teacher, was always a storybook, which I had usually finished reading by dinner time.

When we four youngest were a bit older, we were allowed to pool our few pennies for gifts for each other and include a small order, along with Mother's, to Eaton's catalogue. For a few winter evenings, after supper, after dishes and homework were done, as our parents sat in the front room reading, mending and listening to the radio, we four would sit around the kitchen table with the coal oil lamp and the catalogue, luxuriously picking out all the wonderful toys we wished we could have. Finally, however, we had to count our money and choose accordingly. Each would be sent out of the kitchen in turn while the other three discussed and chose that one's gift and Howard filled out the order form.

It was hard to find things for our parents that our finances would cover. Some years we went to Runyan's Hardware Store after school, where we timidly asked for a calendar for our mother. These were usually very beautiful, often with cut out areas, or little pull-out cages filled with lovely decorated paper birds or flowers and a frosting of brushed-on glitter. I felt terribly intimidated by Mr. Runyan, as he told us sternly to take the calendar straight home to our mother. We never told him it was to be her Christmas present from *us*.

Dad had a pipe, which he smoked only occasionally, but often at Christmas. Somehow we had the idea that he also liked an occasional cigar and so, these being available at the grocery store and costing only five cents, that was often his gift.

Even though Christmas dinner was almost always shared by only our own family, the day was treated as a holiday, with dinner in the front room, the table covered with the best white tablecloth, and all of us wearing , if not our *best* clothes, at least something clean, with everyday chores kept to a minimum. Sometimes there was popcorn and nut cracking later, and some years the special treat of a box of mandarin oranges, with the individual wrapping papers carefully smoothed and saved for future uses, even for very inadequate handkerchiefs!

Weather permitting, neighbours did visit each other during Christmas week, and then out would come leftover turkey, buns, pickles, *The* Christmas cake on the best plates – much discussed by the women as to flavour, ingredients and methods of preparation – mincemeat tarts, coffee, nuts, homemade cookies and candy, and always the playing cards. Card games such as Whist, Smear and Rummy played a prominent part in home entertainment on long winter nights.

I never understood how things happened that night of the dust storm; how Dad managed to appear from seemingly nowhere with a car to get us to THE CONCERT. I later thought that he must have ridden a horse across the fields to Wagstaff's farm to borrow their car, but I also knew that they would have probably been at their own Christmas concert at Acadia, a small country school two miles away. In any case, the time elapsed was too short to include the saddling of a horse. Checking with other family memories, it seems that Dad did hurry across the fields, but on foot, in time to intercept the Wagstaffs, ride with them to Acadia, and then return with their car to get us. "The Wagstaff boys had an old straight backed Chev sedan, about a 1926 or so model. It was the first car they ever had, and it was before the spiffy 1933 model they had later, which could go sixty miles per hour on the gravel highway and beat the train from Huxley to Elnora, as Bill once proved to me."[3]

As soon as our concert was over and Santa Claus had gone, Dad rushed us out, with no time for the usual visiting. He dropped us off at home and proceeded to Acadia School where the Wagstaffs were waiting for their car.

Such was the dependability and naturalness of neighbour helping neighbour in that era of isolated country roads and difficult, time-consuming methods of communication. There was reassurance in knowing that there was someone across the fields, if not at one farm, then at another, whether help was needed in a serious medical emergency or simply with transportation in our memorable year of "Christmas in the Dust."

---

[3] Howard Nash, 1997.

The Maypo Lea Forever

True Confessions of a Five-Year-Old Runaway

I didn't really run away from home, although family legend has always insisted that I did. These many decades later the true story shall be told. It was the dusty warm, bee-humming, barefoot, mosquito-laden summer of my fifth birthday, just when my awareness of the world was beginning. I did not yet know who all these people were, into whose noisy midst I had been thrust. I went about in a haze of discovery of objects, creatures, growing things, places of sunshine and shade, interrupted at frequent intervals by loud voices often directed at me, with instructions or chastisements I tried to understand, but seldom did.

"Mamma," at thirty-four, had six children, all she would ever have, although it is unlikely that she knew that then. It is therefore understandable that never, in my short memory, had I had her all to myself, though I often longed for that. Even then I had begun to have some misty perception that it might never be. There were three older children when I was born, aged eight, four and two, and when I was four months old, Mother became pregnant with her fifth. Added to that, her pregnancy with me was no doubt marked with grief for the recent death in childbirth of one of her loved younger sisters. When I had just learned to walk, there was a new

271

baby in our house.

Along the dusty, empty trail called a road, that ran north past our farm, between the fields, grew tiny wild strawberries, hidden in the grass beneath the few stands of poplar trees. Also a few yards up that road was the barbed wire gate into the Lindeman farm, with its small house visible on a rise a half mile up the lane to the east. Close in age (and with children close in ages), Mrs. Lindeman and Mother had become friends, an occurrence precious and rare in those lonely, labour-filled years of isolated prairie farm women.

These two mothers, somehow, without aids such as telephones or mail delivery, had planned a day out for themselves. They were going to walk through the countryside, looking for wild berries to pick. That our mother would go anywhere without a few children along was unusual enough to be an Event in our fairly eventless summer. We watched her hurry through her housework and pack a lunch. We heard Dad giving opinions and advice on the best places to look for berries, and we saw her walk out the gate with her berry pail to meet Mrs. Lindeman. Dad went back to his farm work leaving Milly, age twelve, in charge of one year old baby Donnie, and more or less in charge of the rest of us – Harvey, eleven, Howard, seven, me, and Bertie, four.

I have often wondered about that berry-picking day and whether they really expected to find any, as they actually did come home with empty buckets. To my young mind, berries meant the sweet little wild strawberries; the most we children had ever come home with was a half tin cupful. I thought that was what they were going to pick. Years later I realized that the large buckets they carried meant that they hoped to find saskatoon bushes. Each year there was at least one family berry picking excursion, at first with wagon and horses and later in Dad's old truck. We always, however, had to go far afield to find the bushes – never within walking distance. I have since reflected on those young women's need for a strongly legitimate reason to avoid guilt for deserting children, husbands and farm work for an afternoon in which to nourish themselves with each other's company.

Howard, at seven already my hero, said later that I had, earlier in the day, bragged that I could walk to Lindeman's all by myself. I possibly did, since that is where I was found, but I have no memory of saying or thinking that, and it was certainly not what motivated me.

I remember so clearly my surprise when the idea popped into my head. I didn't know where it came from, but it presented itself fully formed, as a wonderful way to have Mamma all to myself for a short time. I would walk up the road to meet her coming home! I knew, of course, that I couldn't tell the others or they would all come too, so in the late afternoon, when I heard talk of, "She should be coming soon," off I went, alone. I fully expected to see the women before I got the short distance to Lindeman's gate, and my

273

vivid imagination saw their pleasant surprise at being met. After leaving Mrs. Lindeman, Mamma and I would walk to our house, I holding her hand, she talking only to me - - -. Alas, for the best of childish dreams.

From Lindeman's gate I could see clearly a long way up the road, far past the wild strawberry patch, and the women were nowhere in sight. I stood around for a little while, becoming anxious and sad. It didn't occur to me to abandon my plan and just go back to the house, or to sit down and wait. The road remained deserted. I couldn't think where they could be. Then the answer came! Mamma had walked up the lane to Mrs. Lindeman's house and would be coming back any minute! Off I went, crawling under the barbed wire gate, following my latest logic, but becoming more and more anxious as no one appeared on the long half mile. Finally I was in the yard and there were all the children, but no Mamma, and no Mrs. Lindeman. Nevertheless, the children were happy to see me, and said I should come play with them until our mammas arrived. I was immediately comforted.

At five years, my sense of daily time related to the sun coming up, the sun going down, time to wash for supper, time to go to bed, time to feed the chickens, time to go for the cows. And so, perhaps a short time, perhaps a long time later, along came Mrs. Lindeman, hugged greatly by her children, -- but where was Mamma? She had gone home, Mrs. Lindeman told me, surprised that I expected to find her there. Anxiety returned, but Mrs. Lindeman, warm as always, told me not to worry; I should stay for supper and someone would take me home afterwards. Things looked a little better. I pushed down the apprehension in my stomach; Mrs. Lindeman would make things all right.

Nothing was to be relied upon. Galloping into the yard on the pony, "Little Teddy," came Harvey, and he was not happy with his little sister. Maybe they had got into trouble for not watching me more closely. No one ever told me. Mrs. Lindeman kindly repeated her offer of supper for both of us but, "No," said Harvey, "we are to get home RIGHT NOW," and he switched Little Teddy all the way as he told me repeatedly how I was "really going to get it!" And I hung on behind the saddle, while terror filled my being.

Having thus had my expectation of a major spanking thoroughly reinforced, I felt only a slight abatement of anxiety to be just severely scolded and sent to bed with no supper. My father, as with most fathers then (raising children was traditionally considered the mother's responsibility), was silent through all of this. Even had there been any opportunity for explanation, by then I knew that I could not say or explain that I had planned only to have my mother all to myself for a few minutes. I understood, with sad surprise, that it was an unacceptable wish, not to be admitted – kept forever secret. I *did* walk to Lindeman's all by myself, but you couldn't really call it "running away."

275

Fairy Godmother

For Nancy

If I had not had an older brother to take me places, my social life would undoubtedly have been much more limited than it already was, just by distances, weather and available transportation. At fifteen, Howard was obviously considered responsible enough to look out for a thirteen year old sister and get us both, on horseback, to and from a few of the narrow range of functions open to us. I also realize my good fortune in his willingness to have me along. Though we were good friends for all of my growing years, there was no expectation on my part, nor requirement from our parents, that he take me with him when he began to ride out to a few events on weekend evenings.

Most adolescent boys that I have known since have been more concerned with escaping from a younger sister than with inviting her along. A few times Howard interceded for me with our parents and, as we were always home when expected and had obviously neither caused nor come to any harm, they began to relax and allow us more freedom to choose our outings. Since neither we nor most people we knew had telephones, parents had to rely on the common sense and judgment of their children in most instances, and the help of their neighbours if anything went wrong.

It was very seldom that we were allowed to take more than one horse, but I didn't care about that at all, I was so happy to be taking part in this brand new, exciting social life. Off we would gallop, I always behind the saddle, across the fields to the Barnes' farm, three or four miles distant, stopping only to take down and put back the barbed wire fences we had to cross, or to water our horse at a creek. My best friend Cicely and I would sit on her bed and talk thirteen year old girl talk while Howard visited with her brothers, or played a game of checkers with her mother.

Other times we would ride the four miles to town for choir practice at the school, though I don't think we were able to attend regularly enough to ever actually sing in the Huxley church choir. I really liked to sing, and did so a great deal, as I went about my chores, mostly mournful cowboy songs, loudly in the wind as I rode through the coulees rounding up the milk cows. I always looked forward to hearing and learning the songs the choir sang. I was in awe of the full, rich voice of Muriel McCook, which seemed to me to reach the heavens she was singing about.

Howard was going to dances for some time before I was allowed to go with him, after I turned fourteen. He would come home and tell me about his adventures, the people he met and the places they went. I was fascinated, but I didn't really understand; it

278

seemed such a different world than any I had experienced up until then.

And then my Fairy Godmother appeared. I don't know exactly where and when I first met Nancy Fraser and her tall husband, John. I had heard so much about them from Howard that it seemed I already knew them. Nancy and John were an attractive young couple with two little boys, who lived on a farm several miles to the southwest of us. In some way, probably through their generous, cheerful and fun-loving natures, they had gathered a large following of young people, many, like my brother and I, in their adolescent years. I had heard from Howard of large gatherings for winter sleigh rides, tobogganing parties, wiener roasts, schoolhouse dances and other get-togethers. It all sounded like so much fun, and then suddenly and unexpectedly it was my turn.

Until then, the few dances I had gone to with Howard had been on the saddlehorse, across the fields to Loyalty School or to the Huxley Community Hall in town. Nancy and John had a car and soon, almost every Saturday night, we were hiking the mile across the field out to the highway to wait for them to pick us up. Away we would go to dances in the hall at Elnora, to Doris School and many other little country schools, of which I had previously never heard, though most of them could not have been more than twenty miles away. We had wonderful times! Whole country communities crowded into the tiny one-room schools. Desks had been moved out

279

and chairs or benches set round the walls, babies and small children had been put to sleep on the piles of coats in the closet- sized cloakroom and men were sprinkling soap flakes on the newly washed wooden floor.

The band, tuning up on a low platform especially constructed for them, consisted of whatever country musicians were available, those who were either too young or too old to go to war, or were exempted for other reasons. They played violins, accordions, harmonicas, sometimes guitars, often pianos and occasionally even drums or clarinets. Sometimes they had a vocalist. It was wartime, 1942, and patriotic songs like *White Cliffs of Dover*, *Comin' In On a Wing and a Prayer* and *When the Lights Go On Again* were prominent. We danced to Glenn Miller's *In the Mood*, *Elmer's Tune* and *Don't Sit Under the Apple Tree*. I learned to foxtrot and to schottische, to square dance to *Turkey in the Straw* and *The Arkansas Traveller*, polka to *Red Wing* and *Tavern in the Town* and waltz to beautiful old tunes like *I'm Forever Blowing Bubbles*, *Springtime in the Rockies* and *My Little Gray Home in the West*. There were plenty of partners and none of us ever sat out a dance unless we chose to.

Best of all I liked the old-time waltzes and, with his long legs, nobody could dance these so well as my brother Howard. I felt like Cinderella at the ball as we whirled around the room to the music of Johann Strauss, or a reasonable facsimile. No matter the anxiety and the bitten fingernails over algebra and geometry not understood, no matter the fickleness of adolescent friendships; tonight the Royal Ballroom glittered with crystal chandeliers, my dusty shoes had turned to shining glass slippers, and my blonde, blue-eyed Fairy Godmother smiled lovingly at me as she danced by.

All too soon it was time for the "home waltz," as the band swung into *Goodnight Ladies* or *The West, a Nest and You* and young men, caught unawares, rushed to dance with the girl they had been too shy to ask all evening, or the one they wanted to escort home. Then out came the pots of steaming coffee, plates of sandwiches, pickles, cakes and cookies, all made at home and brought by the community women and girls; everybody would sit around eating and visiting before getting into heavy outer clothing, wrapping up babies and starting for home in cars, horses and buggies or sleighs.

Though dances were held throughout the year, particularly in the larger centres, which had community halls, farm people attended mostly in the winter or late fall, after harvesting was done and there were a few leisure hours at the end of the day. At other times of year farmers and their families worked from before daylight until dark, or often later, and were much too tired for more than very occasional social activities.

Many times through that winter Howard and I plodded willingly through snow up to our knees, I with my dance dress tucked into my heavy wool snowpants and muffled to the eyes with toque and scarf, to wait on the dark, freezing gravel highway for our chariot to transport us to the ball. I seldom knew or cared where we were going. I would have gone anywhere with Nancy and John. I had never met such wonderful people, and I immediately fell under the spell of Nancy's warm and loving large-heartedness. To my great sorrow, the magic all came to an abrupt end with our family's move away from the Huxley area a few months after my fifteenth birthday. Though we found friends, and dances to attend in our new home in the Fraser Valley of British Columbia, and though I still sometimes had Howard to dance with between his longer and longer absences in Alberta, nothing in my life has ever replaced or diminished the enchantment and the happiness of that year, and nothing has dimmed the memories.

Medicine Men – and Women

The kitchen was stifling hot and the door to the front room was closed. Our mother was not at the breakfast table as we ate our "mush," and the security of our regular routine seemed disturbed. After breakfast Bertie and I, two and a half and three and a half years old, were bundled into warm outdoor clothing by Milly, just over eleven, and a hired girl. We were put outside to play in "The Sawdust Pile" and told to stay out of the house until we were called in. Howard, six, and Harvey, not yet ten, went off to the fields to see if any gophers were yet out and about and ready to give up their tails.

It was March 31, 1932, an unusually warm, sunny day for March in Alberta, with melting snow and many bare brown patches in yards, roads and fields. The Sawdust Pile was just the residue from the yearly stack of limbed, thin trees Dad had cut down by hand and hauled by team and wagon from some distance away, then sawed up, again by hand, for summer fuel. It was a favourite play area when we were small, and Bertie and I kept busy there until eventually called in for dinner at noon.

The kitchen was still hot, the front room door still closed and Milly was stirring a pot of stew on the stove. There was a strange man sitting in a kitchen chair against the wall at the end of the table. Someone said, "This is the doctor." I didn't know what that meant, but I did wonder if he had a headache, as he sat looking toward his feet, with one hand over his forehead, saying nothing.

Chairs were pulled up to the table, our "Daddy" came in and lifted Bertie into the old wooden high chair, while Milly dished out stew onto our plates. Then the doctor, looking at Bertie, spoke. "I guess you'll have to give up that chair now," was what he said. I wondered what he meant. Bertie, shy as we all were with strangers, turned her face toward the back of the chair, short brown hair falling over brown eyes.

Dad lifted her out, stood her on the floor and took her hand, saying, "Come with me; I'll show you something," and he opened the door and led her into the front room. Very aware that I had not been invited, I tagged along anyway. The front room also was boiling hot, with a great fire blazing in the big wood and coal heater. There, beside the stove, in the large black wood and leather rocking chair which had been lined with soft blankets, lay a very red, totally naked, brand new baby boy, yelling his head off – our little brother.

Further small, transient events from that day, from days and weeks that followed, present themselves selectively – clear, whole, complete – to memory's childhood eye. Bertie and I were sent for naps. Excited, we spent the whole time peeking through the hall door (and being sent back to bed) to watch the hired girl bathing the

284

noisy new little person in the dishpan on the dining room table. Perhaps that day, perhaps another, we were allowed into our mother's room to see her, still in bed. She was holding the baby, who was fussing. "Maybe he is thirsty," said some female adult standing near the foot of the bed. I left the room, went to the kitchen, got a thick white cup from the Cabinet, filled it half full of water from the water pail, and carried it to the bedroom. My mother asked what it was for.

"She said he was thirsty." Everyone laughed at me. I felt humiliated.

"He can't drink out of a cup," said someone. How would I know that? Bottle feeding was visible, breast feeding never was, not discussed, carried out in private, especially away from children's eyes.

Our mother sat in her tan coloured wicker rocking chair in the front room, the bundle of baby in her arms, while we all clustered round. "He needs a name," she said. "What do you think about 'Donald?'"

"Donald Noodles," said small Bertie, and everyone laughed at that as well.

A few weeks later, "Here comes the doctor with his little black bag, to get the baby," said the adults, and didn't seem to care. Why wouldn't we believe them? We had been told the doctor *brought* the baby, in his little black bag.

285

While playing in the yard, we saw the doctor arrive, friendlier this time, "Well, I've come to get that baby!" as he headed for the house. Teasing children was quite customary in that age, when children were not thought to have the same kinds of feelings as adults, or none that mattered. If thought about at all it was, on the surface, considered to be an expression of affection, though children, then as now, seldom felt it in that way.

That winter someone, perhaps our aunt, knit our fat baby a beautiful royal blue wool suit – sweater, toque and drawstring leggings with feet, which perfectly befitted his blonde hair and blue eyes. Mother was baking bread one sunny late spring day the following year. Donnie was cautiously taking little steps round the edges of the front room, holding on to the furniture. Mother set a little blue empty yeast cake box on the overturned chair, used to block the baby's entrance to the kitchen. He wanted it. He let go of the piece of furniture and took his first few steps.

I was more directly involved in my third encounter with a doctor, later in that year of 1933. I now have learned that Dad had been having problems with infected tonsils and had been advised to have them removed. Medical science had not yet discovered any useful purpose or function of tonsils and adenoids and therefore, deciding that nature had given us these bodily bits on a whim, advised the surgical removal of them whenever possible, especially in children. It had been decided that since Dad was to have his tonsils out, some of the rest of us might just as well have ours out at the same time. This, it was widely believed, would avoid later complications and colds.

Other than Dad, none of us had been medically examined. I'm not sure why Milly and Harvey escaped; Donnie was too young, and so Howard, Bertie and I were targeted for the procedure. I don't think any of us, at ages seven, four and five, had any idea what it all meant. We were excited to be travelling to our aunt and uncle's farm, then near Castor, Alberta, and close to the hospital in the larger town of Stettler. We did then have a visit to a doctor's office, he looked down all our throats, and we all went into hospital at once, with our mother and baby Donnie staying at Auntie's. Mother did stay two or three nights in a hotel in Stettler, visiting us each day, after the operations.

We were put to bed, strangely, in the daytime, in a large room with several women, also in bed. My bed was so high that I could not reach the floor, and Bertie was in a crib beside me. When a younger little girl came in, she was put in the crib and Bertie was put in the opposite end of my bed. The next morning the doctor came in and carried Bertie away, and a nurse told me it would be my turn soon. When someone brought Bertie back she was asleep, and smelled strange. I hoped the doctor was going to carry me, too, but he didn't come, a nurse did.

She laid me on a table and the doctor showed me a little

287

rubber cap with elephants round the edges, which they then put over my hair. Then I had a dream. I saw a deep, deep pit with light in it beside the table and I could see my mother far down at the bottom but there were no stairs for her to come up or for me to go down. At the same time I could see in front of me a large, beautiful circle filled with shining coloured stars – the whole thing whirling round.

I woke up in bed and my throat was very sore. On a table beside my bed was a glass of water with little squares of ice in it. This I had never seen before. When I poked the blocks of ice they went down and then popped back up. Bertie, awake and sounding sick, wanted to play with them too. On my stomach, I slid my legs over the side of the bed until I found the floor. I was surprised to find that my legs felt very shaky as I carefully began to carry the water glass to Bertie's end of the bed.

Suddenly a nurse appeared (rung for by another patient, I later found out) and hustled me back to bed, mildly scolding me for being out and showing me a button to push if I wanted something. No one understood or even listened (a characteristic of grown-ups, I was beginning to realize) when I tried to tell them that Bertie wanted to play with the ice. I viewed the lady who had rung the bell as something of a tattletale.

We were given ice-cream to eat and a not very nice tasting jelly. Our mother brought us each a little celluloid kewpie doll, and the mother of the little girl in the crib brought her a big doll. The

288

mothers promoted a brief exchange of dolls so that we could look at each other's. One day Howard came to see us. We were allowed up part time by then, and he took us out into a hallway and weighed us on a big scale. We each weighed forty pounds. I did not see a doctor again until I was sixteen, when some routine check was required by the British Columbia high school I attended.

Home births were customary in that era, at least in rural areas. A need to go to hospital for a birth would have caused concern and alarm in friends and neighbours. All our births were at home, except for Milly, the oldest, who was born in the Rowley Hospital before our parents had moved to the Huxley District. Our births were also all attended by doctors, though that was not so for many rural people at that time. Many a farm woman of my parents' generation helped to deliver a neighbour's baby.

Our father, in our adult years, could usually tell us which doctor and what circumstances had accompanied each of our births. "Let's see," he would say, "that would have been Dr. Dean. July - - - hmm - - - yeah. I had to ride to Elnora for him - - - it was before noon. We were haying and I had to leave that kid from Ireland in the field - - - he didn't know much about horses - - -," and off he'd go on a different story.

Treatments of illnesses and injuries, except in severe cases, were of the trial-and-error, heirloom variety, passed along in families, and shared with friends and neighbours. There were certain accepted remedies for various ailments, and every household had its favourites. Head colds were a widespread, winter-long fact of life, and were not treated much at all, unless they progressed to ear or chest infections. Mustard plasters for heavy chest colds and even pneumonia and pleurisy were common, though I don't recall our mother ever making any of these burning hot "cures." She did rub camphorated ointment on our chests (later Vicks VapoRub). For earaches, I well remember sitting with a high fever, bundled in blankets by the kitchen stove, holding a bag of hot salt to my ear until the abscess broke and ran, relieving pain and pressure. A school friend once told me that when they had earaches, their father blew pipe smoke into their ears for relief.

Visible infections such as boils, or blood poisoning resulting from infected scratches or cuts, were also treated with poultices, usually of wet, hot tea, salt, or bread soaked in milk and sugar, also applied wet and hot and changed frequently. Bathing or soaking the infected part for long periods in hot, salty water was another commonly used method. Similar treatments were used for aching or abscessed teeth. Children or adults with high fevers were kept in bed, sponged often and given hot lemonade or other hot drinks to "break the fever." Aspirin was available, but probably expensive, and seldom used for children.

"Mamma! My eyes are pasted shut!" was a cry heard often in the night or early morning in our childhood, and Mother would come with a soft cloth and a cup of warm water into which had been dissolved some boracic powder, to wash away the crusty matter clinging to eyelids. It took me until almost adulthood to realize that these were eye infections that we had, and not a necessary or particularly usual part of every child's life, as I thought. The same mistake in understanding held true for leg aches, with which we seemed to regularly wake crying in the night. The remedy for this was just a warm leg rubbing by Mother. (One wonders if she ever got a full night's sleep.)

Iodine was the painful antiseptic used on cuts and scrapes and even severe wounds. We were very happy when Mercurochrome was later produced, as it didn't hurt at all. Peroxide also was a staple antiseptic in most homes. Vaseline, carbolic ointment, and various liniments for aching backs and muscles were usually to be found in the medicine cupboard. My hives were treated with lukewarm baking soda baths, and bed, and my fainting spells (probably caused by an undiagnosed childhood anemia) by just being carried to some shady place to lie until I recovered.

For the perennial attacks of vast swarms of mosquitoes by which we were plagued, there was little to be done except build large smudge fires in the yard in the hot summer evenings, stand around in the smoke, and scratch, then leap into bed and swelter with head under the covers, accompanied by the occasional persistent, whining mosquito. Other biting and stinging insects

291

were prolific. Horseflies, as large as bees, carried a painful bite to both horses and humans. Flies in general were such a torment to horses that most had to be equipped with mesh nosebags to keep the pests away from their tender lips and nostrils.

One day when I was about four, while playing in the grass outside our gate, a bee flew up and stung me on the wrist. Frightened and hurt, I ran screaming to the house, with brothers and sister yelling, "A bee stung her! A bee stung her!"

Mother was in the yard, churning butter. "Where?" she asked, and when I pointed, reached down, picked up a handful of mud and slapped it on my wrist. The pain stopped instantly and I was so surprised, my tears did too. I was in awe that my mother knew such magic. "Go play," she said.

Though we heard about sulphur and molasses, used by many as a tonic in the springtime, it was not a custom in our home. We did, however, have a variety of laxatives with which Mother dosed us regularly. I'm not sure why she thought this was necessary, but each evening before bed we had to line up while she held the big blue glass bottle of *Milk of Magnesia* in one hand, pouring out a spoonful of the chalky, thick white, gagging liquid for each mouth. It was vile. Anyone who has ever had a Barium X-ray will understand the taste and texture. It is hard to say which was the more difficult to swallow – *Milk of Magnesia* or *Mineral Oil*, a clear, thick, unpleasant tasting oil that Mother switched to later on.

In between we once had a terrific tasting medicine called *Scott's Emulsion,* but were soon back on the old awful ones. It may be that Mother subscribed to the prevalent idea that if it didn't taste bad, it wasn't doing you any good, but more likely it was just that *Milk of Magnesia* was probably cheaper.

We often tried to avoid these sessions by hiding out, usually in the outhouse, but Mother always knew who was or was not in the lineup, and we couldn't stay out there all night. The other attempted escape, "I've already gone to bed!" called out from the bedroom, only elicited, "Well, get up and get out here and get your medicine!"

There were bottles of *Epsom Salts* and *Listerine,* and little round red and black boxes of pretty red, egg shaped pills – *Dodd's Kidney Pills,* taken daily by Mother for years. We were not supposed to touch any of this, but we smelled everything and tasted much. The big bottle of *Eno's Fruit Salts* was a particular temptation. It was probably some kind of mild antacid. The way to sneak a bit was to take the lid off the wide-necked bottle, lick one palm, hold the wet hand over the bottle and flip it over quickly and back, leaving a thin layer of the white crystals on the wet palm, which could then be licked off with a fizzy pleasantness on the tongue.

Most of these salves, ointments and medications came from the large suitcases of the travelling salesmen who came to the farms on a regular basis, once or twice yearly. So did most of Mother's spices, flavourings and other small baking and household needs, as well as thread, needles, embroidery threads and all manner of small household goods and knick-knacks. The visits of these representatives of the Raleigh and the Watkins companies were looked forward to by Mother as well as us children, and when we saw the car drive in we would run yelling to the house, "The Rawlyman is here! The Rawlyman is here!" Then we stood around, fascinated, while he opened the large cases, lifted out trays and exposed the many wonders inside.

It was Mother's time to pick and choose, ours to look and covet. She became friendly with some of the long-time salesmen, and though they worked to demonstrate and sell her "extras," she seldom bought anything not strictly needed. She knew exactly what she could spend, and it wasn't much. Only occasionally could the salesman persuade her to try a new pudding mix, or some "improved" ointment. Sometimes there would be a new hairbrush or comb, one for the household – we did not have individual toiletries until into our teen years. Raleigh products had a good reputation, and though the travelling salesmen disappeared from rural areas along with the horse and buggy, Raleigh representatives were still being searched out by our father through newspaper advertisements in the 1970's, and could still be found with their spices and flavourings in the mid 1980's at large flea markets.

In grade four or five we learned in school about microbes,

294

pictured in magazine drawings to somewhat resemble large ants that talked to each other about how to make us sick. Promoted at the same time was a new product, cellophane, that would supposedly keep these malicious creatures out of our food. Two or three years later, some government, many years late, began to recognize that there were large numbers of children in the country who did not get adequate food or nutrition. They then dispensed to schools boxes of little football-shaped, brown gelatin pills filled with fish oil, vitamin D. The contents were very smelly, green and oily. Each morning one was placed on each child's desk and we were supposed to swallow it at once, without water. Many boys did not swallow them at all. It was much more fun to squeeze one until the end popped open, squirting the stinky contents onto your neighbour's clothing, hair, face or, if lucky, an eye.

When I was nine or ten, at the recommendation of a teacher, I was taken to an optometrist and fitted with glasses, ugly little round things with silver frames, which improved my eyesight but not my popularity or self-esteem. Around the same time I had my first visit to a travelling dentist, working from a trailer in Trochu, a town several miles to the south of us. This was not a productive trip. Dad took me in and left me, but just as I got into the dentist's chair I passed out from both the strong smell of anesthetic and, no doubt, fear. I was revived with smelling salts and sent home and my parents gave up the idea of dentists until I was fourteen, when, in

295

preparation for our move to British Columbia, Howard, Bert, Donnie and I were all taken the thirty miles or so to Red Deer, to a dentist. He sat me down in the chair and began pulling teeth, minus adequate anesthetic. Four molars quickly vanished. I don't know whether any others were filled. Though helped immensely by some very kind and sensitive dentists since, that early trauma has never altogether disappeared.

We ran around with rags tied on our cut fingers and toes; our mother pulled slivers and thorns from our hands and feet, and our father, with pliers, pulled porcupine quills from the nose of our dog. Children came to school with measles, mumps, chicken pox, impetigo, tuberculosis, styes, warts, bedbug bites and head lice. Fortunately, and due in large part, I believe, to our mother's innate and insistent cleanliness, we escaped almost all of these things, except measles and chicken pox.

After Dad's leg had been broken and the heavy plaster cast was due to come off, many weeks later, he decided he was not going to give up a day's farm work and drive many miles to pay someone to do what he could do himself. He instructed a reluctant Howard, sixteen, to get the saw and start sawing. Howard nervously began."How will I know when I've sawed far enough?" he wanted to know.

"Just keep sawing," said Dad, "I'll tell you when to stop." After a few minutes the saw plugged up with plaster, and stuck. An anxious Howard took it out and, to his horror, saw blood on it. Of course Dad's skin had become numb inside the plaster for so long. Unperturbed, Dad somehow broke off the rest of the cast. This incident has now become a funny story and an indication that our father was something of a "character." To his neighbouring farmers and friends at that time, however, this would have been considered the practical and sensible solution and, self-reliant, as Depression-taught, just what they probably would have done themselves.

The Maypo Lea Forever

Mammy's Little Coal Black Rose

David Wagstaff ran over Mammy's Little Coal Black Rose. Of course he didn't mean to, and I think he probably didn't even know that he had done so. If he should read this now, nearly sixty-five years later, I'm sure he will be greatly surprised. Though David was probably then no more than nineteen or twenty, most of the Wagstaff children, Bill, David, Norman and their older sister, Laura, were several years older than we were and so, in my eyes, always "grown-ups." Only the youngest, Norman, was close in age to our older brother and sister, Harvey and Milly.

Handsome and shy, the "quiet one" of the three Wagstaff boys, as they were always called, David whirled into our yard in a fancy car to give Mother a ride to town. I don't suppose it was a *new* car, but almost all cars looked fancy to me, compared to our father's old red International truck (circa 1930) with its "ba-*goo*-ga!" horn, activated by a small, stiff, handle-less lever outside the driver's window. Because the circumstance of Mother going to town without Dad or any of her children (a rare escape for her) was so unusual, it was classed as an Event, and we children were all out in the yard to watch her go. David backed out as quickly as he had driven in and, unfortunately, the tiny black kitten, newly brought to

299

the house from its birthplace in the hayloft, had just run under the car. Mercifully, it was an instant death. I remember feeling more shock than sorrow.

Howard and Harvey, who were often allowed, and sometimes required, to sleep in the hayloft when their bed was needed for visiting relatives, always were the first to see new kittens, and so had the advantage in naming them. There were many mice on the grain farm, and therefore many cats, but the number of kittens allowed to grow up was carefully and quietly regulated without the knowledge of most of us when young.

I was impressed with the name, "Mammy's Little Coal Black Rose." It sounded like the name of a song or a poem, but I assumed that my brothers had made it up. Howard was the one with his ear literally squashed to the cloth-covered speakers on the old battery radio, long after the batteries were so weak and the sound so faint that none of the rest of us could hear anything. He went around saying things like, "Who-oo knows? - - - The *Shadow* knows!" and giving the barn cats strange names such as *Joe Louis* and *Tommy Farr* (prominent boxers of the era), and *Pepi Lomoco, King of the Casbah!* He told me all these radio adventures as we sat on our stools in the cowbarn, milking, long after Dad and Harvey had taken their pails of milk to the house. Most of the time I had no idea of what he was talking about. *The Lone Ranger* and his faithful friend, *Tonto* ("Hi-yo, Silver! - - - Away!" – clop – clop – clop –

300

"Who *was* that masked man?") and *Fibber McGee*, with everything falling out of his infamous hall closet each week, to great laughter from listeners, were much closer to the realm of my understanding.

We named all the animals on the farm, with the exception of pigs, calves and poultry, none of which were around long enough to require names. Sometimes Mother helped with suggestions. I puzzled for years about *Little Bob*, a small cow with no horns and an attractive, dark reddish brown, curly-haired face – and a boy's name! *White Face,* a reasonably placid cow which, with my child-sized fingers, I found easy to milk, seemed to have a much more appropriate name. Grown animals that Dad purchased from neighbours or at auctions, often had already been given names.

Such was the case with the two large, bony Holstein cows he brought home, informing us that their names were Bessie and Sadie. This caused a little stir of irreverent but restrained giggling, as we had an Aunt Sadie, our mother's sister. Some of us had never seen Holstein cattle before and, since these two were mostly white, when young Donnie, out somewhere in the truck with Dad, saw in a field a few mostly black cows he logically decided they were "Half-steins." (A family story: Farmers routinely set blocks of salt in their pastures for cattle. At first these were white, always the kind we had. Later, there began to appear some iodized ones of a reddish-brick color. When Donnie, who travelled everywhere with Dad when small, first saw a field dotted with both white and red blocks,

301

he exclaimed, "Oh, look at all the cow salt and peppers!")

Bessie's idiosyncrasy soon showed itself. The milking practice was to release each of the seven or eight cows from her stall out into the barnyard after she had been milked and, when all were out, herd them into their night pasture. As each milk pail was filled, Dad set it out of the way outside the cowbarn door. Imagine his surprise one evening to find that the full buckets he was about to carry to the house, were empty! No one could imagine what had happened and an intensive investigation ensued to determine whether some child had tipped them over and was not admitting it. All children's presences were verified as elsewhere. Within two or three days the puzzle was solved. Bessie, who drank anything contained in a bucket, was caught in the act.

This distinctive peculiarity of Bessie's nature had more memorable consequences some time later. The pails of warm, frothing milk had been strained and all poured together into the big metal separator bowl; someone, possibly me, was turning the handle when several people noticed a strong odour of gasoline in the kitchen. Clothing and footwear were checked. Finally Mother tasted the milk. It all had to be thrown out. With some mind searching, Dad remembered a half pail of gas he had left by the tractor. He checked. It was upright and empty. We were all impressed (except Mother, who was annoyed), by the imperviousness of Bessie's stomach, which showed no outward

302

signs of ill-effects.

"The Momma Cat," aptly named, was the only cat tolerated at the house, though seldom inside, for many years. She was a small Calico and the tips of her ears had been frozen in some fierce winter, so that her face resembled that of a young lion or tiger, with little rounded ears. Since she was older than I was, and since we were quite sheltered from the barn and barnyard animals when we were small, when I first saw a cat with pointed ears I was quite disappointed to be told that this was their natural state. The Momma Cat, well-fed on table scraps and milk, plus some of the numerous mice which liked to find homes with us, produced countless kittens, most of which some of us never saw, and she lived to at least age fourteen.

We were not allowed to have cats further inside the house than the anteroom (which today would be called a "mud room") where they and the dog were fed in winter. Bertie and I, therefore, were frequently scolded for sneaking the current house cat into our bed at night. One consequence of this practice (and our parents own fault for *never* telling us any facts of life whatsoever) was for us to come home one day from school to our mother's wrath and a fresh litter of kittens under the sheets, inside our bed. How were *we* to know what the cat's fat tummy meant?

If Mother took a liking to a kitten, that one could be our next house pet. (They *did* help to keep the mouse population down.)

303

When Ginger, our big, thick-furred orange tomcat, came limping home one day with a shotgun hole through his front paw, already festered and full of maggots, Dad wanted to put him out of his misery, but Mother, with few resources, covered the paw liberally each day with powdered lime (kept for the outside toilet), until it eventually healed and Ginger again squashed himself, each wintry night, against our bedroom window pane through the large hole in the rusty screen, meowing piteously. We always got up and, along with a cold blast of blizzard, let him in and under the covers, where he immediately shook his coating of ice and snow all over our bare feet.

There was so much adult talk of the fierceness of bulls, the danger of bulls, the possibility or the reality of bulls chasing people, attacking people and having the superability to leap every gate or fence with ease, that I was terrified of bulls long before I ever saw one. It was futile then, to tell me later on, as I was about to leave to return the borrowed sugar, butter or yeast cake, "Watch out for Wagstaff's bull. He might be in the field, but don't worry. He won't hurt you." What kind of message was that? If he wouldn't hurt me, why was I to watch out for him? And what was I supposed to do if I saw him? I *did* see him occasionally, never very close, grazing on a hillside, and what I did was step off the hard-packed dirt trail that led through the field, and into the soft, newly ploughed earth, and make a long, wide, nervous circle around him, sinking in

304

the powdery dry soil over the tops of my shoes.

The bull, called by the Wagstaff brothers, "Old Beefsteak and Onions," never looked at me. He couldn't really, because he had a narrow little board, like a visor, over his eyes, hanging from his horns by a piece of wire. This, I guess, was to deter him from attacking, or at least from *seeing* what he was attacking. It provided no reassurance for me. I knew he was endowed with the omnipotence to know exactly where I was at every moment in my trek and I sometimes dreamed of him at night, coming through our small bedroom window to attack us in our bed.

Our neighbour, Olaf Vik, whose farm adjoined ours to the southeast, also had a bull, who was also the subject of many fearsome (and possibly exaggerated) tales. He, too, had the reputation of laughing (snorting?) at all pens, gates, and fences, and of having a particular passion for chasing humans. One summer afternoon, some time after Milly was working away from home, her school friend, Inga Jensen, walked from their farm one and a half miles south to consult with Mother about something, possibly some sewing. After supper Mother and I started out to walk Inga part way home. The gate from the main road into Jensen's fields lay at the bottom of a steep gully, out of sight of their farmhouse. By the time we had walked this far, dusk was deepening and we could see little. On the opposite side of the road lay the fenced fields of Mr. Vik, whose bull had been the subject of uneasy conversation between

305

Inga and Mother on the walk. Suddenly they thought they heard him snorting and galloping down the hill, and Inga was sure he was inside their fence.

The two women turned and began running up the opposite steep hill, back along the road we had just walked. I was exhorted to hurry, to keep up with them, but my legs were short, and my breath was short; my lungs felt as though they were going to burst through my chest. I could hear the women in front of me, "He's still coming! I can hear him snorting! Keep running!" Only their voices in the pitch dark kept me running in the right direction, over unseen stones and ruts in the dried out clay of the road. Finally, at some distance beyond the top of the hill, we all stopped, exhausted, and listened. A nighttime chorus of frogs was the only thing that broke the silence.

We could see nothing, not even each other, in the thick blackness. Inga was sure the bull was still across the fence in the field, just waiting his chance to leap across and demolish us. We clambered through the deep, weedy ditch on the other side, feeling our way under a barbed wire fence, and rolled into the lower field of grain (and thistles) on our own farm, where we lay listening, recovering our breath. When the two women judged that the danger was over we all trudged the remaining mile back to our house, where Inga spent the night. I didn't ever really know if Vik's bull was abroad that night, and whether or not we had been chased by

306

him. Inga and Mother said they heard him and for many years I didn't question that. The next morning, before Inga left again for home, I was given the task of picking hundreds of burrs out of her and Mother's stockings.

Newborn piglets are among the most charming of all young animals, though they very soon grow to be just as bristly and muddy as their many older relatives. To us, they were the cutest little things, all pink and clean and new, running around the pen with their curly little tails while we peered at them through the big wooden gate. We knew enough to keep well away from their huge, sometimes ferocious, mother. There often seemed to be one piglet in a litter that was smaller and weaker than the others. This one was always called "the runt." Occasionally, if Dad thought it could survive, it was brought to the house, wrapped in old cloths and placed in a box behind the kitchen stove, then fed from a baby bottle until judged strong enough to rejoin its family.

We were all introduced to saddle horses and riding by the age of four or five, at first behind the saddle with an older sister or brother, lifted there by our father and told to hang on. I never learned to ride bare-back, that is, with no saddle, as many farm children did. My only experience of that had been discouraging. Bertie and I were not more than five and six, perhaps younger, when we five oldest had trooped out into the pasture about a mile from home on a Sunday afternoon, for reasons which I have now

307

forgotten. We may have been searching for birds' nests, or perhaps we had been sent to pick wild gooseberries. In any case, Bert and I were either tired, or our older siblings were tired of looking after us and decided we should go home. The older ones had been trying to catch one of the horses roaming free and were finally successful.

I believe it was our school horse, Darky, onto whose back we were eventually hoisted, with instructions to "Hang onto her mane!" This we tried to do, but Darky's black mane was sparse and far in front of our short arms. With a slap on the rear from someone still on the ground, she took off, heading for home, barn and food. We had no way of stopping her or steering her and when she came to the closed gate between pasture and barnyard she applied her own brakes, abruptly. Bertie and I, still holding tightly to each other, promptly fell as one with a thud into the dirt. Since we were able to pick ourselves up and get to the house, those watching from inside offered little sympathy and, in fact, seemed to think it was very funny.

I once, when I was twelve, had a simulated ride, bare-back, on my Uncle Ed's mule, along with three cousins. The four of us climbed onto the back of this very tall animal by standing on a barrel and, after about ten minutes of smacking his tough hide with our hands, were treated to a slow, lumbering ramble halfway round the yard, at which point the mule, for reasons of his own, stopped, not to move again that day – or at least not until his supper was served.

Some foals were born on our farm, infrequently enough to make their appearances very special events for us. We loved these beautiful little animals and sometimes had a say in naming them. Information from Howard is that Liz and Bess, both adult in my memory, were daughters of Pinto, an early saddle horse of Dad's. Liz was both saddle horse and school cart horse. She also gave birth to several foals, one of whom was Judy, named by Bert for a character from a storybook. Judy was very neurotic, and this was probably partly our fault, as we petted and spoiled her from the time she was born. She was a small horse of a pretty, soft grey colour, and her first (I think her only) foal died at birth in a steep coulee in the pasture. She would never afterward willingly go into the coulee, whinnying and acting spooked if we took her near. Often the milk cows were near the creek at the bottom of the coulee and the only way to round them up with Judy was to try to take her down backward, an awkward and difficult process.

Another characteristic that made Judy an unsatisfactory riding horse was her insistence that she must, each time she came to any slough, puddle or patch of water, lie down and roll over, regardless of any saddle and rider upon her back.

Shorty, probably our most well-ridden and longest lived saddle horse, carried Milly, Harvey and Howard to school for many years, as well as Dad and the children around the farm. One early evening, a long time after Harvey, perhaps fifteen, had left on Shorty to bring in the cows, we saw him trudging through the field toward home, carrying the heavy saddle. In the pasture, a mile from home, Shorty had suddenly stopped, fallen over and died. ✓

The horse I liked best to ride, and rode most often as I grew into early adolescence, was Blondie, a tall, long-legged horse, slightly more grayish in colour than his white-coated mother, Liz. When very young we walked with Mother to bring home the milk cows; later we were sent in pairs and by the age of seven or so, alone. By age eight or nine, I was allowed to take a horse. There wasn't much to do. As soon as the cows saw us coming they headed up the lane toward home, eager to be milked. I might have been given this chore more often had I not taken such a long time about it. There was a wonderful sense of freedom in galloping all over the fields, looking for cows, singing loudly every Wilf Carter and other cowboy song I'd ever heard. If the cows were distantly visible from the house, of course I had to get them rounded up and on the trail home without delay, but if they were out of home view in the coulee or avoiding flies in some bushes, I could ride around longer, making the later excuse that it took me that long to find them. By the time I was eleven I was also entrusted to ride the four miles to town, on an occasional Saturday errand. Blondie and I were quite compatible and his long stride suited me well.

In 1938, an epidemic of sleeping sickness (enzootic

310

encephalomyelitis), an infectious viral disease of horses, later linked to poliomyelitis in humans, swept the farms of North America. It caused an inflammation of the brain and paralysis. The death rate was high. In that summer there were 184,662 recorded cases in the United States. Canada, especially the already Depression and drought-ravaged prairies, did not escape. Horses on farms around us were becoming sick and dying daily, and we heard the anxious talk of adults. We knew when one horse on our farm got sick and then died, but it was when our dependable school horse, Darky, became ill that we really took notice. There was little to be done, no veterinary to help. Darky lay immobilized in the barn for weeks. Dad cared for the sick horses as best he could, at first rigging up a canvas sling under their bellies to keep them on their feet, later pouring warm water and some kind of gruel mixture down Darky's throat each day with a funnel. No one expected her to live. Slowly, slowly, however, she began to recover. The day came when she was able to stagger weakly to her feet and Dad let her out of the barn into the fresh air and sunshine. We watched her begin to walk, round and round the large barnyard each day for hours, rebuilding her muscles, healing herself, until eventually she was able to again do what she did best – stand patiently to be harnessed, then pull four children in a cart to and from school each day, a trustworthy job for a horse.

Mickey, also a son of Liz, was the last foal born on the farm before we left, and was petted much by all of us. It was King, a high strung horse, who was partly responsible for us leaving the farm. He and Dad had an interaction in the barn one blizzard-filled afternoon, the details of which possibly none of us ever knew, resulting in a severely broken leg for our father, with ensuing complications, which made further prairie farming for him difficult and perhaps impossible.

I never saw my mother on a horse, or even near one, though I can't imagine that our father did not ever try to get her to ride, either in his cowboy days when they both worked on the Imperial Ranch or later, in their early years of marriage. This circumstance seems a little strange until further examination. Though Mother grew up in rural settings, there was no indication that horses were used for anything except field work or pulling wagons and buggies. When her family lived at Mt. Olie (Little Fort, B.C.) the children walked down the mountainside to school, in contrast to my growing years, where children on the larger farms of Alberta frequently lived much too far from school to walk. Probably a stronger reason for Mother not riding was that almost *no* women then rode horses. It was unusual, considered not quite "ladylike." *Men* rode horses. Possibly some farm women rode when necessary on their own farms, but they would have had to wear a pair of their husband's pants to do so, and would have been highly embarrassed had anyone seen them dressed like that. We girls rode in our dresses, and it was not until I was ten or eleven that I inherited from Milly a pair of pants actually made for girls. My mother was over fifty before she bought a pair of pants for herself, which she used for gardening, though she never seemed to feel very at ease in wearing them.

I was well past sixty-five when I last rode a horse, and I had not been on one for years. It was something of a surprise to me to be riding this one and I think the horse, Lady, may have felt the same. We quickly discovered that we did not like each other. I was visiting my long-time good friend, Nancy Fraser, in my old home town, and had been reminiscing about how much I had liked riding in my growing years on the farm, and bemoaning the fact that I would probably never ride again.

Nancy (sneakily!) phoned her daughter-in-law while I was out for a walk and I came back to find, not only a small sorrel horse, saddled and bridled, tethered to Nancy's garden fence, but also the expectation that I would now be overjoyed to "put my money where my mouth was." With a little assistance to aging leg muscles, I attained the saddle. Bev's parting advice as we started down the street was, "If you want her to stop, take her on the gravel. She doesn't like that."

Having grown up with horses that stopped when I pulled on the reins and said, "Whoa!" I became a little suspicious, especially as Lady's ears, at first perked forward to acquaint herself with the situation, were now flattened backward, where they remained

313

throughout the ride. I remembered enough horse-human communication to know that this meant, in horse language, "Who invited *you* to get on my back? Don't for a minute think I'm going to do anything *you* want me to!"

I took her into the long grass growing alongside the remaining grain elevators and the railroad tracks, hoping for a good gallop. "You want a gallop?" said Lady's ears, treacherously. "*I'll* give you a gallop!" and off their owner bolted headlong, with an unpleasant sideways gait designed to jolt me flank-side out of the low saddle with, she hoped, one foot caught in a stirrup, while my head got the bashing she thought it deserved. When this manoeuvre failed, Lady, still travelling at full speed, stretched out her neck, and I quickly saw that her aim now was to suddenly stop short, flinging me forward over her head, when she would then stand with lowered visage, reins down, gazing in mock innocence and grief at my broken body. Lady had been watching too many old cowboy movies.

We were now far past the elevators, into an open field of grass and, even though I applied both voice and reins, Lady showed no signs of slowing down. There was little choice. I turned her back to town and into the gravel, which stopped her at once, just as her owner had said, but also made her *really* mad, and she consequently tried to wipe me off under every tree we passed on the few blocks walk homeward. As I dismounted and watched Lady being led away, her ears twitched at me, "I guess *that* will teach you greenhorns not to come here and mess around with us old-timers!"

The Maypo Lea Forever

How I Helped Win the War

There we were, two thirteen year old girls, swinging our bare feet and legs out the back end of the wooden box of Barnes' little old truck, bellowing out songs into the prairie sunshine as we jolted down the dusty dirt road –

> Just remem-ber--Pearl Harbour!
> As we go-to-meet-the-foe!
> Remem-ber--Pearl Harbour!
> As we did-the-A-la-mo!
> We will al-ways--re-mem-ber
> How they died for li-ber-ty!
> Just remem-ber--Pearl Harbour!
> And go on-to Vic-tory!

Not that we knew what the Alamo was. We didn't even really know what and where Pearl Harbour was, though we knew it was part of the United States and that it had been attacked some months earlier, December 7th, 1941, by Japanese war planes, stunning and frightening everybody in North America, precipitating the U.S.'s entry into World War II and heightening our own silent fears.

Ignorant and naive though we were, we were certainly patriotic, as we had been taught to be. Cicely Barnes was my best friend, and though her brothers were not yet old enough to be in the armed forces, my sister and brother, Milly and Harvey, the two oldest in our family, were in the Army, both eventually to get as far as Belgium, Milly to Germany and both finally safely home.

I was eleven years old when World War II began officially on September 1st, 1939. It was then more commonly called "The Second World War" or just "The War," distinguished in that way from World War I (1914-1918), known always by those in the generations above us as "The Great War." Even more than fifty years later World War II is still referred to as "The War" by anyone who was around in those days and the innocent question, "Which war?" by a younger person will often evoke exasperated or incredulous looks from those who remember first hand.

By 1942, many changes had taken place in our lives and it was beginning to feel like nothing would ever go back to the way it had been, as indeed it did not. Fear is contagious, especially unspoken fear. World War I was not very far in the background of our parents' and grandparents' generations. They had lost sons, brothers, fathers, husbands and friends to its horrors. Their fears were of the known. Mine were of the unknown. Though I now realize that it may not have been so, I just assumed, without giving it any thought at all, that all my contemporaries felt the same anxiety that I did. I would not have expected them to talk about it. Feelings were not discussed freely and analyzed then as they are now and fear was certainly not something to be admitted to. Some of this fear, I believe, would have been relieved had we been given any concrete facts about war in general and this one in particular.

Though the war and any news about it that came through in the few media sources we had – radio, a handful of weekly or monthly farm papers and magazines, often several weeks old – was discussed daily and anxiously by the adults around us, situations were not ever really explained to us in ways we could understand, not even by our teachers, who perhaps did not understand very well themselves. The result for me was that I felt, all through the war, that I never knew the what or the why of any of it. I was probably not as alone as I thought in this, though children whose families had daily newspapers in their homes were no doubt much better informed than I was.

We heard a great deal about Hitler, Winston Churchill and President Roosevelt, and not nearly so much about Canada's own Prime Minister, William Lyon Mackenzie King. We learned who were the good guys and who were the bad guys. Besides Britain's Churchill and Roosevelt in the U.S., the good guys included General Douglas MacArthur, Field Marshall Montgomery, King George VI and Queen Elizabeth. The bad guys, along with Adolf Hitler, were Joseph Goebbels, Hermann Goering, Italy's Benito Mussolini and Emperor Hirohito in Japan. There was much ambivalence about Joseph Stalin, dictator of Russia. At first no one was sure whether he was a good guy or a bad guy, then he became a good guy, and at

319

the end of the war he became a very bad guy and remained so until his death in 1953. Though I was aware, as was everyone, of when France fell to Hitler's troops, I was always very hazy about whether General de Gaulle was one of the good guys or the bad guys.

Radio announcers talked about "fronts," as they do now with the weather, causing, for me, very similar bafflement. We knew people were out killing each other in countries far from us. We knew airplanes were dropping bombs on cities and people, including children, but my impressions of most of this were vague and unclear and therefore anxiety-making.

We heard mostly about the suffering of Britain, particularly England, a country with which many of us identified. Canada was still very much a British Empire country. We were proud of our flag, the Union Jack, and of our King and Queen. Much of our school literature originated in Britain, and our feelings toward England as our "Mother Country" were reinforced in many ways. (I was once "Brittania" in a Christmas pageant and got to wear a gold crown and a beautiful blue satin ribbon across my white dress, while all the other British Empire "countries" sang, very stirringly, "Rule, Brittania!")

We also heard much about the evilness and the power of Hitler and talk of "what if they come here," and when war news was not good, which seemed almost always, adults looked very grim. In March, 1943, Milly was sent "overseas" to England and later that

320

year Harvey came home on leave before also embarking on a troop ship. He looked very adult and important, at twenty-one, in his army uniform. As we said goodbye to him in the farmyard and he left, my mother burst into tears and rushed into the house crying, "He's gone! And we'll never see him again!" That incident really solidified my fears. For one thing, I had never seen my mother cry before and, secondly, it sounded as though she knew something we didn't. All the talk of "what if they come here" suddenly seemed real and possible, perhaps imminent, and I began to feel even more powerless, believing totally that if that happened there would be no place to escape to, no place to hide.

I thought much about that, as I rode the horse for the cows through the wide and open prairie fields, under the immense prairie sky. I felt totally visible and vulnerable. We had almost never before seen airplanes, but now they began to fly over occasionally, high in the sky, and each one, to me, became a threat until it had passed innocently beyond the horizon. As more and more countries became involved in the war and as Hitler took over more and more of Europe, things got more and more scary. It seemed that no one could stop him.

I was about thirteen when I planned the assassination of Adolf Hitler. My reasoning had convinced me that this would solve all of the world's problems. It seemed to me to be so simple, and I couldn't understand why no one had done it. I knew that if I could get a gun and get to Germany, *I* could do it. I knew that no one would suspect someone my age, so I could just go to where Hitler was making one of his big speeches to thousands of people, get myself up toward the front and then just shoot him. Of course I also knew that I would be immediately shot as well, but it seemed to me that it would be worth it. I really could not understand why some adult didn't go do that, and be willing to make that sacrifice to save the world, particularly since it began to sound as though we were all going to be killed, tortured or enslaved anyway.

A lot of emphasis was put on patriotism and "The War Effort," both at home and in school. We were taught to recite, "In Flanders fields the poppies blow/between the crosses, row on row/that mark our place; and in the sky/the larks, still bravely singing, fly/scarce heard amid the guns below - - -. "[1] My understanding of fields included wheat, hay, cows and horses, and Flanders was puzzling. For a long time I thought it was the name of the farmer who owned the fields. Mr. Flanders. Most of us had very limited personal experience of death, funerals or graves.

Government messages came by radio, by newspapers and magazines and by large colored posters which began to be seen everywhere – at school, in the Post Office, in railway stations and stores – exhorting everyone to do their bit to help win the war and

---

[1] *In Flanders Fields,* John McCrae, 1915.

outlining what even the smallest child could do. Scrap metal was gathered. We were urged, as our patriotic duty, to collect tinfoil, something we didn't see much of in those days before household foil wrap, waxed paper or plastic.

Foil came on chewing gum, cigarette packages and certain kinds of chocolate bars, but since few or none of these things were a part of our household, we, like most of our classmates, pounced on every tiny scrap in the ditches or along the wooden sidewalks in town, carefully peeling away any paper and adding the foil to our growing ball, which was presented periodically to teachers. When I saw the balloon-sized balls of foil produced by some of the older children in school with, I seem to remember, some kind of prize incentive offered by teachers, my own egg-sized lump seemed a good deal less than adequate.

And then there was the knitting class. When some well-meaning and enthusiastic townslady or teacher decided we should knit scarves for the soldiers, I expected personal disaster. There was no way to avoid the class. How totally ungrateful and unpatriotic! I could sew a bit (well, I had learned to hem dishtowels on the faithful Singer sewing machine, through tears and thread tangles and my mother's grim determination); I could embroider a bit; I could crochet a bit. I didn't really like any of it and I knew I was not very good at it. I also knew that knitting would be even worse because, for all her household skills and talents, the one thing our mother

323

could *not* do was knit, so I could expect no help at home. Violent inward and a few tentative outward protests did no good. "Of course you can learn to knit!" said my mother, as she bought my sister, brother and I the required wool and knitting needles, though that must have been a hardship for her. She fully supported all school endeavors toward The War Effort; two of her children had gone to war.

As expected, I hated it. My fingers would not do what my brain and my teacher commanded. My humiliation and guilt at not contributing to The War Effort were increased by the awareness that no soldier would ever wear what these protesting fingers produced. In all too visible contrast to the soft, symmetrical scarves some of the other girls and boys were knitting so effortlessly, mine, while starting out at the regulation width, quickly narrowed down to a hard, tight little mat about four inches wide. Every knitting day, under the teacher's unbelievably patient supervision, I would unravel what I had done at the last session and redo it. Each time it came out the same. Finally the teacher gave up and let me go ahead. I did finish it, but I knew it was useless. I was too embarrassed to turn it in with those of my classmates. I didn't remember what happened to it, but my brother Howard recently told me that I gave it to him, and he remembered the shape of it, too!

So far I seemed to be failing my classes in "War Effort." The next challenge was War Savings Certificates. These, along with War Bonds, were issued and promoted by the Canadian government as a means of raising money to finance the war. The War Savings Certificate promotions were aimed at those with little money to invest, including school children. Strong and ongoing appeals were made to us to use our pennies to buy War Savings Stamps, which we could get from our teachers or the Post Office. Four dollars worth of stamps in smaller denominations were pasted in a booklet which, when full, could be redeemed for a five dollar War Savings Certificate. These, in turn, could be redeemed at a certain date, presumably at the end of the war. Competition with friends and schoolmates was also promoted and encouraged.

For many of us, getting enough money to buy a stamp was a long process and our booklets filled slowly and discouragingly. Our mother prodded our efforts and probably bought us each our first stamp, but pennies were few and far between in our household, as in many. "Allowance" was a term and a custom never heard of, and a nickel was a monumental sum. We did our expected share of home and farm chores, like most other farm children we knew, and shared in whatever occasional treat was presented, but we had few opportunities to earn money of our own. A five dollar certificate seemed to me to be a totally unattainable goal. I hardly knew what that amount of money looked like, and I didn't feel very patriotic about using any precious pennies that came my way for stamps to paste in a book which, I truly believed, would never get filled.

It was really not helpful to be told, "At the end of the war you will get five dollars for your certificate." They might as well have said, "At the end of your life you will get five dollars." It was not a time frame that I could visualize and anyway, according to the talk of adults, there wasn't going to *be* any end to the war. And since my book was never going to get full I was never going to get anything for my infrequent and grudgingly parted with pennies except a few sticky stamps.

Not understanding the process, I didn't know that each of my pennies and nickels had already been handed over to the Canadian government, added to the thousands and millions of pennies, nickels and dimes of all the children in Canada and turned into supplies for the armed forces. Our vacillating enthusiasm dwindled along with our pennies and the books lay dormant somewhere in our mother's care for some time. After the four of us who were still left at home moved with our parents from Alberta to the Fraser Valley of British Columbia in late 1943, we began to have a few opportunities for earning – child minding, bean and berry picking – and the War Savings stamp books, almost forgotten by us, were brought out once again by Mother. Eventually, with some necessary nagging, they were filled and redeemed. Five dollars was still a healthy sum for us in 1946 or so, and would have bought at least a pair of shoes or a dress. I always felt, though, that they were our mother's War Savings Certificates. Certainly without her tenacity and determination they would have long before fallen by the wayside.

Our bone collecting summer must have occurred early in the war, perhaps 1940 or 1941, as I had no idea, in all these years, until Howard told me recently, that this project of Dad's was actually part of The War Effort. At first it seemed like it would be fun, a novel change in our fairly routine and predictable summers. We were going to gather bones from our fields. Even Mother came along for a day or two, but it was not long until her household duties demanded her presence. It was also not long until I began to hope that she would really need me at the house.

We certainly gathered bones; cow bones, horse bones, coyote bones, bird bones, badger bones, gopher bones, weasel bones, skunk bones, mouse bones – who knows, maybe even one or two buffalo bones – as we trudged through the sharp stubble fields, the hayfields, the sloughs, crisscrossing most of the whole six hundred and forty acres of the farm. All that dry summer we gathered dry bones, throwing them in the wagon that our father drove ahead, as the sun got hotter and the dust got dustier. When Dad decided we had found them all he nailed high racks onto the box of his old red International truck and piled in the mountain of bones. The strange load got even stranger looks as Dad, Mother and I (my turn for the trip) rattled the hundred or so miles down the gravel highway and into Calgary. Dad enjoyed the attention, but I

327

was old enough to be somewhat embarrassed on only my second visit to a city, as Mother and I climbed out at Eaton's store. The bones were deposited somewhere, Dad got a bit of money for them and, as I have since learned, they then went on to be made into glue and explosives to be used in the war.

As the war struggled on, certain household items became very scarce. The government issued ration books for some things, among them sugar , tea, coffee, meat, butter and gasoline. Permits were given for a certain quota of alcoholic beverages. This was such an intriguing move that some people who did not drink, and never bought anything in a liquor store from one year to the next, would go buy something just to make sure they got their quota. Cigarettes and chocolate were hard to get and anything containing rubber or silk almost impossible. This meant no silk stockings or clothing for women as all the silk was being used for parachutes. Nylon was just invented but was hardly known and was almost totally unavailable to civilians. Even in 1948, three years after the war had ended, women and girls, I among them, were still standing in half block long line-ups to buy a pair of nylon stockings, with often no choice of colour or size.

Enterprising cosmetic manufacturers put out various kinds of leg paint to simulate stockings and as we grew into our teens my sister and I tried some. In those times, stocking seams were of the utmost importance, meaning *straight* stocking seams, so, not only

328

did we have to be able to get the leg paint on smoothly and evenly, with no blotches and both legs the same depth of color, we then had to somehow draw, with a good sharpened eyebrow pencil, a fine, straight seam up the back of each leg from heel to fashionably short skirt. I never achieved any of this. There were girls who claimed that they drew on their nice, straight seams by themselves but I still have doubts about whether it is really possible.

One time, with no sister around and in a hurry to go out with friends, having managed what I thought was a passable leg job, I somehow cajoled my younger brother Donnie, then about eleven, into drawing on some seams for me as I stood on a chair. All I had was the stump of a poor quality eyebrow pencil, and the very squiggly result was a good deal less than convincing. I had to wash everything off and revert to my old mended cotton stockings, and I'm afraid I was neither very grateful nor gracious.

Shortages of meat and butter did not affect us when we lived in Alberta, as the farm had always supplied us plentifully with both, but the lack of sugar was noticed, especially by Mother, who could not do her usual baking and the preserving of fruit that saw us through the winter. Sugar rations included jam, honey and syrup; if you used up your coupons on one you would go short on the others and Mother, as no doubt most mothers at that time, had to use a lot of ingenuity to fill the painstakingly wrapped, steady stream of parcels that made their way across the Atlantic Ocean to her children fighting in the war.

Permits were also required to get tires for vehicles and I was somewhat aware of that, but the scarcity of rubber affected me in a much more personal way. Sewing elastic was not to be had and as a result of this a whole new type of women's and girls' underwear came into being. Our mother had always made most of our clothing at her treadle sewing machine, one of the most valued of her household possessions. Our summer underwear was made of soft, bleached, fine cotton flour or sugar sacks, with, of course, the traditional elastic waist. Now patterns had to be changed to resemble a skirt top, with a waistband and a button fastening at the side. These were very uncomfortable, with no give in sitting and moving or room for expansion and, when the button inevitably popped off, as it did with no regard for where we were, school or dancehall, we were forced to beg, borrow or steal a safety pin. This was much harder than it sounds. Buttons and safety pins were also scarce and precious and if a friend had one she was not going to give it up in case her own button popped off.

I have an unplaced memory of sitting in school most of one day and, whenever I was obliged to stand, clutching my left side at the waist in what I imagined was a casual and unobtrusive manner. There were also popular, though unconfirmed, stories of buttons

330

popping when girls were swung off their feet in our usual rowdy square dances, and a pair of unclaimed panties sailing across the dance floor. Though I didn't know it then, I now realize that button underpants were mostly what was available, through stores, catalogues or homemade, as almost every woman I have questioned recently, who remembers the war years, knows exactly what I am talking about.

"V for Victory!" was the slogan and the inspiration of the war. The words and the two finger "V" salute, attributed to Winston Churchill, were seen and heard everywhere, were drilled into us on a daily basis and became the rallying cry and the antithesis to the Nazi's "Heil, Hitler!"

We loved the war songs, both the old and the new. Patriotic, stirring, funny or sentimental, we listened to them, learned them, danced to them and sang them, fervently and often. In school we learned *It's a Long Way to Tipperary* and *Pack Up Your Troubles in Your Old Kit Bag*, from an earlier war, and we heard our mother singing quietly, "Keep the home fires bur-ning, while your hearts are yearn-ing/though your lads are far a-way, they-eyy dream-of-home - - -." It was a long time until I understood what either I or she was singing about. "Tipperary" was an unknown as was "kit bag." I wondered often what it was I was supposed to pack my troubles in and it wasn't until my sister and brother came marching home with *their* old kit bags that a light finally dawned. As for "a

331

Lucifer to light your fag," – *What?*[2] I figured the teacher didn't know what that meant or she would have told us and, therefore, nobody else in the classroom knew either, so there was no point in asking anyone. On the other hand, maybe she *did* know what it meant, and so maybe everyone else knew, too. Maybe she had explained it when I wasn't listening, so I couldn't reveal my ignorance by asking.

Just as war songs helped some people to deal with the war, so they helped me, and possibly others of my generation, to better understand some aspects of the war. ("- - -We're comin' in on a wing and a prayer/look below-there's our field-over there/though there's one motor gone/we can still carry on/comin' in-on a wing-and a prayer - - -.") Romanticized though the songs may have been, through them I began to visualize what might be really happening to the young men and women, all friends or schoolmates of my brother and sister, who had left our community to go to war. News of the deaths of some of these young sons of our parents' friends, our schoolmates' brothers, which was immediately known by all in such a sparsely populated community, was much harder to understand. We were not given details, probably because there were none to give. Actually, we were not even told; we just heard adults tell each

---

[2] "Pack-up-your-troubles in your-old-kit-bag and smile, smile, smile!/While you've a lucifer to-light-your-fag/Smile, boys, that's-the-style- - -!" "Lucifer" is slang for match, and "fag" for cigarette.

other, "So and so was killed," or "One of the so and so boys was killed; I don't know which one." The fears and the hush in households would deepen. There were no songs that told about the deaths and the possible deaths.

> - - - We are the Dead. Short days ago
> We lived, felt dawn, saw sunset glow,
> Loved and were loved, and now we lie
> In Flanders fields - - - .
>
> John McCrae

There'll Always be an England! (-and Eng-land shall-be-free!-); (There'll be blue-birds o-ver-) *The White Cliffs of Dover* (-to- morrow, when the world is free-); *When the Lights Go On Again* (-all over-the world/and the boys are home again/all over-the world-) stirred and rallied people as cold, hard, depressing newspaper facts never could. In England Vera Lynn had become the sweetheart of the armed forces and was singing for them, "We'll meet again/don't know where/don't know when - - -," in the United States Kate Smith was singing, *God Bless America!* and we were singing, *I Left My Heart at the Stage Door Canteen*, *Don't Sit Under the Apple Tree* (-with any-one else but me/'til I-come-mar-ching home), and *The Vict'ry Polka* with Bing Crosby and the Andrews Sisters. We wore out shoes dancing the new *Beer Barrel Polka* and jitterbugging to Glenn Miller's *In the Mood*.

Had there been a popularity poll among young women and

girls about armed forces uniforms, probably the Navy would have been voted the most romantic and we dreamed teen-aged dreams as we sang "Bell bottom trou-sers/coat-of-na-vy blue!/She-loves-a-sai-lor/and-he- loves-her-too - - -.""

When I complained recently to my friend Mary, about my seeming lack of any contribution to The War Effort, she asked, "Didn't you write to any sailors or airmen?" No. I didn't know any. Not that I and my friends wouldn't have liked to know some. (Mary ran off with an airman from New Zealand stationed in Vancouver and became a War Bride to New Zealand.) There was a Naval Station about a half mile up the road from our house in Aldergrove and sometimes on Sunday afternoons some of us would saunter by the gates and back again, hoping that some cute sailor would just happen to see us and start a conversation (– leading to a date, leading to a wonderful romance - - -). We never actually saw anyone.

A few times, when several of us were walking to a dance in Aldergrove, or to Aberdeen Hall three miles down the road, the Naval Station truck would come along and give us a ride. It was usually filled with sailors also going to the dance, and they were always polite and friendly, but we were very young and unsophisticated and they were not interested. I don't remember any of them even dancing with us.

As near as I can figure, this is about the same time that Mary

334

and her friends in Vancouver (Mary and I first met thirty years later) were throwing food over the fence to guys in uniform quarantined for mumps at Jericho Beach. We did write to Milly and Harvey from time to time and letters would come back to the whole family, which Mother would read out loud. Sometimes there would be a card from some exotic sounding place where they had gone on leave, Paris or Scotland, with pictures of the Eiffel Tower or castles.

I should have called this story "How my Mother Helped Win the War." Her last big effort to dredge up some patriotic enthusiasm in her younger children was to make us have Victory Gardens. This project, as nearly as I can remember, was inflicted only on my sister Bert and me, then fourteen and fifteen. Howard, seventeen (with his own story to tell about the tortures of bean picking in the Fraser Valley), had gone back to sunny Alberta to work in the harvest fields and Donnie was probably exempt because of his age (eleven) and possibly his paper route.

Victory Gardens, at that time being strongly promoted by the government and schools, were supposed to help The War Effort by providing families with their own food, thereby leaving more for the armed forces. It seems that there was some incentive provided through our schools, so Mother persuaded Dad, under protest as I recall, to plough up some small patches of ground near our driveway on Jackman Road. I should explain that my attitude toward gardening fell somewhere between my feelings about knitting, on

335

the low end, and cleaning out the chicken house (which I never actually had to do). As well, I didn't see any sense in duplicating Mother's vegetable garden.

On the farm in Alberta, my parents had always had very large vegetable and flower gardens, as well as a field of potatoes, and a small field of rhubarb, all of which, along with the farm's production of beef, pork, poultry, eggs, butter and milk provided most of our food, supplemented by a few bought staples – flour, sugar, cases of dried prunes in the winter, plus canned saskatoons from summer berry-picking. Part of our farm chores was to help in the gardens, planting, weeding, thinning out the carrots and harvesting. Completed weeding of a garden row would earn us, when small, a coveted big penny, about the size of our present twenty-five cent piece. We liked them better than small pennies, I suppose because they were rare. They gradually disappeared altogether.

Those garden rows, to me, looked as long as the four mile road to school and I don't believe I ever in my life got to the end of one. I did like the planting and the harvesting, partly because these were usually family affairs, with Mother showing us where and how to drop the seeds and make the rows straight, or the whole family going out on a beautiful burnt orange fall day to get in the potatoes for winter. Dad would walk along behind a one horse plough, turning up the rows of potato hills, while the rest of us followed, picking up the nice, new potatoes, filling our buckets and emptying them into the large farm wagon that stood waiting. It was hard work; the buckets were very heavy, but Mother had usually made a picnic lunch, which we would eat in the shade of the wagon, so there was a bit of an air of festivity about the day. Tired and grubby at sunset, we all piled onto the wagon for the ride back to the house, where Dad then had to unload all the potatoes into bins in the dugout cellar below our house.

Victory Gardens on Jackman Road at Aldergrove were quite a different thing. This was not the rich, black loam of the farm. This was a patch of fist-sized rocks with a little dry brown dirt in between, all held together by the prolific and impenetrable root system of Fraser Valley weeds and grasses. I hacked with dull hoes, planted seeds under rocks, trying hard to avoid any contact with soil that might contain bugs and worms. If I had known how to swear yet, or dared, I would have; instead I cried in anger and frustration.

I could cook and bake from the age of seven onward, I could saddle and ride a horse anywhere I was sent, I could milk cows, I was responsible and efficient at housecleaning, laundry and ironing. I could harness and hitch a horse to the buggy or drive a team pulling the hayrake (which last I loved but didn't get called upon to do too often, as my traitorous body had a way of sometimes passing out in the hot sun, and I was always having to be carried somewhere and revived). All of these things I liked doing, in varying degrees,

337

but I was not a gardener. Nothing came up in my Victory Garden. It was not until I was in my forties that my mother's attempts to pass on some of her satisfactions in gardening began to materialize in my own life.

As the war in Europe began to turn in favour of the Allies, attention became more focussed on the war in the Far East and this was even more frightening. We, as yet, knew almost nothing of the concentration camps in Germany, Russia and Poland; it would be years until we learned of the horrors of Auschwitz and Buchenwald and read the shocking statistics of the war dead and missing, including civilians. We were, however, beginning to hear stories of the tortures of Japanese prison camps, of Kamikaze pilots and of the Japanese determination to never surrender until every last person in Japan was dead. Scary, indeed.

People began to visualize the war going on for interminable years, as had the Japanese-Chinese war, with inestimable loss of life. Men already overseas who volunteered to go fight in the Far East were promised a few weeks home on leave in Canada before being sent. To Mother's great distress we had word from Harvey in early 1945 that he had volunteered and would be home shortly for his leave.

Overseas there-came-a pleading,
"Help a na-tion in dis-tress,"
and we gave our glorious laddies,
honour made us-do-no-less.

Let no tears add to their hardships,
as the soldiers pass a-long,
and although your heart is breaking
make it sing this cheery song:

Keep the home fires burn-ing,
while your hearts are yearn-ing,
Though your lads are far a-way
they-ey dream-of-home.

There's a sil-ver li-ning,
through the-dark-cloud shi-ning,
Turn the dark-cloud in-side-out
till the boys-come-home![1]

On May 7, 1945, Germany surrendered unconditionally to the Allied Forces. With the signing of the necessary papers the next day, the war in Europe was finally over, and May 8, 1945, was officially declared V.E. (Victory in Europe) Day. Harvey did not have to go to the war in the Far East. The atomic bomb intervened. Japan surrendered on August 14, 1945, and many Japanese citizens committed suicide outside the palace of the Emperor because of the dishonour. All papers were signed on September 2, 1945, making

---

[1] *Keep The Home Fires Burning,* Lena Guilbert Ford; Ivor Novello. 1915.

that day officially V.J. Day. Celebrations were subdued, as they had certainly not been when western victory was declared in Europe.

On V.E. Day, my sister Bert and I, just coming up to our sixteenth and seventeenth birthdays, daringly hitchhiked across the Patullo bridge to New Westminster and joined the thousands of people dancing, shouting, laughing, crying and singing the full length of Columbia Street, with musical bands blaring joyously every half block or so, all day and into the night. I finally danced with a sailor. Maybe I danced with several, but I remember one because I wore his hat. My friend Mary thinks it would be really stretching it to include this as part of my contribution to The War Effort.

Prairie Ghosts

Five towering spaces

          loom against a harvest sky

rising silent round long vanished grain

          above the fallow village

five winds keening

knock and clatter

          within their shadow walls

call back   call back

the desecrated spine bones of the town

in weedy bereaved lots between the quiet houses

phantom buildings stare from mindless eyes

there the Railway Station

the Boarding House

there Runyan's Hardware

and here along the wooden sidewalk

the Post Office

the Red and White Store

and shimmering faintly from long past

a blacksmith shop

a livery stable

but oh, the schoolyard!   oh, the schoolyard!

too many dead
                    shout across the ballfield

noisily slap chalkdust from worn blackboard erasers
                    on misty red brick walls

rattle the bones of cart and horse
                    across the railroad tracks

the terrible times

the wonderful times

rustle and rise from dry leaves underfoot

crowd boisterously

pushing   shoving   swarming loudly
                    through the caragana hedge

violently shake the poplar trees

laughing   calling   weeping

swoop through old grass

swish round
                    swirl down

            murmur   whisper

                sigh

            and settle

                                    K. Nash 1997

343

L'Envoi

Where our Depression farmyard and buildings stood, wheat shimmers golden in August, a few gnarled maple trees that we once climbed stand twisted, ready to fall, and Yellowleg Hall is overgrown with young poplars. With the five grain elevators – the spine bones of the town – the railway station, the stores, the post office, and now the school all gone, the shrunken village is barely discernible across the fields, but the stair steps of the roads are still the same – one south, one east, one south, one east. Many of the people are gone, too, and a few new ones are growing up there, but for a little time yet, on hot summer Sunday afternoons, memory shadows of four barefoot children will still troop down the trail to the pigpen roof.

ISBN 155395202-2

9 781553 952022